California Angel

California
Angel

NANCY TAYLOR ROSENBERG

A DUTTON BOOK

DUTTON
Published by the Penguin Group
Penguin Books USA Inc., 375 Hudson Street,
New York, New York 10014, U.S.A.
Penguin Books Ltd, 27 Wrights Lane,
London W8 5TZ, England
Penguin Books Australia Ltd, Ringwood,
Victoria, Australia
Penguin Books Canada Ltd, 10 Alcorn Avenue,
Toronto, Ontario, Canada M4V 3B2
Penguin Books (N.Z.) Ltd, 182-190 Wairau Road,
Auckland 10, New Zealand

Penguin Books Ltd, Registered Offices:
Harmondsworth, Middlesex, England

First published by Dutton, an imprint of Dutton Signet,
a division of Penguin Books USA Inc.
Distributed in Canada by McClelland & Stewart Inc.

REGISTERED TRADEMARK—MARCA REGISTRADA

ISBN: 0-525-93945-8

Printed in the United States of America

PUBLISHER'S NOTE
This is a work of fiction. Names, characters, places, and incidents either
are the products of the author's imagination or are used fictitiously, and
any resemblance to actual persons, living or dead, events, or locales is
entirely coincidental.

To Amy Rosenberg and Janelle Garcia: miracles come to those who believe. And to my own little angel, my first grandchild, may your journey through life be safe and smooth.

ACKNOWLEDGMENTS

Many people assisted in this book becoming a reality, and I would like to offer my appreciation. My agent, Peter Miller, at PMA Literary and Film Management, Inc., expressed enthusiasm after only listening to me spin this tale one evening; my editor and very special friend, Michaela Hamilton, at Dutton/Signet, who made the suggestion that my angel be a teacher and supported this project every step of the way; and to my husband, Jerry Rosenberg, who handled the kids, the business, the everyday details of our lives while I worked night and day. To Jennifer Robinson, of PMA, for her continual support and advice, and to my precious mother, LaVerne Taylor, who first introduced me to the world of angels. To Barbara King, a teacher at the Willard Middle School in Santa Ana, who served as my inspiration for the character of Toy Johnson, and to all the wonderful students at Willard, who have convinced me that they can make their way in the world regardless of the obstacles they must overcome. Of course, I must thank the man upstairs for providing me with the inspiration to create such a story. Next, I must thank Rabbi Bernard King for developing the "Adopt a School" program at our temple and making me believe that I could make a difference.

But the one person who inspired me the most was Janelle Garcia, a child I have grown close to over the past three years. Janelle suffers from a rare disease known as MMA, and is presently the oldest living survivor with this condition. One day when she was very ill and confined to bed, I told her and her younger sister, Nettie, this story and was rewarded with radiant smiles of delight and wonder. From that day forward, I was determined to see *California Angel* in print, and was certain that within the pages was a special magic—not my own of course—but Janelle's. In her room, in her house, in her presence, the angels are always gathered to assist her in her battle against her illness. I should point out that she is doing quite well, even though each day is a struggle. With her tenacity and courage, her loving family and friends, her enthusiasm for life, and her celestial helpers, I'm certain Janelle will have a rich, full life.

I'm grateful to have such a wonderful family: Forrest and Jeannie, Chessly and Jimmy, Hoyt, Amy, and Nancy Beth. So many other wonderful people also work on my behalf: Alexis Campbell, my publicist and assistant; Elaine Koster, my publisher, as well as Peter Mayer, Marvin Brown, Judy Courtade, Maryann Palumbo, Leonida Karpik, Arnold Dolin, Alex Holt, Lisa Johnson, Neil Stewart, and the complete staff at Penguin USA, I offer my appreciation for your hard work and support.

To my suspense readers, I thank you for taking this brief sojourn with me and hope you find it entertaining and meaningful. After looking hard at the dark side, I wanted to play on the other side of the fence a few moments before returning to my customary terrain. We may be in the midst of despair, but shouldn't we hold on to our hope for the future?

PROLOGUE

October 29, 1982: The leaves on the towering maple trees surrounding the Hill Street Baptist Church in Dallas were tinged with brown. Because the parking lot was full and the Gonzales family was late as usual, they had to park their ten-year-old Ford Fairlane on the street.

He was in the backseat, his eyes glued on the shiny mirrored strip of chrome running along the door frame. He wasn't looking at it but through it, or even into the chrome itself. Yesterday he had touched it with his thumb and now found himself fascinated with the outline of his fingerprint—fuzzy and milky on the outside, shiny and reflective on the inside. In his mind the fingerprint became something else, just as everything he touched or saw became something else. He was looking at a large lake, frozen solid, snow piled high all around. Overhead, the sky was gray, heavy clouds ready to spit forth more snow, and a fierce wind whipped across the icy surface. There were no people in his imagined landscape. There were never any people.

Noises drifted by his ears. He felt the vibration of the sounds against his cheek. In the front seat his parents were fussing, trying to find their prayer books, rushing so they would not have to walk into the sanctuary after the service had begun.

"Rosie," his mother said. "Hurry, get Raymond out of the car. We're going to be late."

Madonna Gonzales was a thin, dark woman who always seemed to be in a hurry, always late, always anxious. She no longer allowed people to call her Madonna, including her husband. Since her separation from the Roman Catholic church two years ago, she asked that she now be called Donna. She didn't like the connotations of the name Madonna, she told people. It sounded too Catholic; Donna was now a Baptist.

Rosie circled to the rear passenger door and peered at her brother through the window. At eleven years old to his thirteen, she was smaller and far more childlike. Her golden brown skin had a warm, healthy glow, and she was wiry and active like her mother. She reached for the door handle and then sighed, watching her brother's face, the detached look in his eyes, the pronounced stare. Why couldn't he talk to her? Why couldn't he share things with her? Why couldn't he go to school like she did every day, maybe even walk with her to the bus stop?

Ever since she could remember, Rosie had been asking her parents the same questions. "Raymond is sick," her mother would say. For Rosie this was a difficult concept to grasp. Her brother's body was strong and well developed. He was big for his age, while Rosie was small and delicate. He never coughed or upchucked in the bathroom. He never ran a fever or broke out with spots as Rosie had last year when she had come down with the chicken pox. But Raymond was sick. And Rosie knew he was sick. He was sick in his head.

"Get out, Raymond," Rosie said softly, taking his hand and pulling, while his eyes remained fixed on the door frame. Quickly she moved her free hand in front of his eyes, breaking his eye contact. Sometimes this worked. His eyes would follow her hand, and his body would follow his eyes. Today it didn't work. She leaned back with all her weight and pulled on his hand. "Momma," she yelled, frustration and annoyance in her young voice, "I can't do it. He won't move."

While Roberto Gonzales stood by the driver's door, his arms limp by his side, an unconcerned look on his face, his wife ran to the back door and tried to get her son out of the car. Her eyes would find her husband's and narrow, as if to say, Why can't you help me? Then she would yank Raymond's arm with all her might. "Please, Raymond," she exclaimed. "Get out of the car. We're late for church. Don't you want to go to Sunday school? You can color. You know how you love to color."

He didn't answer. She didn't expect an answer. Her husband always gave her that look when she tried to communicate with their son. He had long ago given up.

The pond disappeared from his mind like a slide from a projector, and he quickly found another vision: a forest, a blur of vibrant emerald green mixed with a soft cocoa brown. His lips spread in a smile as he dived inside the colors, felt the warmth of the brown caress his skin, heard the rushing of the green like water in a small stream. Then his eyes expanded and his breath came faster. Sounds were echoing around him, but he didn't hear them.

"Raymond," his mother said. Her voice was loud now, insisting. She had managed to pull him to his feet, but he was still firmly planted and would not move, his head tilted back and his eyes trained on the leafy branches of the maple tree.

Inside the tree was a blue bird. He had never seen anything so lovely in his life, so mesmerizing, so blue. The bird was perfectly still, strangely undisturbed by the people beneath the tree. He let the blueness fall over him like a blanket on a cold winter day. Suddenly the blue changed to many colors, all of them fluttering. The green rushed and twittered, the brown throbbed, the blue shook as the bird cleared the tree branches and took flight.

"Roberto, help me," his mother pleaded. This time her husband responded, slowly walking around the front of the car and grabbing his son around the waist. Roberto Gonzales was a large, heavy-set man who made his living with the strength of his body as a furniture mover for Bekins Van Lines. He had a look about his face like a beagle, long and sad, his eyes large brown orbs in his expressionless face. Carrying his son under his arm like a sack of potatoes, his eyes down in embarrassment as other congregants hurried to the sanctuary, he set him down on the steps in front of the church and walked away. Roberto had done his job, done what his wife had asked. That was all he was capable of doing. He'd yearned for a son to help carry the workload of the family as he had done when he was thirteen, a son to laugh with and discuss the things a man should discuss with his son. Sometimes on sleepless nights he found it difficult to believe that this strange being was really his child. He had even gone so far on one occasion of accusing his wife of being unfaithful.

Rosie was dressed in her best dress, the white one with the red sash at the waist that she was allowed to wear only on Sunday. It was almost too small now; she had received it several years ago, a gift from the social worker who came about Raymond. And her skinny legs were getting longer. Tugging at the hem of her dress, she shuffled along behind her mother and Raymond, her father having gone on ahead. They would drop Raymond off at the Sunday school classroom; Rosie would go inside the sanctuary. She would have preferred the Sunday school class but her mother insisted that she listen to the preacher. That's where it would occur, her mother always told her. If it was going to happen, it would happen inside the sanctuary, during the prayers.

Rosie had liked their old church. She had liked the smell of the incense, the robes of the priests, walking to the altar with her hands in a praying position to take communion at the rail. Right after her First Communion, when she was so proud and happy, her mother had suddenly decided to attend the Baptist church. She had sat Rosie and her father down one day and told them why.

"I have prayed and prayed," she told them, tears streaming down her face. "I have asked God for a miracle for Raymond. I have asked the priests to pray for a miracle, but they tell me I have to accept this —the way he is—that it is God's will. I cannot do that," she said, her head jerking upright and the tears drying on her face. "I can't accept that this is God's will, that God wants my child to be this way."

A week later, a doctor recommended by the Social Services Agency had diagnosed Raymond's illness, giving it a name none of the family had ever heard before: autism. Rosie couldn't pronounce it. Her father shook his head; his son was not right. That's all he knew. Names meant nothing. But his mother was certain her son's affliction was a curse, a possession by evil spirits—that only by being close to religious people, only by prayer could her son ever be free of the demons that held his soul captive. If they believed, she told them, if they prayed for a miracle, then possibly it would occur. The people who attended this church believed in miracles. They also believed in the devil and his power to destroy innocent lives. Within these walls, Raymond's mother was certain she would find God and He would cure Raymond.

After depositing Raymond in the Sunday school class, Rosie and her mother made their way to the sanctuary. Her mother liked to sit in the front row. Her father's job was saving them a seat. One of the church's deacons nodded to them as he walked in the opposite direction, accompanied by a strange-looking young woman. Donna Gonzales stopped and stared. For a second, her eyes met the woman's and she felt a chill, wrapping her arms around her body and clasping Rosie's hand even tighter. She had never seen this woman before today. She knew most of the members now for she tried to attend every function possible: the Wednesday prayer meetings, the coffees held for the altar guild, the Friday morning gathering that was specifically for the purpose of healing. She had even learned how to pray for a miracle. She had been told that she should not ask, but rather thank God as if the miracle had already occurred. This way she was affirming it, Reverend Whiteside had said, demonstrating her faith.

While Rosie was pulling her toward the door leading to the sanctuary, the church's organ already playing a hymn, Donna stared at the young woman and the deacon. The woman wasn't dressed appropriately for church, even for someone her age. Wearing a navy blue T-shirt with the words California Angels emblazoned on the front and a large letter *A* crowned by a halo, blue jeans, and house slippers, the woman looked very different from the women and girls who attended the church every Sunday in their finest dresses, their best shoes, carrying their nicest bags. The woman's bright red hair flared out around her face as though she was standing in a strong wind. The face, however, was enthralling. Donna stared, watching as the woman's lips moved, her words too soft to be heard.

Her skin was soft and pink, unlined and unblemished; her eyes were distinctly green, not blue-green or gray-green or hazel, but the very essence of green. Her prominent forehead showed a widow's peak, a little point in the front where her hairline dropped down. Donna thought it was like an arrow, pointing at the rest of her lovely face. Her nose sloped evenly but was small, almost snipped off at the end. It was the kind of nose that sometimes made an Anglo person look stuck-up, as if they thought they were better than everyone else. Her mouth was pale pink, like the skin of her face, and as compact and perfectly formed as a rose. High cheekbones delineated her face, and in the center of her chin was a small dimple.

"Mom," Rosie pleaded, pulling harder on her mother's hand, "I hear the preacher talking. Everyone's going to look at us when we walk in. Please."

Donna pulled her eyes away from the woman and followed her daughter into the sanctuary.

Deacon Miller pulled Mrs. Robinson out of the Sunday school class after entering and depositing the woman in one of the small chairs designed for children. "Who is she?" the teacher asked, puffing up her chest, thinking Deacon Miller was bringing in a new teacher.

"She didn't tell me her name," Deacon Miller said. "She just walked in off the street, and someone found her roaming around in the halls. She says she's from California. She wanted to see the children."

"Why are you leaving her here?" Mrs. Robinson could hear the children laughing and making a ruckus inside the classroom. She needed to return before complete pandemonium broke out. She was an older woman, in her late sixties. A retired schoolteacher, she had been teaching the Sunday school class at Hill Street Baptist Church for over fifteen years, never once missing a Sunday.

"Look at how she's dressed. I don't think it's a good idea to take her into the sanctuary. She may have walked away from a mental institution or something. She doesn't appear to be coherent. All she said was that she was from California and she didn't know why she was here, and then kept asking me to take her to the children."

"Well," Mrs. Robinson said, sighing, her hand on the door to the classroom, "maybe she's drunk or on drugs. How old is she anyway? She looks so young. Why don't you call the police?"

Deacon Miller grimaced. Tall, emaciated, dressed in a dark suit, the sixty-nine-year-old man resembled an undertaker. His skin had a pasty, almost waxy appearance. "This is a church, Mildred. If a person can't come here when they need help, where can they go?"

"Did you offer her money?"

"Yes," he said, running his hands through his thinning gray hair. "She said she doesn't want money. She only wants to spend time with the children."

Mrs. Robinson wrapped her arms under her heavy breasts and gave Deacon Miller the kind of look she reserved for unruly children. "But if she's mentally unstable, she sure shouldn't be around the children. That doesn't make sense, Bob. Get her out of here. Take her someplace else."

"You can watch her, Mildred. What can she do? She appears harmless, just lost and confused. I didn't smell alcohol on her breath."

"Oh, all right," she snapped, the noise in the classroom getting louder every second. When Mildred Robinson entered the room, she was mumbling under her breath, "Now I'll never get them to sit still."

The first thing she did was clap loudly to bring the class to order. She glanced at the young woman and then looked away. Just let her sit there, she thought, seeing the blank look in her eyes. She wasn't a psychiatrist. She had no idea what to say to a mentally disturbed person, and she resented Deacon Miller's invasion of her routine. "Get in a circle," she ordered the children, "it's story time. Today I'll be reading to you the story of Jonah."

"Jonah and the whale," a little boy chirped, obviously liking this story, squatting on the floor in the front row.

The woman was sitting in the back of the room next to Raymond Gonzales. A pair to draw to, Mildred Robinson thought. The boy's head craned to the side at an unnatural angle as he studied the designs in the wallpaper while his palms moved in small circles. Any moment she expected to see the woman do the same: start staring at the wallpaper. She looked dazed and disoriented, and her eyes were swollen as if she had been crying. Mildred couldn't stop herself from gawking at the funny bedroom slippers on her feet, the baseball T-shirt, the wild, bushy red hair. Normal women didn't dress like that in Dallas, particularly when they attended church, entered the house of the Lord.

"Okay," she said, opening the small biblical storybook and reading, "Jonah was . . ." Soon she was into the story, the children's eyes all on her, the woman forgotten. Mildred had read this story hundreds of times but she never tired of it.

As Raymond looked at the woman, he experienced a strange sensation. It was as if he and the woman were suddenly wrapped in soft white cotton, as if they were the only people in the room. Just then, a child squealed from the reading circle across the room. The sound was no longer jarring and frightening, but instead became a perfectly pitched note in a beautiful serenade that only Raymond could hear. His breath rushing in and out of his nostrils became an instrument, along with the familiar sound of his heart beating inside his chest. But the rhythm was not the same, and Raymond knew the sound well. His heartbeat was the only sound that never changed, that remained constant and recognizable.

He held his breath and listened, trying to figure out what it was that was different. Then he heard it. His heart would strike a beat and then instantly, another identical beat would follow, as if someone was walking directly behind him on a cobblestone street, following in his footsteps. Raymond became alarmed, finding the sensation uncomfortable.

No one could enter his world, he told himself. It wasn't possible. It had never been possible. But Raymond's instinctive urge to retreat vanished as he dived into the vibrant red of the woman's hair, fascinated by the way the strands twisted into shiny loose curls, so airy and light that they seemed to float weightless around her head. As his concentration intensified, his pupils expanded and he saw a montage of brilliant, dancing colors. The woman's head was turned away but he could see her face looking directly at him, feel the green of her eyes wash over him. Somehow he knew. He knew it wasn't her physical face he was seeing, but the visage of her soul. He wanted to drink it, touch it, smell it, preserve it. The image was so pure, so perfect. His lips trembled. His mouth opened and then shut. The beating in his chest was stronger now, and he could no longer hear the secondary heartbeat. He had never felt this way, never seen this way, never heard this way. His joy became a gurgling, pulsating sensation in the pit of his stomach, an enormous humming engine that was pushing him to speak, act, be.

His eyes jerked to the ceiling, but he didn't see the water spots, or the dirty glass of the light fixture, the graveyard of dead flies trapped inside. He saw magnificent images and enthralling scenes, wanting to stare at them forever, study them, add new images to the existing ones. But his vision suddenly strained and the images became fainter, the colors dull and fading. Something wasn't right, he thought sadly, as a solitary tear escaped and made its way down one side of his cheek. He saw jagged cracks, thinking the images were withering and dying right before his eyes. Heavy strokes had been layered over delicate strokes, trapping microscopic particles of dust and dirt between them and distorting the once flawless images. Many of the colors were now too bright, too harsh, so much so that they burned into his eyes and caused him to look away.

Near the part in the story that related how Jonah is swallowed by the whale, Mildred Robinson observed the woman on the floor with Raymond. To her surprise, she thought she heard them speaking to one another. Raymond was making no eye contact with the strange woman but his lips were moving, and what appeared to be words were coming out of his mouth. Mildred leaped from her seat, abandoning the story and the children, and immediately crossed the floor to the woman and child. She shoved her eyeglasses tight on her nose, wondering if her eyes had deceived her. She knew Raymond Gonzales was autistic. The only sounds she'd ever heard the boy make were grunts and groans. He didn't speak, he didn't make eye contact, and from all appearances, he didn't hear when people spoke to him.

"He's talking," she said, as if God had come down and performed a miracle. "I heard him. Wasn't he talking? What did he say?"

The redheaded woman ignored the teacher, mesmerized by the child. She stretched out on the floor, grabbing a handful of crayons and a sheet of paper. As the stunned teacher watched, she began to draw images on the paper with the crayons. Raymond's head drifted to the left and then to the right, but never did he focus on his new playmate, and no sound now came out of his mouth.

"Please," the teacher pleaded, "talk to him some more. He said something, didn't he? He's never spoken."

Like a child herself, the woman gazed up at the teacher and then dropped her eyes, proceeding to draw more images on the paper, filling them in with bright colors. The teacher's chest fell. She must have been mistaken. The woman was obviously an escapee from a mental institution or deranged in some way, and the child was the same as always.

She returned to the now unruly and rambunctious crowd of children she had previously abandoned, vowing to have both her eyes and her hearing checked next week.

With her back turned, Mildred heard the same sounds again and instantly spun around. This time there was no mistake. Not only did she hear a voice that had to be the boy's, he was staring directly into the woman's eyes, only inches from her face. Returning quickly to the two, the teacher knelt down on her hands and knees. What she heard completely amazed her.

"My name is Michelangelo," the boy told the woman in a clear, distinct voice. He snatched the crayons out of her hands and started drawing circles within circles. A few seconds later, he handed the woman a crayon, and she filled in the circles with red, then blue, then green, each time receiving the color in her outstretched hand from the boy, like a surgeon accepting a scalpel. The teacher was awestruck. She didn't speak, too fearful to disrupt the magic that was happening right before her eyes. She'd known other autistic children during her long career as a schoolteacher. She was all too aware of Raymond's handicap and resulting limitations.

"Here," he said to the woman, removing an orange plastic ring shaped like a pumpkin from his little finger.

The woman acted like this was a common occurrence and promptly removed a ring from her own finger and placed it on Raymond's. Just as casually she slipped on the pumpkin ring and continued coloring. Raymond immediately flashed a smile like no other, a smile that released small bubbles of saliva from his mouth. "I love you," he said through the bubbles.

"I love you, too," the woman said, briefly letting her eyes drift up to his in exquisite gentleness and then dropping them again to the paper. "But I have to go." While the teacher watched, still kneeling on the floor beside them, the woman stood, dusted off her pants, and walked out of the Sunday school class.

The teacher's eyes darted from the woman to Raymond. The children were running around in circles on the other side of the room, chasing one another and screaming. "Raymond," she said. "Can you hear me? Do you understand? You spoke. Praise God. You did speak, didn't you?"

"Yes," he said calmly, staring deep into her eyes.

"Oh, Raymond!" the teacher exclaimed. "You can talk. You can hear." Few, if any autistics, would look a person directly in the eye. This was a major breakthrough, Mildred decided, a spectacular act of divine intervention. It had to be nothing short of a miracle, particularly as it had occurred in a church, in God's house, in her own Sunday school class.

She suddenly saw Raymond's hand and the ring. On his little finger was what appeared to be a genuine piece of jewelry: a tiny ruby ring surrounded by diamonds. The teacher's heart fluttered. No matter what had happened, she couldn't let the boy keep something so valuable. She stood and went to look for the woman, carefully slipping the ring off Raymond's finger. "I'll be right back," she told him. "Keep coloring. I'm going to get your parents."

The woman was gone. The teacher searched the entire building and she was nowhere to be found. The ring pressed in her hand, she found Mr. and Mrs. Gonzales, the pastor, and several deacons in the church, insisting that they follow her to the classroom and observe the miracle.

Over the next six months, Raymond made remarkable progress. He spoke: first in disjointed sentences consisting of a few words, then in more sophisticated sentences involving verbs and adjectives. And he drew. Circles became scenes of life: trees, clouds, grass, flowers. From crayons he graduated to pastels, donated by a member of the church. With these, he drew lovely images of pastoral scenes with delicately shaded hues. The scenes were almost surreal and possessed of an unnatural breathtaking beauty. The church, the school, the Gonzaleses, and their friends and family were astounded.

Having no way to find the woman and return her ring, everyone decided it belonged to Raymond. She had given it to Raymond; it had to remain with him. In the beginning there was some discussion that the ring should be sold, the money used for Raymond's education and future treatment. Mr. and Mrs. Gonzales refused. Like a visit from the Virgin Mary, they began to think of the strange woman as a messenger from God, the ring physical proof of the existence of the divine.

The church and its members, even Mildred Robinson, although overjoyed at Raymond's progress and recovery, quickly delegated the entire incident to the unknown and uncharted nature of autism itself. Raymond had simply snapped out of it.

He wore the ring every day. He went to school in it, bathed in it, slept with it on his finger. To make certain that he didn't lose it, the family wrapped the back with masking tape so it fit snugly. Like a person possessed, Raymond drew, colored, and painted almost incessantly.

At the end of two years, he was reading and writing almost at his grade level. Placed in the public school, his progress was remarkable. But his progress in speech and language, as well as subjects such as mathematics, was minor compared to his rapid growth as an artist.

Raymond was acclaimed, even if on a small basis. Many of his fantastical images hung on the school walls and in various classrooms, framed and covered with glass, his distinctive scrawl at the bottom.

At age eighteen, Raymond was awarded a scholarship to the prestigious Willard Art Institute. The ruby-and-diamond ring had been enlarged to fit his growing fingers, and Raymond still never removed it. In the beginning he claimed he didn't remember the woman at all, nor the orange pumpkin ring he had given her. But a few years later her image began to appear in his paintings.

Raymond was no longer painting landscapes, he was painting human beings. And the human being he painted again and again was the redheaded woman wearing the California Angels T-shirt.

ONE

October 15, 1994: The halls of Thomas Jefferson Middle School in Santa Ana were empty and an ominous stillness had replaced the deafening sounds of hundreds of rowdy youths as they pushed and shoved their way outdoors at the end of the day. The school's security officer, Adam Leonard, a robust man in his late twenties who was attending college at night to become a teacher himself one day, stood patiently by the front door waiting for the last of the teachers to leave the building. When he saw a slim, delicate redhead making her way to the door, he pushed his shoulders back and quickly slicked his hair down with his hand. He knew she was married, so it wasn't as if he wanted to impress her. But there was something about Toy Johnson, something unique that set her apart from the other teachers. Not only were the students affected by her charisma and sense of purpose, but almost everyone who came in contact with her felt it. In her presence Adam experienced a strange urge to stand straighter and taller, to smile in spite of himself, and to speak more softly and with more patience when he interacted with the students. In one way, her presence uplifted him, and in other ways she made him feel inadequate, as if he, along with everyone else, were not doing enough.

Out of the corner of his eye he watched her, slowly approaching as she chatted with a fellow teacher, her bright red hair tumbling onto her face in big, sloppy curls. She reminded him of someone out of a picture book, similar to the kind his mother had bought for him as a child. She wore no makeup and her features were so soft and delicate that they looked as if they had been sketched with a pencil and could easily be erased. To Adam, Toy Johnson was both incredibly beautiful and painfully plain. When she was among the children, her face was radiant and her eyes turned an electric, almost glowing shade of green. But when the children were gone, she appeared to be nothing more than a simple young woman, one you would see but soon forget.

"No guns today," Toy said cheerfully as she passed through the double doors with her friend and fellow teacher, Sylvia Goldstein. People around the school sometimes joked about the close friendship between the two women, for they were so drastically different in appearance. While Toy was tall and willowy, her skin fair and her voice soft and lyrical, Goldstein was short and dark, never hesitant to speak her mind, her opinions uttered in a loud, grating New York accent. Toy dressed in simple cotton dresses that fell below her knees, dresses he had heard she made herself, while her friend favored more contemporary apparel: tailored jackets, pants, platform shoes, an occasional suit with a designer label. They were just so mismatched that seeing them together all the time struck a lot of people as comical. Terms like "Mutt and Jeff" and the "Sledge Sisters" abounded.

"Nope, no guns today," Adam answered, returning Toy's smile. "Tomorrow's another day, though."

"Yeah," Sylvia replied quickly. "Were you here the time some kid almost took a shot at us from the apartment complex across the street?" She stopped and pointed. "He was standing right there, on the second floor of that apartment complex. You know, on the little balcony. The police said he had an AR-15 assault rifle pointed at the front door to the school."

The security guard shook his head and proceeded to link a heavy steel chain through the door handles, then secured it with a padlock. "I've only been here six months. Guess I missed that one. I was here when we had the stabbing in the boys' bathroom, though."

"See you tomorrow, Adam," Toy said abruptly, suddenly yanking her friend's arm to get her to leave.

"Why do you do that?" she said as they continued on to the parking lot.

"Do what?" Sylvia said.

"You know," Toy said, stopping and shielding her eyes from the sun, "talk about negative things all the time."

Sylvia carried far too much weight for her height, most of it bunched unattractively around her midsection. She wore her straight dark hair in a short bob that made her face appear even fuller than it was, and in the last year or two a faint mustache had appeared above her lip. "Well, it's not like it didn't happen," she said, scrunching up her fleshy face. "What are you trying to say?"

"Just that talking about it solves nothing," Toy said earnestly. "All it does is create negative energy. I think when you talk about bad things all the time, it's almost as if you will them to happen."

Sylvia tossed her hands out to her side and then let them slap back against her thighs. "Negative energy, huh?" she said sarcastically. "And pointing an assault rifle at someone isn't negative? Give me a break, Toy. You live in la-la land. This is a war zone here."

"These are kids," Toy said firmly. "They're just children, Sylvia. Kids learn from their surroundings, have to adapt to whatever environment they find themselves in or they can't survive."

"Well," Sylvia answered, "what do you want us to do? Give them all guns or something so they can shoot at us?" She stopped and smacked her lips. "Most of them have them anyway."

"That's not true," Toy said, refusing to allow the other woman's remarks to upset her. She'd known Sylvia Goldstein since they'd attended UCLA together, Sylvia's family having migrated to the West Coast when she was in high school. Toy had finally talked her into transferring to Jefferson from a squeaky-clean school in the suburbs two years ago. She knew her friend was a good person and a dedicated teacher, but she had failed to see beneath the surface as Toy had. Too many dark faces stared back at her from the classroom, many of which were hostile and troubled.

"We have to give them love," Toy said, "show them we care about them, accept them on their own terms. The boy they arrested across the street was one of my students, remember. I know him. I know what he's been through, what kind of life he leads. All he did was pick up a gun that belonged to his father. He was only goofing around, and now he's caught up in the system, serving time in juvenile hall." She stopped and took a deep breath. "His father is the one they should punish for bringing that gun into the house, but he's probably out robbing someone while his kid pays the price."

"Goofing around," Sylvia said, appalled. "Well, excuse me, but I don't consider pointing an assault rifle at someone's head goofing around."

"See," Toy said quickly, "that's just what I'm trying to say. Kids play with whatever they find in their home. These kids grow up with guns, live with guns, so they—"

Sylvia interrupted, her expression grim, "You can save the speech, Toy. I've already put in a request for a transfer."

Toy's eyes dropped and she fell silent. A sudden breeze brushed past her, picking up the hem of her cotton print dress, but she didn't

notice. Her knees were scraped where a group of students had accidentally knocked her down on the sidewalk earlier in the week.

"There you go," Sylvia whined, her face flushing with frustration.
"I knew you'd make me feel guilty." Then her voice elevated several
octaves. "I can't handle it here, okay? I tried, but I just can't. I want
to teach, Toy. I want to teach normal children from normal homes
who have the ability to learn. I don't want to be a prison guard. I
don't want to lock myself in my classroom during recess, fearful
some thug will rape me or shoot me." Seeing the disappointed look
still on her friend's face, she added more fuel. "I don't want to listen
to foreign languages all day either. This is America, you know. Half
the kids here don't even speak English. They're Hispanic, Vietnamese, Haitian, whatever."

"You have to do what makes you happy," Toy said softly, shrugging her shoulders as she slowly raised her eyes. "But the kids like
you, Sylvia, even though they don't always show it. You're good with
them. You could make a difference here."

Sylvia laced her fingers through her hair and pulled. When she
removed them, strands of hair were wrapped around her fingers.
"See this," she shouted, waving her hands in front of Toy's face. "I'm
not only ready to pull my hair out, it's falling out on its own. If I stay
at this stink hole another month, I'm going to be bald. It's bad
enough to be fat and divorced, but I'll never get a man if I'm bald."

Toy laughed at the thought of her friend without hair, breaking the
tension, and soon Sylvia was laughing as well. "I have to go," she
said a few moments later. "I want to see Margie this afternoon."

Sylvia fell serious. "How is she?"

Toy made a wavy motion with her hand. "You know, she's in remission, but she's so weak from the chemotherapy that she can't
come back to school. And let me tell you, if the leukemia comes back
before she's had a chance to recover from this last round of treatment, I'm not sure she'll make it."

"Are you still giving money to the family?"

Toy blanched and started back-stepping toward her Volkswagen a
few feet away. "Sort of," she said self-consciously, uncomfortable
with where the conversation was heading.

"Does Stephen know?"

Toy made it to her car, unlocked it and ducked inside. "See you
tomorrow," she said out the window.

"So, he doesn't know," Sylvia said, frowning.

Toy cranked the engine and waved at her friend, trying to get her to move away from the car window so she could leave.

"You're making a mistake," Sylvia cautioned, shaking a finger at her as though she were one of her students. "He's going to find out, Toy. If I was married to a handsome doctor, I wouldn't do anything to jeopardize my relationship."

"Look," Toy said, her voice louder than normal, about as close to shouting as she ever got, "you have to do what you have to do, and I have to do what I feel in my heart." As soon as she finished the sentence, she started backing up the car, forcing the other woman to step away.

"It's not fun being divorced," Sylvia yelled out as Toy drove off. "Believe me, you're not going to like it."

Toy steered the Volkswagen a few blocks away to Dorado Street and parked at the curb in front of a modest stucco residence. The paint was cracked and peeling, and the yard consisted of a mass of unruly weeds. A small Hispanic woman pushing a baby carriage loaded down with groceries passed her, and several low-riders were making their way down the street, rap music blasting out of the windows.

Toy thought it strange how the area had changed in such a short time. The city of Santa Ana is located in Orange County, only a few miles away from Disneyland. At one time, it had been predominantly white and Protestant, but today it was far from it. The Hispanic culture was dominant, but there was also a large Asian community made up of Vietnamese and Koreans who had fled their own land for the promise of America, many of them boat people. When Toy was growing up, there had been no exit on the freeway marked "Little Saigon" like there was today.

She started to get out and head to the house when she suddenly felt overwhelmed and placed her head on the steering wheel, Sylvia's words playing over in her mind. She knew her friend's admonitions were right. Stephen had completely forbidden her to give the Roberts family any more money. The father didn't work, he said, and he wasn't about to support another man's kids, particularly since he and Toy were unable to have children of their own. She'd tried to explain the family's sad situation—that if the father worked a regular job, the family would no longer qualify for state assistance and would be unable to pay for Margie's treatment. And the mother was worse off than the father, confined to a wheelchair with rheumatoid arthritis. They had their own bills to pay, her husband argued, promptly reminding her of the enormous debts he had incurred while attending medical school, debts they had as yet to completely satisfy. Her husband had his own surgical practice now, and as far as Toy was concerned, the money he earned every month amounted to a small fortune. Why couldn't they use some of it to help people in desperate need? A few months ago, her husband had bought himself a brand-new Mercedes. When he had wanted to buy Toy a new car as well, she had quietly declined. Her ten-year-old Volkswagen would do just fine, she told him. Children were starving. She could forgo the delicious scent of new leather that he found irresistible and make do with what she had.

Toy could not comprehend her husband's miserly attitude when it came to helping others. The loans he always talked about had been outstanding for over ten years. Couldn't they wait a little longer? She wasn't providing luxuries for this family, only the dire necessities: food, clothing, shelter. What she prayed was that it would all add up to hope. Hope for a dying child. Hope for the future and the other children still in the home. Hope to make it through one more agonizing day.

Lifting her head, Toy glanced at her own image in the rearview mirror, seeing a pale, drawn woman that she no longer recognized. She had to start wearing makeup, start taking care of herself. Maybe they were right. Was she hopelessly idealistic? Was she letting her own life slide through her fingers in her quest to help others? Could she stop? She shook her head, answering her own question. Sylvia could transfer to another school, even drop out of teaching if she so desired, but Toy didn't consider that an alternative. Something else drove her, something her friend couldn't understand and she could not bring herself to share with her.

It had first happened in Toy's senior year in high school, the illness striking suddenly and fiercely. At first they had thought she had the flu, but when her condition worsened in the middle of the night, her parents had rushed her to the emergency room of a local hospital, where the doctors diagnosed her illness as pericarditis, an inflammation to the sac surrounding the heart. Only seconds after she arrived at the hospital, Toy had gone into cardiac arrest. Her mother was certain that she would not be alive today had she not been in a hospital when her heart stopped beating. But Toy seldom thought about that aspect to her illness. To Toy, her illness had occurred for a purpose and that purpose was to change her life forever. In the few short seconds she had been technically dead, she had never felt more alive, more vital. She'd felt connected to the universe, to the trees, the wind, the earth, as if she were part and parcel to the whole.

It was then that she knew administering to the needs of children must be her life's work.

While the doctors were working frantically to revive her, Toy had seen herself in a room full of children. One boy in particular had spoken to her, reached out to her. She remembered the pain and loneliness sparking all around him, and developed the feeling that he was trapped in a place he could not escape. But before the dream ended, Toy sensed the presence of boundless hope and unlimited beauty, so awesome in its dimensions and scope that she would never forget it and would more than likely spend the remainder of her life trying to find it again. She didn't know who the boy was, but she was certain she had helped him in some way.

The strange part about it was Toy had returned from her sojourn to the other side minus something tangible—the ring her parents had given her for her sixteenth birthday, one she distinctly recalled giving to the boy in her dream. Instead she awoke wearing a plastic ring, the kind that sometimes come in cereal boxes, and the small, worthless trinket instantly became her most cherished possession. When the world caved in on her, Toy would retreat to the bathroom and remove the ring from the bottom drawer where she kept her shampoo and other personal items, placing it on her finger and waiting. She never knew what she was waiting for—to be carried back to that moment perhaps. To Toy, the ring was like a talisman that had mysteriously fallen from the sky. It had to have some meaning, some mystical connotation. She had brought it back with her, brought it back from the brink of death. She didn't know how and she didn't know why, but she knew wearing it made her feel better, calm and peaceful. By the time she removed the orange plastic pumpkin and put it back in its hiding place, she was ready to tackle the world again.

Her parents played down her strange experience, elated that their daughter had survived a terrifying ordeal. They insisted that the ring had simply been lost in the confusion, possibly even removed by the emergency room staff when she had first been admitted. But Toy knew differently. She had been terribly ill when she'd arrived at the hospital, and they had rushed her immediately to the team of doctors waiting to treat her. She was certain the ring had been on her finger, just as she was certain that something miraculous had occurred that night, something she could not explain or fully comprehend. As the years passed, she studied near-death experiences and other related phenomena, trying to put her own incident into perspective, but the articles and first-person accounts she read indicated the people saw visions of Christ, long tunnels, and blinding bright lights. Some people claimed they saw long-dead relatives and loved ones.

All Toy had seen were children's faces.

Pulling herself from her thoughts, she opened the car door and headed up the walkway to the front door. It was the fifteenth of the month. Toy knew that meant the bills from the first of the month had not been paid and were now past due. If the rent wasn't paid by tomorrow, the family would be evicted. How could a desperately ill child survive in a filthy and crowded public shelter, where half of the occupants were mentally ill or drunks off the street? Once Toy had placed a family with several children in a shelter and had been devastated to learn that the youngest boy had been molested by an older man. She just couldn't allow it to happen to Margie or one of her brothers or sisters. Fate had been cruel enough to this family. What they needed was a break, and the only break she could find was herself.

Before knocking on the door, she opened her purse and checked the balance in her checkbook, chastising herself for not going to the bank. If she wrote another check, Stephen would find out. She should have brought cash instead. She closed her purse with a feeling of doom, knowing she had made her decision, and promptly knocked on the door. If Stephen valued a new Mercedes over human life, then he'd just have to trade her in for a flashier model.

She could change her hair for him, even let him buy her fancy dresses for exclusive parties with his fellow doctors and their wives, but she couldn't change what was in her heart.

Toy arrived home before her husband and rushed to the kitchen to prepare dinner, careful to remove her shoes and leave them in the entryway on the little mat she had placed there for that purpose. Stephen had insisted on decorating the house in black and white, and the plush carpet under her feet was difficult to maintain. Walking through the living room in her bare feet, she saw all the dust on the shiny black surfaces and wondered if she would have time to dust before her husband came home. Sometimes when she got really annoyed at him, she gave thought to dumping ink all over the white carpets and taking a carving knife to the black lacquered furniture. She detested it. She wanted her home to be just that—a home, a place of warmth and comfort, not sterile and forbidding. She wanted knicknacks and other collectibles, warm, rich woods and colorful prints, but Stephen didn't like clutter, and he hated bright colors. She wanted a dog, but with the white carpets, Stephen said it would be a disaster.

Sometimes she thought she lived in an operating room.

In the all-white kitchen, Toy tossed several potatoes on the cutting board and started chopping them, but her thoughts kept returning to Margie and the time they had spent together. Even though the girl was doing well and the cancer was in remission, she was desperately fragile, so weak and wasted that she could not get out of bed. Today she had brought her fears out in the open, talking to Toy about death and the feeling she had that her own was imminent.

"You're fine," Toy had insisted, sitting on the edge of her twin bed. "You're not going to die, Margie. You're going to beat this and have a wonderful life."

"I don't think so," she said softly. "I feel it, you know. I know it's waiting." Then the child's voice dropped to a whisper as she leaned close to Toy's face. "Sometimes at night," she said, "when everyone is asleep, I look by my bed and I'm certain I can see it. It's like a big, ugly shadow just standing there staring at me."

"That's your fear you see," Toy told her, her voice soft and consoling. "That's not death, Margie. Death is beautiful, painless, magical. Can't you see? It's living that's tough. Death is our reward."

"I know all that," the girl answered weakly. "You've told me that before, but I don't believe it." She stopped speaking and looked out the window by her bed. A few moments later, she turned back to Toy. "I got you a present. It's supposed to be a Christmas present, but I want to give it to you now."

"Save it," Toy said. "I'd rather open it with you on Christmas morning. You know I'll be here. I was here last year, wasn't I?"

The girl's lips compressed and she shook her head. She didn't have to tell Toy what she was thinking, that she wouldn't be there for Christmas, that by Christmas it would all be over.

"Don't think like that," Toy said quickly, gently stroking her thin arm. "Did I tell you what I dreamed the other night? I dreamed I saw you in this beautiful white dress, a wedding dress. And listen, Margie," she said, "you were the most gorgeous bride I've ever seen."

The girl ran her tongue over dry and cracked lips, her voice wheezy now when she spoke. "Get the present. It's on top of the chest."

Surfacing from her thoughts, Toy dropped her knife on the kitchen counter and went into the bedroom, removing the small package the girl had given her and lovingly touching the contents. Margie had given her a California Angels baseball T-shirt, exactly like the one she had been wearing the night she became ill. One of her boyfriends had taken her to an Angels game and bought it for her. Toy had ended up using it as a night shirt. It was such a strange coincidence, she thought, that Margie would give her the same T-shirt. Of course, she told herself, the child hadn't bought it. One of her relatives had given it to her as a gift, and she in turn had wanted Toy to have it. Suddenly she decided to wear it, and removed her dress, hanging it up in the closet. Then she pulled the T-shirt over her head and stepped into a pair of faded Levis. Padding barefoot to the kitchen, she remembered the bedroom slippers she had been wearing that night when she went to the hospital, and wished she still had them. They had been funny actually, those big, silly slippers made to look like animals. Hers had been penguins. She decided to get Margie a pair next week. She'd get a kick out of them, and a smile was worth everything right now. She had to get the little girl's spirits up and dispel her fears of impending death.

"What's going on?" Stephen said from the doorway. "Is dinner ready?"

"Not yet," Toy said cheerfully, walking over to embrace him. Although Toy was five foot eight, her husband was over six three and completely engulfed her. He had the lean, hard body of a runner, dark hair and eyes, and an always confident look on his handsome face. She inhaled the musky scent of his aftershave and nuzzled her head against his chest. "How was your day, honey? Are you tired?"

"Don't ask," he said gruffly, pushing her away and then yanking his tie off. "Remember the gallbladder I did about three months ago? Well, the stupid woman is suing me for malpractice. I saved her life, and all she's worried about is how she will look in a bikini. She thinks the scar is too big."

"I'm sorry," Toy said, kissing him tenderly on the forehead. "It'll be okay. You know how the courts frown on these kinds of lawsuits." But she knew there was cause for concern. Every time Stephen was sued, his malpractice insurance went up, and lately everyone he touched had wanted to sue.

"How long before we eat?"

"Maybe thirty minutes," she said, returning to put the potatoes in a pot to boil, trying not to respond to the annoyed expression on his face. When they had first met, Stephen had been an intern and the life of the party, always cracking jokes and making Toy laugh. They'd sat for hours talking about their hopes and dreams, about how they wanted to make the world a better place. Nowadays they seldom talked at all. But Toy knew it wasn't easy being a surgeon. Even when you did your best, people didn't always appreciate it, and over the years Stephen had become tense and rigid. The carefree young man she had fallen in love with no longer existed. Now her husband was demanding and strident, barking orders at home just as he did in the operating room. He never seemed to be able to relax. Even when they made love, she could feel the tension coursing through his body.

"You know I like to eat at six o'clock," he snapped. "I have to digest my food before I go to bed. Is that too much to ask?"

"No, Stephen," Toy said, lighting a burner under the wok so she could prepare the vegetables. "I just got home. I had to do some things after school."

"What things?" he asked.

"Errands," she lied. Then she smiled brightly. "Hey, if you're hungry, I can make you a snack."

"I don't snack," he said flatly, disappearing from the doorway.

Five or ten minutes later, he came back. "Something peculiar happened today. Do you know someone named Rachel McGuffin?"

Toy stiffened. Rachel McGuffin was the name of one of Margie's aunts, the one who normally cashed checks for the family because the Roberts' didn't have a bank account. "Why do you ask?"

"Why don't you just answer the question, Toy?"

Her eyes roamed around the room. "What question?" Then she giggled. "I thought we were just making small talk. I didn't realize this was an interrogation."

"Stop this," he said loudly. "Do you know this woman or not? The bank called my office this afternoon, claiming she was trying to cash one of our checks for six hundred dollars. I told them it was a forgery."

Toy let the dish towel in her hands fall to the floor. "You what? How could you do that? They probably arrested her. Good Lord, Stephen, I gave her the check. She didn't forge it." She started walking to the wall phone to call the Roberts' and apologize for the confusion, praying the bank hadn't called the police, but her husband blocked her way.

"No one," he said angrily, "and I mean no one, is going to walk off with my money unless I say they can. Do you hear me, Toy? Who is this person and why are you writing checks to her? I demand to know, and I want to know right now."

Toy's upper lip was trembling, and she had turned as white as the wall behind her. She hated arguments and nasty scenes. When she and Stephen got into a disagreement, she simply walked out of the room and stayed in the bedroom until he calmed down. She seldom raised her voice, and she despised friction of any kind. But this was a fight she couldn't avoid. The time had come to settle it once and for all.

"It's not just your money," she told him, meeting his harsh gaze with one of her own. "I bring in an income, too. The money that you managed to keep in your precious bank account today was supposed to keep Margie Roberts out of a homeless shelter. But you ruined that, didn't you?"

He tossed his hands in the air. "I should have known," he said. "The damn Roberts family again. Don't you know they're using you, Toy? How can you be so naive?"

She planted her feet and stood her ground. "How can you be so callous?"

"I resent that," he snarled, his hot breath on her face. "I forbid you to give those people another cent. You do the cooking and cleaning, and I'll handle the money in this family. I told you it would be that way when we got married."

Toy stomped over to the stove and turned it off. Before she knew it, he would go into his "only one boss in the family" diatribe. Toy decided it really was like the psychologists say. People emulate their parents, whether they were good parents or not. Stephen's father had been a surgeon as well, and he had run his household with an iron fist. Even though Stephen had balked against his father's rigid rules and dominating manner, he felt compelled to run his own home in an identical fashion.

She grabbed her purse and pushed her way past him.

"Where do you think you're going?" he barked.

"I have to take them another check now. The rent has to be paid tonight. They already got an eviction notice."

"That's their problem, not yours," he said, following her to the front door.

"It's everyone's problem," Toy said. Then she spun around and faced him. "When a child is sick and in need, we're all responsible.

You're a doctor, Stephen. I would have thought you would know that."

He grabbed her arm and squeezed hard, making her wince. "You walk out that door, Toy . . . I . . . Don't come back."

Suddenly she felt locked inside a dreadful cocoon of silence. Stephen had turned the television on in the living room earlier, but she didn't hear it. Cars were passing outside on the street, but she couldn't hear them. All she could hear was her own heart pounding inside her chest. In a whisper she said, "Do you really mean that?"

"Yes, I mean it," he hissed. "I can't feed and clothe the whole city." He began pacing back and forth in front of her. "I was in surgery by five o'clock this morning, and how do I know I won't be called out again tonight. I work hard for my money. These people . . . they're lazy . . . loafers. They want a free ride. That's what we've got in this country now, people that expect other people to pay their way. Well," he said, puffing his chest out before he yelled at her, "they're not getting any free rides from my bank account, and they're certainly not taking advantage of my wife. I won't tolerate it."

He stopped pacing and collected himself, seeing the look of dismay on his wife's face. Toy always came around, he thought, feeling confident that the situation was resolved. "Don't you see?" he said in a normal tone of voice. "It's all because we can't have children. You've developed some kind of psychosis relating to children. Just like these crazy dreams you're always talking about, telling me that you imagine you're saving children from some terrible fate. It's a form of hysteria, I believe. I think you need treatment."

Once Stephen had established his practice, he'd asserted his desire to start a family. But Toy couldn't conceive. There was no physical basis for her infertility. Her husband had made certain. She had been tested, probed, poked, and studied. She'd even undergone exploratory surgery. Stephen had also been tested. Nothing was wrong. His sperm count was normal. They had to wait. Eventually, the specialist had said, it would happen.

"Now that we've got that settled, let's eat," Stephen said, heading for the kitchen. "I'm starving."

When he reached the door to the kitchen, he stopped and turned back, expecting Toy to be behind him. The front door was standing open, and a chilly breeze whisked into the room bringing a few leaves to rest on the marble entryway.

TWO

By nine o'clock Toy had delivered a replacement check to the Roberts family, and was sitting in Sylvia Goldstein's living room. Sylvia lived in Mission Viejo, a thirty minute drive south of Santa Ana. Toy lived in Laguna Beach, a few miles closer to the school and considerably more affluent. Whereas her house had been custom-built, her friend lived in a tract where all the houses were identical and fairly affordable. But Toy was always comfortable in Sylvia's home. It was messy and cluttered, almost every solid surface covered with mementos and pictures. Several Siamese cats crawled wherever they wished, and one black one that Sylvia called Simon was perched on the back of the chair right next to her friend's head.

"I can't stop," Toy said, tears streaming down her face. "I can't let Margie go to a shelter. Maybe she only has a few months left. How could I put her through that?"

"Why don't they just put her in the hospital?" Sylvia asked.

"Because she's in remission, and as a Medicare recipient, they won't admit her to an urgent-care facility unless her leukemia is in an active state."

"I see," Sylvia said slowly. She was clasping a steaming cup of coffee with both hands, seated on a leather recliner directly across from Toy. Wearing a black sweatsuit and tennis shoes, she'd been ready to walk out the door to go to the gym when Toy had suddenly appeared in tears, telling her she had nowhere else to go. "Well, have you ever considered that the guy is right?" she said. "It's more than Margie, Toy, and you know it. I see you digging in that beat-up plastic thing you call a purse every day, handing out money to the kids like candy. Look at yourself. How old are those shoes? You've had those same black flats since God knows when. Really, I think you even had them in college."

"I don't just hand out money," Toy said defensively, swiping at her eyes with the back of her hand. "I give them money for coats and shoes, things they have to have to come to school."

Sylvia leaned forward, setting the coffee cup down on the end table. "What kind of coats? This is California, Toy. No one's going to freeze here. I mean, this isn't Idaho where there's two feet of snow on the ground." Then she smirked, her double chin resting on her chest. "Did you give Jesus Fernandez money the other day? Did he come crying to you, claiming he needed a winter coat?"

Toy nodded meekly, lacing her hands together and placing them in her lap.

"Well, next time you see him, get a look at what he bought. He bought a leather coat, woman. No one *needs* a leather coat. A cloth coat or a cheap jacket I can understand. He's a gangster, Toy. He took advantage of you."

"He's twelve years old," Toy said. "Maybe that coat made him feel important. Maybe he won't rob someone or kill them to get what the other kids already have."

Sylvia shook her head. "Forget it. What are you going to do about Stephen? Are you going home?"

"No," Toy said firmly. "He doesn't want me. He made that perfectly clear tonight."

"Did he say those exact words?" Sylvia asked, tilting her head to one side and staring at Toy. "Did he say, 'I don't want you, Toy'?"

"Not exactly."

"I didn't think so," Sylvia said, thinking Toy was exaggerating the severity of the situation. "Look, Toy, you just had an argument. Go home and seduce him or something. That always worked on Sidney." She saw the look on Toy's face and added, "Well, maybe it didn't work that well. He divorced me." Then she laughed, a wonderful, full-bodied sound that filled the room and seemed to jiggle the light fixtures. "Lighten up, okay? I was just kidding this afternoon. Even if you do end up in divorce court, you'll find another man. You're pretty as a picture, and of course, you're thin. That's all it takes, babe. Those skinny little twigs you call legs brings them in every time."

"I don't want another man," Toy said. She got up and went to the bathroom, returning with a few squares of toilet tissue to blow her nose. Once she had done so, she continued, "I don't know what I want right now to be truthful. I just want to do something important, something that matters."

"I have tissues, you know," Sylvia said. "You don't have to use toilet paper."

Toy gave her a wide-eyed look. "It's cheaper and thinner. Why waste the paper? Every time you use paper, another tree dies."

"Wow," Sylvia said, rolling her eyes purposely, "I didn't know that. You mean, they make paper from trees? Why didn't anyone tell me?"

Toy wrinkled her nose and then laughed. "You're a case, Sylvia."

"So," she said, "you gonna stay with me? Is that the plan?"

"Can I?"

"Of course," Sylvia said. Then her face came alive, and she sprang to her feet. "I've got a super idea. Why don't you go to New York with me to my nephew's Bar Mitzvah? We have Monday and Tuesday off anyway because of the district meetings, so if we leave tomorrow night, we'll have all that time in the city. It should be a fun trip. You can meet my brother and his wife, my nephews and nieces. The only day we'll be tied up is Saturday, the day of the Bar Mitzvah."

"I thought you were going with Louise," Toy said. The thought of getting on a plane and flying off somewhere suddenly sounded appealing.

"She backed out today. Says she has the flu, but I know she's lying. This dentist she's been after for six months finally asked her out, so she axed our trip." Sylvia stopped and took a sip of her coffee. "Really made me mad, you know. We've already booked the tickets and they're non-refundable. Bet she'll sell you hers for peanuts."

"I'll go," Toy said eagerly, thinking it was just what she needed. She'd get away for a few days, and it would give both her and Stephen time to think, time to put things in perspective.

Sylvia seized the smaller woman in a bear hug, lifting her off the sofa. "Great! We're going to have a ball. We'll do Manhattan and I'll show you all the sights."

Rather than removing herself from her friend's embrace, Toy rested her head on her shoulder and let her continue to hold her. She felt so tired, so emotionally drained. "I love you," she said to Sylvia. "You're my best friend in the world."

"Mine, too," Sylvia said, reaching up to pat her on the head like a child. "Everything's going to be all right now. You're with me now, kid, and old Sylvia knows how to have fun. Just let that pompous creep you married sit and think about what a louse he is. By the time you get back, he'll be begging."

"Do you really think so?" Toy said tentatively.

"You bet your britches," Sylvia said, hugging her to her chest even tighter. "Who in the world could walk away from an angel like you? The man would have to be crazy." She pushed Toy back with her arms and glanced at her clothing, a broad smile on her face. "Hey, you even have an Angels T-shirt. Well, get ready to sweat, Ms. Goody Two-Shoes. You made me miss the gym. Now you have to chase me around the block about five times or I'm never going to forgive you."

"What would I ever do without you?" Toy said, crying and laughing at the same time.

"Exactly like Sidney did—move away, make a million dollars, and forget you ever knew me." She pulled on Toy's arm. "Come on. It's time to run."

Later that evening, Toy couldn't sleep and the two women sat in the dark on the floor in the living room, talking until all hours of the morning. "Remember when we used to do this at school?" Sylvia said, munching on potato chips. "Want some?" she said, extending the sack to Toy.

"I'm not hungry."

"You're never hungry. What? Do you think you're saving the food of the world or something by limiting your intake? Sometimes I think you really are loony, you know." She tossed the half-empty sack of chips aside, disgusted at herself for eating them. "You're the only skinny person I've ever trusted. Thin people are weird. They aren't wired the same as fat people. When I was a kid, I was even fatter than I am now. I was certain all the toothpick kids in school were from Mars or somewhere. Heck, everyone in my family is fat. How did I know?"

"You're not fat," Toy said offhand, her thoughts drifting to the past and her own childhood. "Did I ever tell you that I used to pretend I was a nun?"

"When was this?"

"I don't remember exactly. I think I was thirteen."

"How did you pretend to be a nun? You prayed, you mean?" Sylvia chuckled. "Did you walk around chanting? Hey, tell me already."

"No, I made a nun's habit. I took sheets and wrapped them around my head, then draped them around my body, tying them with a cord. I had this big iron cross I used to wear on my neck. I bought it at a garage sale for a dollar."

"You never told me your parents were Catholic," Sylvia said, grabbing the bag of chips again and tossing a handful in her mouth, then crunching them loudly with her teeth. So much for willpower, she thought, wondering if it would help any if she ate the chips while running in place.

"They weren't Catholic," Toy answered. "My father's an agnostic. I went to church only once in my life. It was somebody's wedding. I don't know what my mother believed. We never talked about it."

"What did your parents think when you dressed up and pretended to be a nun? Didn't they think that was a little strange?" Even though Sylvia knew she shouldn't, she added, "Maybe they should have taken you to a shrink back then and you would have turned out normal. You know, mean and uncaring like the rest of us."

"Oh," Toy said, recalling the day her mother had come home and seen her in her makeshift habit. "They didn't know. I always did it when no one was at home. Except one day my mother came home unexpectedly and saw me. She just thought I had made a costume for Halloween."

"Why'd you want to dress up like a nun? I've certainly never wanted to dress up like a rabbi."

"How do I know?" Toy answered, lifting her heavy hair off her neck. It was damp and sticky. Sylvia had never been into fresh air. She was certain if she opened her window, someone would crawl in and murder her in her sleep. "I was a kid. It was a fantasy like boys pretend to be firemen. There was a Catholic church on the corner, and the nuns wore old-fashioned habits then. I used to hide in the bushes and watch them."

The two fell silent, and Toy was soon roaming through other memories from her childhood. She'd been a happy, bubbly little girl, always running and jumping, full of energy. When she was eight, she decided to emulate the tightrope walkers at the circus and had strung a clothesline across her swing set. Once she stepped onto it, hands spread at her sides for balance, it snapped and she fell to the ground, breaking her arm. It was one in a long line of injuries: broken bones, bumps and bruises, sprained and twisted limbs. Her mother called her a tomboy. Her father went further, nicknaming her Roy. "We just missed your name, tiger," he would tell her. "Instead of Toy, we should have named you Roy." Calling this rough-and-tumble little girl Toy had been a misnomer from the word go. If she had resembled any toy, it wouldn't have been a doll. It would have been a spinning top.

For Christmas one year her mother had gone to the Salvation

Army and purchased a complete assortment of costumes someone else had discarded. Toy would dress up in one of the costumes almost every night after supper and perform for her parents, doing tap dances and making up ballet steps. They couldn't afford for her to take lessons. Her father was a postal worker and her mother didn't work, so money for extras was scarce. Toy didn't realize there was such a thing as lessons, or that a person could really learn to do something so natural.

But things began to change around her thirteenth birthday. Toy became quieter and more introspective. Her mother assumed it was simply puberty, that she knew she was too old now to dance around the living room in silly costumes. Once she had done her homework, Toy would retire to her room and read or just sit there quietly thinking. Eventually, her reflective states extended to school hours, and her grades started to plummet. When she became ill in her senior year, she had been no more than a B student. After her experience at the hospital, though, she had poured herself into her school work and managed to graduate at the top of her class.

"You think there's some deep-rooted underlying psychosis because I once liked to dress up like a nun?" Toy asked after a long silence.

"No," Sylvia said, her eyes half closed, the entire bag of chips history. "I'll tell you what I think, okay? I think we need to go to bed and get some sleep. God, I ate so much salt, I feel like I could float to New York like the Goodyear blimp."

Toy ignored her and continued. "Stephen isn't a bad person, Sylvia. He's just developed the typical surgeon's attitude: thinks he's God, orders me around, treats me like I'm inferior. When I talk to him about something I'm interested in, he just walks away."

Sylvia stuck her hand in her glass of ice water and patted her face to stay awake. "How do you feel about that?"

"I don't like it," Toy said. "No one would."

"Then I guess your marriage is over," Sylvia pronounced with a sense of finality. She pushed herself to her feet to head to the bedroom before she passed out.

Feeling downcast and empty, as if she'd just had four teeth extracted, Toy silently followed her friend down the dark hall to the guest room, flopping face first onto the bed.

Why had she walked out? She'd never walked out on Stephen, no matter how severely they had argued. Toy didn't believe in going to bed angry, and always forced herself to make up, even if she had to give in to her husband's demands. Life was too short to be angry, she always told herself. And in every relationship someone had to compromise, acquiesce to the other's needs. She didn't mind that the person was her, as long as Stephen didn't interfere in the things she wanted to do.

But tonight was different, and Sylvia was right. It was more than Margie Roberts and a penchant for charitable endeavors. Stephen had brought up the dreams, made Toy feel foolish for telling him about them. She'd known better, but the man was her husband. How could a person be married to someone who intimidated her so badly that she was afraid to share her inner thoughts, her dreams? She had always thought that was the purpose of being married, but evidently, her husband did not agree.

Had she become angry because he had mentioned the dreams? Toy asked herself. Once she had told Stephen, the dreams had stopped. It had been at least six months since she had had one, and she longed for the blissful feeling that accompanied them, the feeling that she had saved some child's life. She knew they were just dreams, fantasies, grandiose delusions, as Stephen called them. She'd never tried to tell him they were real, just how good they made her feel.

Did she blame Stephen because she didn't have the dreams anymore? In some way, did she think telling him had interfered with the magic?

The phone loomed in the corner of the room, but Toy refused to call her husband. If she was childish, foolish, and naive like everyone told her, she simply didn't care. She wanted magic, miracles, overnight solutions. She wanted to live in a world where there was hope. Her eyes closed and she tried to recall the specifics of one of the dreams. When that didn't work, she tried to will herself to create a new one. But nothing came—not the dreams, or sleep of any kind. Her heart was racing inside her chest, and there was no way to stop it.

Finally, she made a commitment. She would go to New York with Sylvia and turn over a new leaf, embark on a new life. Instead of trying to save one child, she would try to save them all. If there was such a thing as a miracle, a divine presence, she would search until she found it. She'd waded through the shallow waters of the world long enough. If she had to, she would step outside again. She'd done it before, she told herself, she could do it again.

But tears soon streamed down her cheeks and she curled up into a tight ball, filled with anguish and self-loathing. She was everything they said she was—a loony, a goofball, a dreamer. How could an intelligent, rational mind tender such ridiculous thoughts? How could she possibly think that she alone could ever make a difference? It must be like Stephen always told her, that she was no more significant than a fish swimming upstream in a school of millions.

Then she thought of all the children, the ones with no food, no homes, no parents to care for them. Children who were dying from horrid illnesses like little Margie Roberts, suffering and in pain. From the shadows of the room she could see their soulful eyes reaching out to her, pleading with her. And from the center of her soul she could hear their frail voices crying. Faces from the news filtered into her mind—children slaughtered in senseless acts of violence. How could an intelligent, rational person sit by and do nothing while the world sank deeper and deeper into despair?

She wasn't crazy, she concluded. It was the people who looked the other way who were crazy. With this thought in mind, Toy finally felt her body relax, and in seconds, she fell into a deep, peaceful slumber.

THREE

Francis Hillburn was tall and did not have an inch of fat on his body. He thought of himself as a star maker in the art world, a person who had led many young artists from obscurity to worldwide recognition and acclaim. In his middle forties, Hillburn dressed consistently in black. Black shirts, black pants, a narrow black silk tie. His hair had once been a light brown. Several years ago, he had bleached it almost white. He wore wire-rimmed glasses and in his left ear was a one-carat diamond stud.

A few years before, Hillburn had discovered Raymond Gonzales at the art institute in Dallas where he was a student, promptly insisting that the young man relocate to New York so he could supervise his work, polish his manners, and perfect his technique. But things had not developed as Hillburn had planned, and he was now standing in the loft he owned in TriBeCa, issuing Raymond an ultimatum. "I never said you could live here indefinitely," the agent told him, his eyes scanning the canvases lined up along the walls. "Our agreement was that you could live here until your first show. Tell me, how can I put on a show when all I have are fifteen canvases that are virtually identical?"

Raymond was staring off into space and did not reply.

"Okay," Hillburn said with a sour expression. For two years he had tolerated Raymond's dark moods and extended silences. He had no idea what was wrong with the man, but if he didn't come around soon, Hillburn had decided to wash his hands of him. "Are you deaf perhaps?" he said loudly. "I've been meaning to ask you that for some time."

Again there was no response.

"I'll give you three days," Hillburn said flatly. "If you do not produce something different, or at least start a piece with a new subject, you'll have to find your own studio. I have another artist coming over from France."

Raymond wasn't thinking of where he would go or how he would survive if Hillburn forced him to move out of the loft. The darkly handsome young man with the haunting eyes was staring at the floor thinking of the woman, her bright red hair, her blazing green eyes. He could see her soft, saintlike face as she lay stretched out on her stomach on the floor of the Sunday school classroom, her head braced in one hand, a green crayon in the other. Exactly what had happened that day, Raymond didn't know. All he knew was he had to find her. She had completely taken over his mind. Her image was in every one of his paintings now. No matter what he intended to paint when he began, he always ended up painting her face, her hair, her eyes. His obsession with this woman, this one monumental event in his life, was stifling his creativity, endangering his career.

He saw a flash of black as Hillburn brushed by him, and was assaulted by the strong scent of his cologne.

"So, Raymond," Hillburn said, "have you come up with a new name? If you paint just one new piece for me, I'll organize the show for next month, but I still think you need to come up with another name. Raymond Gonzales is too ethnic, too generic. It just doesn't have the right connotation to it. You need something exotic, a little mysterious, something that gives nothing away."

"Black," Raymond said, just wanting the man to leave him alone, allow him to return to the solitude of his thoughts.

"Not bad," Hillburn said, twirling the backing on his studded earring, causing the diamond to move around in circles. Seeing Raymond's eyes dart to the sparkling stone, Hillburn quickly stopped fiddling with it. He knew his people. Raymond loved things that reflected light. He also liked things that turned. And Hillburn had seen him crawl deep inside himself, completely mesmerized by a simple object, unable to speak or work for weeks on end. "Okay," he said, snapping Raymond out of it. "But it has to be two names. You can't just call yourself Black."

"Stone," Raymond said, gazing at the earring. "Stone Black."

"Hmmmm," Hillburn said, his large, fleshy lips pursed. "Stone Black, huh? I like that. I like the sound of that. It almost sounds American Indian or something. It's mysterious, strong, exciting."

"I have to go to work now," Raymond said softly.

"Of course, *Stone*," Hillburn said, smiling with satisfaction. This was much better. Their little talk had worked wonders. Already Raymond was eager to get to work on a new piece, and he could certainly sell Stone Black more easily than he could sell Raymond Gonzales. "From this day forward, you're Stone Black. That's how you sign your new painting." He stared at Raymond for a few more minutes and then headed for the door. "Call me when it's ready," he tossed out. "Three days, remember?"

As soon as Hillburn had left, Raymond grabbed his coat and raced down the stairs to the street. It wasn't a bad name, he thought, even though he didn't know what his name had to do with people purchasing his artwork. Symbolically, however, it made sense. To Raymond, he had been trapped inside a black stone, unable to get out. The stone had been made of glass. He had become a part of the glass. But he hadn't been able to reach through to the outside. The world he had lived in before the woman had appeared had not contained humans, only colors and designs.

He glanced at his watch and panicked, picking up his pace. It was already three-thirty, and he had to be at work by four o'clock. Under his overcoat Raymond was wearing his work clothes, black pants and a white shirt, and he had secured his long, straight hair in a tight ponytail in order to comply with the health codes. He didn't mind working as a busboy, although he would have preferred to be able to paint full time. No one bothered him, and a busboy wasn't expected to interact with the customers.

A few minutes later, he reached West Street and saw the sign reading Delphi Fine Foods. Quickly stepping through the doorway, he headed to the back of the restaurant. Hanging up his coat, he punched his time card and tied on his apron.

"What's your name?" a dark-haired girl asked him just as he was about to walk out into the main section of the restaurant and check the tables.

"Oh," he said self-consciously, "I'm just a busboy. That woman over there is a waitress. Maybe she can help you."

"Oh, really?" she said, giving him a big smile. "Well, I'm a waitress, too." She pointed at her uniform, wondering why the handsome young man hadn't noticed it. "This is my first day here." She stopped and stuck out her hand to shake. "Sarah Mendleson," she said. "And you're—"

Words seemed to be coming at him like bricks, and his head started throbbing with a splitting headache. What was she saying? Why couldn't he understand her? Sometimes his illness was maddening. There were days when he had no trouble understanding what people said, days when everything seemed to work perfectly. And then there were other days—days when he felt so alienated and bewildered that he wanted to die. "I . . . I . . ." he stammered, unable to find the words inside his mind. He would walk away, he told himself. It was the only thing to do when he got this way.

Then a whiff of her distinctive scent reached his nostrils. She smelled like chocolate and lemons, something incredibly light and delicious. He slowly raised his eyes, looking not at her body specifically but the space around it. Green. Raymond loved people whose auras were green. That color denoted charity, freshness, goodness. When he'd seen the woman in the Sunday school class that day, he had seen her in clouds of green light. But this girl was not his mystery woman, even if she did resemble her somewhat. Long, silky black hair cascaded down her back. Her lips were painted bright red, the focal point in her face, but her eyes were unadorned with makeup, as was the rest of her face. An unusual look, he noted. For shoes she was wearing black, lace-up boots with rubber soles, not exactly the standard shoes for a waitress.

He smiled again, his eyes bypassing her pronounced lips and finding her eyes, shocked that they were green, too. Green. Emerald green, vibrating green. He knew those eyes. He knew that green. It might not be worth the effort to try to communicate with most people, but Raymond suddenly had a burning desire to communicate with the girl in front of him.

Under his intent stare Sarah Mendleson brushed her dark hair behind one ear, and was taken aback when she saw Raymond mimic her gesture. To make certain she wasn't imagining it, she rubbed her palms together and watched as he duplicated her movements again. Even though she found him attractive, Sarah knew now that there was something wrong. "Why are you doing that?" she asked abruptly. When he just stared at her blankly, she added, "You know, copying my gestures?"

"I don't know," he said in a high-pitched voice that was not his own, but the closest imitation he could manufacture of her voice.

"Can you speak, tell me your name?"

"Raymond," he said in the same feminine voice, and then shook his head in confusion. "No, it's Stone." He sighed and dropped his head in embarrassment. "I'm sorry."

"Hey," she said, patting his arm and smiling, "don't worry about it. I like Raymond, though. If you don't mind, I'll call you Raymond.

Stone is weird, if you ask me. Sounds like you're a pet rock or something."

Before he could say anything else, she walked away to wait on some customers. His heart fell. For the first time, he had found someone that really appealed to him, and he had been unable to communicate with her.

Then he decided that it was useless anyway. How could he explain it to her? How could he tell her that sometimes he had to borrow gestures and voices simply to speak? Regardless of what the professionals thought, he knew most autistics did possess language abilities. But their language was unintelligible to normal people, consisting of whistles, chirps, grunts, and various unformed sounds. When people spoke, these were the sounds Raymond heard instead of words. Like a person in a foreign country, he had trained himself to translate the alien words and strange sounds of normal conversation to his own personal vocabulary. But many times he could accomplish this only by pretending to be the person who was speaking, copying his or her voice and body language.

Raymond stared at the pretty brunette with longing. Something told him that she was different than all the others. He'd had many girls before, and had learned to enjoy sex and the physical pleasure it gave him. But he found it impossible to connect emotionally, and although Francis wanted him to find another subject, he simply could not paint these girls. They were too one-dimensional, their faces too worn, their odors too repulsive, their voices grating and shrill. Even though most of them were young, they were void of life, old before their time. Their hair glowed with an artificial luster. Their eyes were flat, the colors dense. Those that managed to linger past one night invariably developed an irrational jealousy of the subject he constantly painted.

"Who is this woman?" they'd ask repeatedly. "She's your girl-friend, isn't she? Why can't you paint me? Why do you always have to paint her?"

It didn't take long before they were gone. In most instances, he was glad to see them go. It was hard to have them in his world: their demands, their mere closeness annoyed him and made it impossible for him to work. Lately he had elected to spend his time alone, but the longer he remained isolated, the more he thought about his mystery woman.

What he recalled was vague and obviously distorted over the years. He made every attempt to keep the memory pure, but knew that was impossible. It was hard to separate what he had felt and experienced from what had been told to him by his mother, Deacon Miller, and old Mrs. Robinson. His mother's last letter informed him that his Sunday school teacher had died. Deacon Miller had died many years ago. The only people left to remember that day were Raymond and his family.

But something had happened. And bits and pieces of that miraculous event were firmly planted in the young artist's mind.

"It was like a silvery thread entering my world," he told his mother repeatedly, forcing her to listen to the story every time they were together. "My world was a solitary world of glass. The thread broke through the glass somehow. I saw it snaking around me and tried to grab it. Like thread through the eye of the needle, the thread touched and entered my body. It was painless. At first I was frightened. You know, when I first saw it in there with me—inside the glass with me. When it left, it took a part of me with it. Like an explosion, I was suddenly outside the glass. Noises were magnified many times over, and the colors, odors and sensations overwhelmed me. That's when I saw her face and everything changed."

In the two years he had been in New York he had spent most of his meager earnings trying to find the redheaded woman, strapping himself so severely that he sometimes didn't eat for days at a time.

The ring was the only solid piece of evidence that she'd even existed. It wasn't that unusual a ring: a one-carat ruby and twenty small, individually set diamonds. But the private investigator he had hired had finally traced it to Weisman's Jewelers, an enormous jewelry chain originating in Israel. The news he had brought back, however, had not been good. They had made over a hundred of the exact rings and had sold them in outlets all over the world. There was no way to identify the owner.

"Why can't they trace the ruby, find out who cut it?" Raymond had pleaded. "Every jewel cutter has a distinctive style."

"True," the investigator had said, "but all Weisman's jewelers cut the same. They're all trained by the same people. I mean, we're talking about a one-carat stone, not the Hope diamond. You're never going to track down this broad. Let it go, guy. Go on with your life. There's plenty of fish in the sea, if you know what I mean."

Raymond saw that one table had finished their salads and rushed over to remove the plates, his thoughts still fixed on the woman and the ring. Everyone told him to forget it, forget the woman, forget the whole thing.

He could not. He had been drowning and she had saved him. She was a mystical, magical creature. All around him he saw violence and despair, sirens screaming all night, the television news so bloody and horrible that he'd picked up a lamp the other day and smashed his screen. She was the key, and Raymond knew he had to find her. If she existed, there was hope for them all, hope for the future.

She would know all the answers.

Just then he smelled the enchanting odor emanating from Sarah Mendleson's body as she brushed past him, carrying a heavy tray. "Table three needs bussing," she said quickly, a line of moisture appearing on her forehead.

"I want to paint you," Raymond blurted out without thinking.

"Oh, you do, huh?" she said sarcastically, thinking he was into some type of kinky activity like body painting. "You gonna paint me all over? Is that it? What color?"

Raymond felt a wonderful feeling fluttering in the pit of his stomach, the nervousness of earlier gone now. He could communicate with her, see through her to the part that mattered. He was certain he could paint her. The more he stared at her, the more he saw how much she resembled the woman. "Green," he said foolishly.

Sarah held her heavy tray over her head with ease, resting her free hand on her hip as she reappraised Raymond Gonzales. She should have known, she told herself. He wasn't retarded or insane, he was just another goofy artist. She'd worked with them before in menial jobs, along with dozens of aspiring actors. It was just as she always told her friends—working in a restaurant wasn't such a bad place to meet men. Raymond was incredibly handsome. For all she knew, he might actually be talented. "You're an artist, aren't you?"

"Yes," Raymond said. "Will you pose for me?"

"I might," she said, winking at him. "But first I think you better bus that table."

Even without her husband in the bed, Toy had slept soundly. She was used to him not being there; all the calls in the middle of the night to rush to the hospital. Waking around six, she retrieved her purse from the floor and pulled out a small black book. It was an Episcopal prayer book that she purchased one day when she'd walked through the cathedral to look at the stained-glass windows. Now every morning when she awoke, she would read a few prayers, but only after Stephen had left for the day. Like her father, Stephen was an agnostic. Toy, however, was curious, drawn. She couldn't go through her entire life believing in nothing. Just touching the book gave her a feeling of comfort, even though she was uncertain what she actually believed. Her recent acquisition of the prayer book was probably one of the reasons she had mentioned her childhood fantasy of becoming a nun to Sylvia.

After reading a few prayers, Toy put the book back in her purse, and went to the guest bathroom to shower and wash her hair.

Instead of getting into the shower, however, Toy just stood there studying her reflection in the mirror. Through the looking glass, she thought, believing at that moment that if she looked long enough, she could see through the mirror, see what was on the other side. Something had happened to her in the past three or four years, and it was threatening her marriage, her very existence. She had always been so happy, so contented, so at peace with herself. While many of her high school and later college friends had lapsed into periods of depression over grades, boyfriends, stress over their future, Toy had not been one of them. She'd always been focused, steady. Other than the stream of childhood accidents and the one instance when she was seriously ill, she had never been sick for more than a few days at a time, and never with anything more serious than a cold, a virus, a mild case of the flu.

She thought of her fears. She didn't fear much. She didn't fear death as most people did. Her experience in the hospital had eliminated that fear completely. As she'd tried to tell Margie, death must be the last mystery, the greatest of all adventures. When her heart had stopped beating and she was technically dead, she had felt no pain, no terror. She thought of Margie Roberts and wished that she shared her experience. The next time she saw her, she decided, she would tell her all about it.

Poverty didn't terrify her as it did her husband. She knew his need to be affluent and respected in the community was his driving force. If he didn't feel important, if someone criticized his work, even something minor like the woman who had complained that Stephen had left an unsightly scar, he would fly into a rage. If not, he would sulk around the house for weeks and make Toy's life miserable.

For Toy, money was insignificant. She didn't care where she lived, what she wore, what kind of car she drove. As long as she had a roof over her head and food on the table, she was satisfied and happy.

If she feared anything, she decided, it would be to wake up one morning and realize her life was almost finished and she had taken more than her share.

Toy liked to think her passing on earth would leave it in as good a condition as the day she was born. She religiously conserved water. She drove a car that consumed very little gas, and when the temperature soared to a hundred degrees, Toy still refused to turn on the air conditioner and waste electricity. Even when she went to the grocery store, she carried her own cloth shopping bags, and she wore the same clothes several times before washing them.

But even with her earnest efforts to protect the environment and the many sacrifices she made for her students, Toy sometimes felt insignificant. The one thing she had always yearned for had been denied—a child. Would anyone remember her after she had died? Would she leave even the smallest legacy behind to make her time on earth worthwhile?

She stepped into the shower, running the water only a few seconds and then turning it off while she lathered her hair. Then she turned it on again and quickly rinsed the shampoo out, telling herself that the only real traumatic experience she had ever had was the one she was experiencing right now. And except for the problems with Stephen, she felt good, felt like she always felt: happy, safe, glad to be alive. Did she really need therapy as her husband suggested, as even Sylvia had implied last night?

Stepping out of the shower, Toy dried herself off and then wrapped her wet hair in the towel, deciding to call Stephen as soon as she got dressed. Seeing the California Angels T-shirt and her jeans folded neatly in the chair, she realized she had nothing else to wear to school. She could never wear Sylvia's clothes.

Besides, she decided, Stephen had to be worried about her and that wasn't right. Checking the clock, she saw it was almost seven. Sylvia's alarm clock was ringing in the next room, and Toy didn't want her to talk her out of calling. By now Stephen should be out of surgery and back at his office, preparing to see patients.

"Can he talk?" she asked the receptionist. "It's me, Toy."

"He's seeing an early patient," the woman answered, "but I can ring him anyway."

Normally Toy would have declined such an offer. She didn't like to interrupt her husband at his work. Most of what she had to say was trivial and could wait. "Get him, please, Karen," she said. "I'll hold."

A few moments later, the woman's voice came back on the line. "I . . . I don't know what to say. He doesn't want to talk to you. Maybe his procedure this morning went bad, and you should call back later.

You know how he is. Sometimes he gets in these funks when things don't go right."

"I don't think so," Toy replied, sighing deeply. He was being obstinate, trying to punish her for walking out last night, trying to reassert his control. "Look, Karen," she said, "I hate to get you involved, but I have to ask you to deliver a message for me. Tell Stephen I'm going away for a few days, that I love him and I'll miss him, but I think we both need some time apart." She paused and caught her breath. It was embarrassing to expose their personal problems to outsiders, but her husband had left her no choice. "Will you do that for me? I'd really appreciate it. We're having some problems right now, as you may have guessed."

"Sure," the woman said. "Are you all right, Toy? Is there anything I can do?"

"No," Toy answered, "I'm fine, but thanks anyway."

Once she had hung up, she sat perfectly still on the edge of the bed, mourning what appeared to be the demise of her marriage. She'd have to go to the house during the noon break and get some of her things.

Just then Simon padded into the room and leaped onto her lap. She picked the heavy cat up in her arms and held him in front of her face. "What I need is a big, fuzzy guy like you," she said, nuzzling her face against the cat's fur. "You wouldn't care how much money I spent, would you, Simon?"

Sylvia's bulky form filled the doorway. Her hair was disheveled, her eyes puffy from lack of sleep, and her mouth open in a wide yawn. "Don't kid yourself," she told Toy a few moments later. "Simon here is no different than any other male. He'd want you to give all your money to the SPCA."

"Well, Simon," Toy cooed to the cat, "I can handle the SPCA." Then she turned to Sylvia and smiled. "As long as he doesn't want a Mercedes, he's my kind of guy."

"Did I hear you talking to Stephen?"

Toy shook her head, placing the cat in the center of the unmade bed. "He wouldn't talk to me, but I left a message with his receptionist that I'm going away."

"Praise the Lord," Sylvia said dramatically. "I was certain you were going to run straight back to him and leave me high and dry. I want you to go to New York with me. We can have a really good time." She fell silent and stared at Toy intently. "If you go back now,

he'll never let you live your own life. Now's the time to assert yourself, Toy, show him you mean business."

Toy simply nodded. She was going to assert herself all right, she
decided. She was going to assert herself right out of her marriage,
end up in an ugly divorce. She knew her husband. He would fight her
for every stick of furniture, every last dime they possessed. While
Sylvia headed to the kitchen to put on a pot of coffee, Toy brushed
her tangled hair in the dresser mirror, her eyes going to the design
on the navy blue T-shirt. California Angels, she thought, seeing the
big *A* with the halo emblazoned on the front of the shirt. Too bad it
was only a baseball team, she thought sadly. Right now she could use
a few angels.

Then she grimaced at her reflection, dropping the brush on the
bureau. Facing an impending divorce was a reality, and thinking of
angels and magical creatures was only fantasy. Toy knew there were
no angels. If they existed, they would have never allowed things to
get this bad.

All night long Raymond had remained awake staring at the ceiling, walking to the window and sitting on the window ledge, smoking,
thinking. At four he had started painting, splashing paint on a huge
blank canvas, then tossing it aside and starting over with a charcoal
pencil. He sketched the face, the first face ever that was not the face
in his dreams, the mysterious redheaded woman. Once the sun
streaked through the windows of the loft, bathing it in a golden, hazy
glow, he found the piece of paper Sarah Mendleson had given him
the night before with her phone number on it.

"May I speak to Sarah, please?" he said when a woman answered.

"Hold on, I think she's still asleep."

A few minutes later, a voice, still groggy, picked up the phone.
"Hello, this is Sarah."

"Raymond Gonzales," he said. "Was that your mother?"

"Oh," she said, laughing, her excitement at his calling noticeable
in her voice. "No, that was one of my roommates."

"You said last night that you'd pose for me. I'd like to see you."

"Really? When?"

"Now."

"Now?"

"Now. Can you come to my loft?"

"I . . . I don't know. Where is it?"

"In TriBeCa," he said.

"I don't know," she said, slightly nervous. She didn't really know this man. Although intriguing, he was strange and dark, and his calling her this early in the morning frightened her. When anyone was too eager, it struck a chord of alarm. "Maybe I better not," she said. "Why don't we get to know each other a little better first?"

"Take a taxi. I'll pay."

"Really?"

"Really."

The line was silent while she thought. Finally she made her decision. A person had only one lifetime, and good-looking single men were hard to find. "Okay. Wait while I get a pencil and write down the address."

When she rang the buzzer later, Raymond raced down the stairs and paid the cabdriver. Then they waited for the elevator. He didn't want her to smell the urine and filth in the stairwell, make her hike up the four flights of stairs to his loft. Normally he avoided elevators, though. He didn't like to be that close to people. "Where do you live?"

"Queens," she said softly, somewhat nervous. "I rent a house with three other girls. That way we can afford the rent."

"This is it."

The elevator door opened directly into his loft. "It's wonderful," she said, walking straight into the center of the room and turning around in circles. Canvases lined the walls, some covered with vibrant images, some blank and expectant. She stepped up close to one and studied it. His style was different than anything she had ever seen. Although from a distance the woman in the painting appeared three-dimensional and lifelike, up close Sarah could see that she was constructed out of zillions of tiny dots of paint, all of them different colors, similar to a mosaic. If she stared at it long enough, she could see the colors swirling and moving on the canvas as if they were mysteriously infused with life. It reminded her of her biology class, studying cellular structure under a microscope.

She was so fascinated, she tilted her head and tried to determine what exactly he was trying to accomplish. Realizing she was too close, she stepped back and saw that the woman looked as if she had wings. But the woman was like no angel Sarah had ever seen, and when studied carefully, she decided he had not intended to paint wings. The painstakingly blended dots of colors seemed to be depicting light, as if the woman was glowing from within.

Stepping to the other side of the room, Sarah then saw a huge board suspended by chains from the ceiling. At first she thought it was a piece of electronic equipment, that the small circles of brilliant colors that covered it were lighted dials. On closer inspection, however, she saw that it was actually an enormous pallet. What he had done, she assumed, was carefully blend various colors in every possible shade. On the floor next to the pallet were tubes of primary colors, but on the pallet were the most exotic hues imaginable.

Then she saw the canvas on the easel, the one he had started working on that morning. The clunky black boots from the day before were gone, and on her feet were black ballet slippers. She stepped closer and closer in tiny baby steps, as if bracing herself for what she was about to see.

For a long time she just stared at the canvas. All that was on it was the outline of a face, some other broad strokes where he thought the movement would be, his initial concept. "Who is she? Is this your model?"

"Yes," Raymond said, compelled to step up behind her, allowing his hands to do as they wished. They wished to find her waist, touch the fabric of her dress, feel the heat emanating from her body. "She's you, Sarah. Or at least she will be when I'm finished. Now she's just a ghost, a shadow. Soon she'll be real."

Sarah put her hand over her mouth and leaned back against him, fully aware of what she was doing, aware that she was now touching him, his breath on her neck, his strong scent of paint, turpentine, and perspiration intoxicating and heady. She sucked it in, her heart racing. He was painting her. Most of the men she dated were arrogant animals, leaving her with nothing but unpleasant memories. This man, as different as he might be, was going to preserve her likeness for eternity.

"I'm so flattered," she said. "I never dreamed . . ."

Sarah was wearing a yellow-and-green-print blouse and black pants. Raymond was certain he could smell the printed flowers. Green. Yellow. Grass and squash. A mossy pond and a yellow field of sunflowers, van Gogh's sunflowers. His now, he thought. "Don't leave me," he said.

She had the eyes of his angel. She had brought all the smells and colors with her, swirling around her head like a halo. "She was an angel. You look like her. Maybe you're an angel, too."

"Not quite," she said, looking away, thinking his statement was rather strange. People had called her a lot of things before, but no one had ever called her an angel. "Do you have any champagne? Wine? Beer?"

Although it was only ten o'clock in the morning, he didn't comment. To Raymond, days and nights were the same except for the light. He needed the light to paint. "I don't have champagne," he said, "but I have a bottle of wine." He crossed the floor to the refrigerator, brushing by her and carrying her scent now on his skin, in his clothes, along the shafts of his hair. All her odors had blended into one, and he instantly knew her. He knew just how her underarm would smell, the dark, moist place between her legs, the nape of her neck, the small of her back, the inside of her thigh. Green. She would smell green.

Finding two glasses on the floor, he filled them both with wine and reached a long arm over to hand her a glass. Then he stood perfectly still and silent, watching as she drank, the bubbles and moisture beading up on her lips. They weren't ruby red today but russet brown. "Why only your lips?" he asked.

"What?" she said.

"Why paint only your lips?"

"Oh," she said. "Why not? I like my eyes the way they are."

"I like your eyes, too," Raymond said. "They're lovely."

"Really?" she said, a pink tongue sliding across her bottom lip, retrieving the dots of moisture and bringing them back inside her mouth.

"Don't you like your lips?"

"Not as much." She held her glass out, both arms extended.

He was several feet away, braced against the back wall. He leaned forward and filled the glass, immediately returning to his previous position. He was studying her, enthralled by her.

"Why not?"

"I don't know. Hey, that's enough questions. Tell me about yourself. How long have you been an artist?"

"All my life. How long have you been beautiful?"

She smiled a coy smile. "All my life."

He didn't feel his feet moving or see her moving toward him. They simply met in space and he placed his forehead against her forehead. "May I touch you?"

"Is that a little like asking me to dance?"

"Could be."

His arms encircled her waist and he pulled her close, burrowing his nose in her hair. It was dark, heavy, moist, slick. It reminded him of his mother's hair, but hers was wood brown while Sarah's was almost blue-black. "Is your father Oriental?" he asked, never having seen hair like hers on a Caucasian.

"He's from Argentina. My mother's family is English."

"My parents are from Mexico."

"Latin," she said, a little smacking noise coming from her mouth. "We're both Latin. That could be trouble, you know?"

The talking had worn him out. He didn't want to hear her voice anymore or his own, or any sounds whatsoever but the ones generated by the colors swirling around her. Pushing her away, he turned to the canvas and picked up his brush. She didn't move. When he stared at her, narrowing his eyes, then dabbing his brush in the paint on his suspended pallet, Sarah tossed her head back and struck an alluring pose.

Time passed, no sounds inside the loft except the traffic outside, the loud voices of people passing beneath them, the ticking of his alarm clock. One hour turned to two hours and then three hours. She moved. Her leg was cramping, she said. He set his brush down and stared at the canvas, knowing instantly that it was wonderful, had the potential to be his finest piece. The figure he had painted was ethereal, gorgeous, the slender young body, the small, perfectly shaped breasts, barely visible through her lightweight yellow-and-green blouse.

"What are you going to call it?" she asked, her voice echoing in the large room.

"I . . . I don't know," he stammered, suddenly agitated and annoyed, the spell broken by the sound of her voice. His face twisting in a grimace, he moved his brush to the palette and swiped it back and forth across the canvas again and again in jerky, violent movements, covering the image he had so carefully created with slashes of black paint. He couldn't paint this woman. She wasn't his angel. She was just like all the others, a smelly, abrasive, loud-mouthed human being. What purpose would it possibly serve to immortalize her? There were millions of others just like her.

"Why'd you do that?" Sarah said tensely, abandoning her pose and walking over closer to the canvas. "Now it's ruined. It was so pretty and I stood for so long." She turned around and faced him, waving her arms in the air. "Why? Tell me why?"

"Leave me alone," Raymond snarled at her, mimicking her arm movements and speaking in a falsetto voice in order to express himself. "It was my creation, not yours. If I want to destroy it, I'll destroy it."

"What's wrong with you?" she said, bewildered. "Why do you copy me like that? You sound so silly. And why are you so moody?" She started walking toward him and then stopped, seeing the dark look in his eyes. "I mean, I know about artistic temperaments, but don't you think you're carrying it too far?"

"Go home, Sarah Mendleson," Raymond said, the look in his eyes flat and unemotional. "There's nothing here for you. The place I'm in is not a place you can ever go."

Tossing his brush to the floor, he threw himself face first onto the bed, overwhelmed with despair and anguish.

"You're crazy," Sarah exploded. "You're not an artist, you're a lunatic."

Raymond did not move or speak. He had crawled deep inside himself, where he felt safe and protected, where existing required no effort, where communicating wasn't necessary. In no time he was reliving that day in the Sunday school class, calling for the beautiful creature who had touched his life to come to him, help him, show him the way again. For weeks now he had felt himself falling into the black hole inside his mind. The glass prison beckoned and he was powerless to resist. It was too hard dealing with his illness, trying to become a part of a world that he couldn't understand, a world that seemed to accommodate every evil that existed, but could not accommodate a person like himself.

Sarah stood and stared at him on the bed, shaking her head in confusion. Several times she glanced at the canvas, trying to see the remnants of her image, but with the black paint it was distorted and depressing. This strange young man had brought her to life and then erased her, obliterated her. He was too unpredictable, too frightening. Looking at the painting again, it was as if he wanted to destroy her, not just the image in the painting. In the slashes of black paint Sarah saw enormous anger and bitterness. She had made a mistake. She should have never come here. But at least it wasn't a mistake she couldn't rectify.

Anxiously she grabbed her purse and left, leaving him to wrestle with his demons alone.

FOUR

———————

Toy didn't go to her house to pick up her things at lunch as she had planned. Learning that the flight to New York didn't leave until seven o'clock that evening, she waited until school was out, thinking she would stop off at her parents as well. She had to tell them she was going away, or her mother would call the house and become concerned.

Tom and Ethel Myers had an unassuming home in San Juan Capistrano, a small, quaint city only a short drive from Sylvia's house in Mission Viejo. But the town was quite different from the row houses and the gleaming modern shopping malls of Mission Viejo. The little town was like something out of the past. The towering spires of the Spanish mission stood alone in the clear blue sky, a beacon to the famous swallows who returned every year, drawing thousands of tourists in buses, cars, pouring out of the coaches at the Amtrak train depot located right across the street from the historical landmark. There were no skyscrapers, and what businesses lined the main thoroughfare had either a Spanish or western flavor, primarily making their livelihood from the sale of incidentals and souvenirs relating to the mission. Hand-painted signs hung in the windows, offering Free Swallow Stories as an inducement to get people to step inside.

Everyone knew the Myers house. In many ways their house was as famous to the locals as the mission was to the tourists. Their house abutted the railroad tracks, and their yard was quite peculiar. Toy always wondered about the passengers on the speeding train and how it appeared to them, thinking it might resemble a backyard amusement park or a day-care center for young children. The yard was terribly cluttered and many people thought it was tacky, with the wishing well, the fake bridge over a nonexistent stream, the life-size stone statues of angels, the wooden forts and hand-carved family of mallards, the fifty-two different birdhouses, all painted in different colors, dangling from the limbs of trees like lanterns.

Pulling into the driveway and parking the car, Toy realized she had forgotten all about the stone angels. It was funny, she thought. Sometimes you looked at something so long, you forgot it was there. When she was a child, the neighborhood kids had all teased her, saying she lived in a cemetery. Some of the kids swore her parents were junk dealers. They were right about the angels, she thought, getting out and slamming the door on the Volkswagen. When they had put in a new housing tract on the other side of the freeway where the old cemetery used to be, her father had rented a truck and salvaged some of the discarded stone monuments. Like Toy, he didn't like to see things go to waste, even things he had no immediate use for.

No wonder she had decided to dress up like a nun, she decided, laughing with relief. With the mission only a block away and the stone angels watching her every move, it was easy to see how she had developed this kind of fetish.

She didn't go to the front door because she spotted her mother in the yard, bent over as she pulled weeds from around the base of one of the stone monuments. "Mom," she yelled, opening the gate and entering the yard. "You're going to break your back doing that. Why don't you use the weed eater I bought you?"

"Oh," she said, standing and removing her gardening gloves, her face beaming, "I enjoy gardening. It's relaxing. I hate that noisy weed thing." She paused and then continued, studying her daughter's face. "How are you, baby? This is a pleasant surprise. We didn't expect to see you until next week."

Toy looked into her mother's tired eyes, so like her own, and stepped into her arms. In her late sixties, she was still slender and attractive, but her hair was now snow white and her face deeply lined. "I'm fine, Mom," she said. "Where's Dad?"

"Where else?" her mother shrugged, squinting in the sunlight. "In his workshop. Since he retired, he's been going at it like a madman. He insists he can sell the things he's making, but I'm not so certain."

"It doesn't really matter, does it?" Toy said. "As long as he enjoys it." Ever since she could remember, her father had spent all his free time woodworking, carving children's forts and birdhouses, most of them now scattered in various locations throughout the yard. His latest project was to set himself up as a custom toymaker, and he spent hour upon hour in his little workshop in the garage, carving miniature trains, cars, trucks, and other items children could play with, then painstakingly painting each one. This Christmas, he said, he was going to put up a sign out front and sell them. This was how he planned to supplement his retirement income.

While her mother went into the house to make a fresh pitcher of lemonade, Toy went to speak to her father. At first she just stood there, watching as he worked over a square piece of wood, shaving it carefully with his knife. Although he was no older than her mother, he had worked hard all his life, most of it outdoors in the sun delivering the mail each day, and it had taken its toll. His skin was leathery and tough, with numerous scars where he had developed cancerous lesions and had them removed. But his hair was still dark, with only a spattering of gray throughout, and he was as strong and fit as many men half his age.

"What's it going to be?" Toy asked softly.

"A toy soldier," he answered without looking up.

"Are you going to come inside and have some lemonade with us?" she asked tentatively.

"Maybe a little later," he said.

Toy knew what he meant. It was her father's way of saying no, that his work took precedence over visiting with his daughter. She knew he loved her, but he was a quiet, reflective man, far happier in his workshop than in his home. He had never been one for small talk or gestures of affection. Toy sometimes thought it was all the years he had worked alone, walking down each street with his mailbag slung over his shoulder, whistling and singing to himself.

"I'm going away for a few days," she said. "I just came by to let you know."

For a long time he continued whittling away with his back turned, curled pieces of wood falling to the floor like potato peelings. Finally he said in a low voice, "That's nice. Is Stephen going with you?"

How did he know? Toy wanted to turn around and run back to her car. As little as they had communicated throughout the years, her father always knew when she was in trouble. In his odd way, she assumed he could sense it. Once when she had been in elementary school, she had swallowed what she thought were Red Hots, her favorite childhood candy, after seeing one of them abandoned on her friend's plate. As soon as she had swallowed it, she became desperately ill and rushed to the water fountain, reddish foam spewing from her mouth and dribbling all over her clothes. As it turned out, little Toy had swallowed another child's worm medication, and had been humiliated in front of the entire lunchroom. But when she had walked out of the school at the end of the day, still nauseous and stinging from the ridicule and taunting of the students, her father had been waiting in front of the school in his mail van. Never before had he shirked his duties to come to her school. Somehow he had just known.

"No," Toy said, deciding that now was not the time to tell him about the problems in her marriage. Her parents were so proud, so proud that she had married a doctor. If she and Stephen did get divorced, Toy knew they would be devastated. "Stephen can't get away, Dad. I'm going with Sylvia. It's only five days, anyway. We're going to New York. I've never been to New York."

"Big city," he said, this time turning to look in her eyes. "You better be careful, Toy. There's a lot of bad people in a city like that. Why don't you wait and go with your husband?"

Toy frowned. "I might be waiting forever, Dad. You know how Stephen feels about leaving his practice." Then she forced a smile, seeing the concern on his face. "Whether you realize it or not, I'm perfectly able to take care of myself. I'm not exactly a kid anymore, you know."

"I know," he said slowly, but Toy could see he was still troubled. "How are you feeling? Have you had yourself checked recently?"

"I feel fine," Toy said emphatically. "Besides, I'm married to a doctor, Dad. I go for a physical every year. I don't even have to pay for it."

He turned his attention back to the piece of wood. Toy felt a strong urge to walk over and throw her arms around him, tell him that she loved him. Tell him that he was a good father, as good a father as he could possibly be. But she could not. Too many years of distance stood between them, creating a chasm that was too wide for her to cross. She stood there for a few more minutes watching him, and then walked off to visit with her mother.

The five-hour flight from LAX was tiring. Toy and Sylvia then had to lug their suitcases from the baggage claim area and wait in line for a taxi.

Dressed in a lime green pantsuit, the jacket tucked in at the waist and then flaring at the hips, Toy had never looked more beautiful. Her red hair was shiny and clean, curl upon curl popping and bouncing around her head. Her eyes were clear and expectant, and other than feeling somewhat bedraggled, she was in great spirits. It wasn't really so bad being away from Stephen. She had managed to survive one whole night and a complete day, even travel across the country without him, and she was still alive. No one had used her, robbed her, or conned her out of her last dime as Stephen would surely be predicting.

"I can't believe there's a line for cabs this late," Toy said, short of breath and panting, looking at the six people in front of them. "How far is the hotel from here?"

"Well," Sylvia said, "we're in Newark and the hotel is in Manhattan. If there's not too much traffic, we should be there in less than an hour." Then a concerned expression appeared on her face. "Are you having trouble breathing, Toy? You look really pale."

"Oh, no," Toy said quickly, brushing her hair off her face and smiling, "I feel terrific. I'm just not used to carrying things. Guess I need to exercise more often."

They finally reached the front of the line and hopped in the taxi, Sylvia telling him to take them to the Gotham City Hotel on Central Park South, near Sixth Avenue. "This is a great hotel," she told Toy enthusiastically. "Wait until you see it. It's right across the street from Central Park, in the same block as the Plaza. I got us a special weekend rate, but Monday and Tuesday are going to cost more money."

Toy was concerned about her finances. She had her credit card but very little cash. She would have to give Sylvia a check for her share of the hotel, and pray there was money left in the bank to cover it. But Sylvia claimed she didn't mind. She'd already paid for Toy's ticket. As long as she got the money back eventually, she'd told her, it would be okay. Her budget was tight, but a loan of a few weeks she could handle.

While Sylvia bantered back and forth with the cabdriver, Toy stared out the window, mesmerized by all the cabs and the towering buildings as they made their way into the city. A few times she felt so exhausted she leaned her head against the window and tried to sleep, but everything was too loud and noisy, and the cab was jerking and bouncing as the driver darted in and out of traffic. Cars honked at one another, sirens squealed, people yelled profanities and shot other drivers the finger out their window. Toy had expected Manhattan to be similar to Los Angeles and was shocked at how different in atmosphere the two cities were. Even though it was big, noisy, and dirty, Manhattan was pulsing with energy and vitality, while Los Angeles had always seemed to be sleeping in a drugged-out haze of perpetual confusion.

"What time is it here?" Toy asked.

Sylvia glanced at her watch. "I'm still on California time, but it's three hours later, so it's almost two."

Toy's mouth fell open. "Two o'clock? It's really two o'clock in the morning? There's so many people out milling around."

"The city that never sleeps," Sylvia said, turning to smile at her friend. "That's one of the things I miss about living here. You know what? You can get a corned beef sandwich any time you want. Are you hungry? We can go to Wolfe's Deli. It's right down from the hotel."

Toy just looked at her. She couldn't imagine digesting a corned beef sandwich in the middle of the night. "I'm pretty tired," she said. "But I'll go along if you want me to."

Sylvia sighed, glancing down at her heavy thighs. "No," she said. "Corned beef is probably the last thing I need."

A few minutes later, they pulled up to the hotel and let the bellman take the bags. Sylvia went to the counter to register. "I requested a big room, view of the park, and two queen-size beds." She leaned over the counter while the desk clerk completed the paperwork.

"We don't have anything left with two beds," he said. "All we have is a king."

"What do you mean?" Sylvia snapped. "I specifically told my travel agent that we needed two beds."

"I'm sorry," he said politely, "but we're sold out tonight. There's a convention in town."

Sylvia stepped away and conferred with Toy. There really wasn't much to confer about. At this time of night Sylvia didn't think it was wise to go out shopping for another hotel. Both women feeling the strain of the long day, they headed up in the elevator with the bellman to the twenty-ninth floor.

The room was nothing like Sylvia had expected. When the bellman unlocked the door and placed the luggage inside, she immediately ripped into him. "This room doesn't overlook the park. What is this anyway? The worst room in the hotel? God," she said, peering into the tiny bathroom, "this is the pits. I could have stayed at my brother's house in Brooklyn if I wanted a crappy room like this."

"Sylvia," Toy said, pulling her into the bathroom. "He's only the bellman. He doesn't own the hotel. Let the poor man go."

Her friend was still agitated. "You don't understand about this city, Toy," she said, placing her hands on her hips. "If they think you don't know the ropes, they'll rip you off in a minute. Well, they're not ripping me off. I'm no country bumpkin. I grew up in this lousy place."

"Let's just get some sleep," Toy said calmly. "Then we'll deal with it tomorrow."

Sylvia reluctantly handed the porter a tip, and the man quickly scurried off. Then she pulled down the bedcovers, wondering how they could both sleep in the same bed. "Hope I don't roll over on you and squash you like a pancake," she told Toy. "If you know what's good for you, you'll cling to the corner all night."

"No problem," Toy said, laughing. "You're the one who should worry. Stephen says I talk in my sleep."

"Oh, really?" Sylvia said, arching her eyebrows. "You can talk all you want, just make sure it's something juicy."

They took turns in the bathroom, and in no time, they were both in bed, the covers pulled up to their chins. Sylvia was wearing a long cotton nightgown with a picture of a cat on the front, and Toy was sleeping in her California Angels T-shirt and a pair of black stretch pants, having forgotten to pack her night clothes in her haste to get her things and get out of the house before Stephen came home.

Toy turned off the lamp on the nightstand and left the bathroom light burning.

"Whatever you do," Sylvia told her wearily, "don't wake me up in the morning. I'm so tired I feel like I could sleep for three days. This is the plan—we sleep in until about eleven or so. Then we'll be adjusted to the time difference."

Curling up in her corner of the big bed, Toy felt an aching loneliness, wanting to have Stephen next to her. But her head sank into the soft pillow, and she quickly fell into a deep, exhausted sleep.

She was walking in a tall field of grass, so high that it reached past her ankles and grazed her knees. Behind her was a group of young children. She was taking them somewhere, leading the way as she did when she took her class on a field trip.

"Hurry," Toy said, going to the back of the line and urging the children to move faster. Thick clouds of black smoke filled the air and the heat was intense; only a few feet behind them was a blazing inferno. Sparks popped and flew through the air, one landing on the ground right next to Toy's feet and igniting the dry grass instantly. She screamed at the children to run faster; they were coughing and choking from the smoke.

Just then a small boy stumbled and fell. Like a wicked burning snake, the fire raced through the grass and started burning all around him. He was trapped inside a circle of fire. Trapped and screaming, crying for his mother.

Toy looked quickly at the children in front of her and then back at the boy. As she raced in his direction, a fiery finger reached up and his shirt erupted in flames. His wail of terror shifted into a horrifying scream of agony; the smell of burning flesh filled the air. Toy lunged, willing her body to pass through the flames, moving as fast as she possibly could, not pausing for even a second. She reached him and swooped him up in her arms, racing back through the wall of fire, trying to shield him with her upper body. Once outside the circle of burning grass, Toy threw herself on top of the boy, felt the searing heat of his body against her own flesh, absorbing his pain as her own.

Behind her the fire was still raging, moving in their direction fast, while the blazing fields of grass lit up the sky with an eerie, unnatural yellow glow. The child's eyes were open, but he wasn't moving, wasn't crying out. Swooping him back up in her arms, Toy started running with him, the flames nipping at her feet. She was coughing and her eyes were tearing from the smoke. She could hardly see anything now other than the tiny spots of blackness in the distance, the children's backs.

"You're going to be all right," she said to the boy as she ran, panting and out of breath. "Everything's going to be fine."

"I want my mommy."

It was a pathetic plea, a thin little voice reaching through the chaos. Up ahead Toy saw fire trucks and ambulances, a crowd of people gathered in a tight group, watching, waiting. She headed for the row of ambulances. A dark figure in a heavy coat met her and accepted the injured child from her arms. "Is this your boy?" he said.

"No," Toy said.

"Are you all right?"

"Yes," Toy said. "You have to find his mother. Maybe she's in the crowd."

"What's his name?"

"I don't know."

Toy was jogging next to the fireman now, the child in his arms. Panting, the man looked down at the boy. "What's your name, fellow?"

"Jason . . . Jason Cummings."

The fireman began yelling. First he yelled for assistance from the paramedics. One rushed over with a large steel case, and another ran behind him with a gurney. In what seemed like seconds they had an oxygen mask over the boy's face and were trying to assess the damage. "His vital signs are good. I don't want to pull away that sweater yet. Let them do that at the burn unit."

Toy bent over the child, sandwiched in between the emergency workers. "Jason, everything's fine now. They went to get your mommy and you're safe."

For a moment his tortured eyes met hers and his lips moved inside the mask. Toy had to lean even closer to be able to hear him. "I'm scared. I hurt really bad. I hurt so bad I can't cry."

His forehead was black and sooty. Toy kissed it lightly, her lips cool against his skin. "Have you ever heard the story about the little engine trying to pull the toys over the mountain?" Toy waited but the boy didn't answer. "I think I can. I think I can. I think I can. Then the little engine says, I know I can, I know I can, I know I can."

She saw recognition in his eyes. It was a popular story; they even made children's records of it, little multicolored forty-five's. Toy had played it over and over as a child. "Jason, you're that little engine. Keep saying that over and over to yourself. I know I can. I know I can. I know I can. Tell your body to heal itself, take away the pain. Tell yourself that you can do it."

"We have to take him now, miss," the paramedic said, ready to lift the gurney.

"You can do it, Jason," Toy said firmly. "I know I can. I know I can. Come on, Jason. Say it."

As they carried him off, the child's lips were moving inside the mask. "I know I can. I know I can. I know I can." He jerked his eyes to the side, desperately trying to find the woman who had saved him, but she was no longer there.

FIVE

At ten o'clock the next morning, Toy started mumbling under her breath, "Run. Hurry. Don't stop."

Sylvia groaned and opened her eyes, glancing over at Toy to see if she was awake. Deciding she had only been talking in her sleep, Sylvia quietly slipped out of bed and paid a visit to the bathroom. When she returned, though, Toy was on her back and her arms were extended at her sides, making it impossible for Sylvia to share the bed with her. She didn't want to wake her, so there was nothing else to do in the small room except continue to rest until her friend woke up, and to do that, she had to get her to move.

First, she picked up one of Toy's arms and draped it over her chest. Realizing she still didn't have enough room, she decided to roll her over on her side. Toy was so still, she thought, her body was almost rigid. Instead of ending up on her side when Sylvia pushed her, Toy's body rolled all the way over onto her face.

Sylvia slipped into the bed and waited, thinking Toy would adjust her position and make herself comfortable. When Toy continued to remain in the same position, her face buried in the pillow, her arms limp and still at her sides, Sylvia became concerned. She'd watched her sleep when they were in college, and if her memory served her correctly, Toy was a restless sleeper.

Something was wrong.

"Toy," she whispered.

There was no answer.

Sylvia poked her gently in the ribs, hoping she could get her to turn over without waking her, but Toy still did not react. She couldn't let her remain that way. She could suffocate. "Toy," she said, her voice louder now. "Wake up. You have to turn over."

Still there was nothing.

Sylvia sat up in the bed and shook her by the shoulder. When she still didn't get a response, she began to panic, and grabbed her arm to check her pulse.

"Oh, God," she screamed, certain there was no pulse. Quickly she pushed Toy over on her back and placed her head against her chest. Nothing. Then she turned her face sideways and tried to feel Toy's breath on her cheek. She felt nothing. Grabbing the phone on the nightstand, she hit the number for the operator and yelled into the receiver, "Call an ambulance. Fast. My friend isn't breathing. I think her heart stopped."

Sylvia took a deep breath and tried to remember how to administer CPR, tried to keep herself calm and focused. "Hold on, honey," she said, her voice shaking, perspiration now pouring down her face. "Please, God, don't let her die. Let me do it right. I can't mess up now."

She ran her finger up Toy's midsection until she located her sternum, then placed one palm on top of the other and began the compressions. Once the first set was completed, she sealed her lips around Toy's mouth and began ventilating. She tried not to think of what was happening, tried only to remember what she had been taught. This was not her best friend, she told herself. If she thought that way, she couldn't do what had to be done.

Sylvia didn't know how much time had passed before she heard heavy footsteps pounding in the hall outside the room. She moved her mouth to Toy's again and suddenly realized that Toy was breathing on her own. Lowering her head again to her chest, she heard the thump, thump, thumping of her heart.

"Thank you, God," she said, and then started jabbering prayers in Hebrew.

Just then the door opened and two paramedics rushed in, carrying a large steel box with their equipment, the hotel manager remaining in the hall as they entered. One of the men was tall and dark, the other smaller and fairer, his blond hair shaggy and long enough to cover his ears. "Her heart's beating now," Sylvia said excitedly. "I gave her CPR."

They rushed to Toy on the bed, and the dark-haired man pulled up her T-shirt and placed a stethoscope there, listening carefully. "Her pulse is weak but steady," he said. "Are you sure she was in cardiac arrest?"

"I think so," Sylvia said, suddenly unsure. "I listened and didn't hear anything, and I'm almost positive she wasn't breathing." She stopped and thought a moment and then added, "She was short of breath earlier in the evening when we were carrying our bags at the airport."

The blonde with the long hair was already ripping open a package, preparing to start Toy on an intravenous drip. As soon as he handed the needle to his partner to insert into Toy's vein, he used his portable radio and contacted the hospital, filling them in on what they had. Once both men were working on Toy, Sylvia stepped to the back of the room and wrapped her arms around her chest.

"Does she have any medical problems?" one of the men asked.

"I don't think so," Sylvia said. Then she recalled what Toy had told her about her illness in her senior year. "She had a virus once around her heart, but that was almost ten years ago."

The paramedic jotted the information down on his clipboard. He then unfolded the gurney, and they both lifted Toy onto it. As they did, one of her arms fell off the side, and Sylvia saw that the inside of her hand was red and inflamed.

"Her hand," she yelled out. "Look at her hand."

They stopped, one lifting Toy's hand carefully and examining it. "Looks like a burn," the dark-haired man said. "Do you know what happened?"

"No," Sylvia said, shaking her head and compressing her lips in dismay. "She didn't even leave the room. How could she get burned like that? This is bizarre. It just doesn't make sense." She started frantically searching the room, jerking the drawers open, then sticking her head in the bathroom. "There's not even a book of matches in here. It's a non-smoking room."

"Your guess is as good as mine," the man said, nodding at his partner and both of them straining as they hoisted the gurney again.

Sylvia became hysterical as they carried Toy out of the room. Seeing her friend so pale and still, she was fearful she would never see her again. "Where are you taking her?" she said, her eyes filling with tears.

"Roosevelt," the man answered, the gurney clearing the door. "Amsterdam and Fifty-ninth."

"I'll be there," Sylvia said, hurrying to get dressed.

Toy opened her eyes to blazing white light and the distinctive odors of disinfectant, quickly realizing she was in a hospital, the dream still fresh in her mind.

"So, you're awake," the pretty blond nurse said, peering down at her. "I'll go get the doctor."

"Where am I?" Toy asked, weak and confused as to why she was here, trying to make sense of the dream.

"You're in intensive care at Roosevelt Hospital," the nurse told her. "But I think the doctor is going to move you to a regular room in the cardiac care wing now that you're stable."

Before Toy could say anything else, the woman left and a few minutes later, a tall, distinguished-looking man with dark skin and intelligent eyes entered the room, dressed neatly in an expensive brown suit.

"I'm Dr. Esteban," he said with a slight accent, stepping to the edge of the bed. "How are you feeling?"

"Fine," Toy replied tentatively. "Why am I here?"

"You suffered a cardiac incident and were brought in by ambulance. I'm a cardiologist, on staff here. The hospital called me in to take a look at you."

"I was with someone," Toy said, unable to concentrate on what the man was saying. She saw there was an IV in her arm hooked up to a bottle by the bed, and she felt something sticky and annoying attached to her chest. Then she jerked her head to the side and saw the monitor. She was hooked up to an EKG machine and could hear it beeping. "A woman, my friend. Where is she?"

"If you're referring to Ms. Goldstein," Dr. Esteban said, "I believe she's still in the waiting room."

"Oh," Toy said, closing her eyes, wanting desperately to return to the dream so she could see the boy again and make certain he was all right. Like all of her dreams, this one seemed so real, so vivid. She inhaled deeply and was certain she could still smell the smoke on her body.

"Can you tell us how you got those burns on your hands?" the doctor asked.

Suddenly Toy felt a thickness to her left hand and lifted it, seeing that it was bandaged. Her other palm was smarting with pain as well, but there was no bandage, only raised blisters. Just like the ring, Toy thought. She had brought something back from the dream. She was elated. "Did my heart stop?" she asked the doctor, her green eyes flashing. "Didn't you say something about a cardiac incident?"

"We're not completely certain, but Ms. Goldstein claimed you went into cardiac arrest in the hotel room. She administered CPR, and more than likely saved your life." He paused a moment and then continued, "I've ordered a number of tests. Once they're completed, you'll be transferred to a regular room. We felt it was better to keep you in intensive care until we were certain your condition had stabilized."

"I don't want any tests," Toy said fiercely. "I'm fine now. I want to leave."

Dr. Esteban scowled at her. "That's foolish. This is a serious situation, Mrs. Johnson. Surely you realize that. Your friend related that you once suffered an attack of pericarditis. That attack more than likely damaged your heart, and that's why you suffered this incident today. We've notified your husband, who I understand is a physician, and he's en route here right now from California."

Stephen, Toy thought, angry that they had called him without her consent. The fact that she had landed in a hospital her first day in New York would only prove his point—that his wife was a weak, naive woman who could not take care of herself. "I don't want to see my husband," Toy told the doctor, trying to sit up. "I'm getting out of here."

The doctor gently pushed her back down in the bed. "Please, Mrs. Johnson. You're upsetting yourself and making things difficult for no reason. I simply cannot release you until we arrive at the proper diagnosis, and see if this recent attack has caused any more damage to your heart."

Toy turned her head away, realizing it was useless to argue. The man was a doctor, no different from Stephen. He couldn't understand the joy the dream had brought her. He would mar what Toy secretly felt was a miraculous event, try to fit it into the narrow and restrictive realm of science.

After a long time, Toy turned back to look at the doctor. "Can my friend come in?" she said.

"Only for a moment," he answered. "They'll be coming soon to take you for the tests. Once I review the results, I'll come back to talk to you."

The doctor left the room, and a few minutes later, Sylvia stepped in. She looked horrid. Her hair was disheveled and standing straight up on her head, while her eyes were bloodshot and filled with concern. She rushed to Toy's side and kissed her forehead. "Thank goodness you're okay," she gushed emotionally. "You gave me a terrible scare this morning. Boy, what a way to start a vacation, huh?"

Toy smiled at her. "I'm fine," she said. Then her eyes filled with gratitude. "The doctor said you saved my life, gave me CPR."

Sylvia's chest swelled with pride. In the few times she had been in a crisis situation, she'd always panicked and done the wrong thing. About six months back, one of her students had severely cut his hand on a jagged piece of aluminum he was using for a science project, and Sylvia had tried to make a tourniquet to stop the bleeding. Unfortunately, she was so hysterical that she'd tied the cord too tightly around his arm and it had sliced through his skin. She'd felt awful, and had sworn she would never try her hand at first aid again.

"I can't believe I remembered to do it right," she told Toy a few moments later. "I mean, it's been at least six years since I took that CPR course, and I never went in for the refresher."

"You're a hero," Toy said, never looking more radiant than she did at that moment. Her eyes were the deepest of green, like priceless glowing emeralds. Her lovely hair was fanned out around her face on the pillow, and her skin was as clear and translucent as the finest silk.

Sylvia's face flushed with pleasure. She had finally met a crisis straight-on and not turned into a bumbling idiot. A few seconds later, though, her expression shifted back to one of concern. "How did you get those burns on your hands? Did you leave the room or something during the night? It's the weirdest thing, Toy. I didn't hear you leave the room during the night, and I'm generally a light sleeper. I'm certain you were in the bed with me."

"Something happened," Toy said, quickly ripping the needle out of her arm and flinching as it smarted.

"Stop that," Sylvia said, wide-eyed with alarm. "You can't take that off. They're giving you medicine, Toy. Now I'll have to go get the nurse and have them put it back in."

Toy sat up and pulled up her hospital gown, bending her head to pluck the suction cups off her chest. "Get my clothes. We're going back to the hotel before Stephen gets here."

Sylvia was standing there with her mouth open, gaping. "I'm going to get the nurse," she said sternly. "You can't just get up and walk away like nothing happened. Damn it, Toy, you almost died."

"I did die," Toy said, a sly smile playing at the corners of her lips. "If my heart stopped beating, I was technically dead. Isn't that right? When your heart doesn't beat, you're dead."

Sylvia threw her hands out to the side. "So, you were technically dead. What difference does that make? It certainly doesn't mean you should get up and walk out of here."

Toy shook her head. "You don't understand, Sylvia. I can't explain it right now, but I'll tell you everything that happened later." Then she stared deep into her friend's eyes, seeing how upset she was becoming. "As soon as we get out of here, okay? I promise."

Sylvia planted her feet and crossed her arms over her chest in defiance. "Tell me now," she demanded. "I'm not letting you leave, Toy. If Stephen comes and finds out I let you check yourself out of the hospital, he'll be furious with me."

"Then you shouldn't have called him," Toy said, stepping onto the cold floor in her bare feet. "Quick, get me my clothes."

Sylvia refused to budge. "Get back in the bed, Toy."

Toy ignored her and found her clothes in a plastic sack attached to the foot of the bed. In seconds she was dressed. All she needed were her shoes. "Where's my shoes?" she said.

Sylvia shrugged, her concern turning to annoyance at the way her friend was acting. Toy had always been so complaisent, so easy to reason with. She had no idea why she was acting this way. "You didn't just walk in here, Toy," she said sarcastically, "you were carried in on a stretcher." Then she pursed her lips and spat out, "Unconscious, remember?"

Toy was dressed now in the baseball T-shirt and her black pants, ready to leave, shoes or no shoes. "Are you going or staying?" she asked Sylvia, walking toward the door.

"Where are you going?" Sylvia said. "Back to the hotel, I hope. Please, Toy, swear you're only going back to the hotel."

"Yeah, sure," Toy said, "where else would I go? Why? Aren't you going with me?"

Sylvia glanced at her watch and saw it was late afternoon already. When she had called Stephen from the hotel, he'd told her he was taking the next flight out of Los Angeles and would come straight to the hospital from the airport. Toy had been unconscious for several hours, and then they had made Sylvia wait outside until the cardiologist had arrived and had a chance to examine her. "Stephen will be here pretty soon," she told Toy. "Maybe I should wait here until he comes. Otherwise, the man will go ballistic when he walks in here and finds out you're gone."

"Suit yourself," Toy said, shrugging her shoulders. She started to leave and then paused in the doorway. "I really appreciate what you did for me, Sylvia. I . . . I just can't stay here. Please try to understand."

"I'm trying," Sylvia said, flopping down on the hospital bed, then leaning forward over her knees with her head in her hands.

* * *

People's heads turned as the woman in the California Angels T-shirt with the flaming red hair rushed past them in her bare feet in the hospital lobby. Toy was oblivious of their stares, lost in her thoughts.

The dreams had finally come back, and she knew her prayers had been answered. Perhaps the dreams had stopped because of Stephen, she told herself, just like she had thought. He was a hardened cynic, distrustful of anything he couldn't pigeonhole into a neat little category or examine under a microscope. Toy felt her hands smarting and instead of reacting to the pain, she felt an intense, overwhelming pleasure. Let him try to explain this one, she thought, stepping out into the damp, chilly air.

She looked up at the sky. It was overcast and dismal, and the scent of rain filled the air. Wrapping her arms tightly around her chest to stay warm, she took off down the street, trying to keep her head down and watch for broken glass on the sidewalk. Hordes of people pushed past her on the street, most of them dressed in raincoats and carrying umbrellas, all of them seemingly in a desperate hurry. Toy had no idea where she was, but she knew she couldn't keep walking or she would surely step on something and cut her feet.

All around her were the sights and sounds of the city. Instead of being overwhelmed with disgust, however, Toy could smell the delightful odor of chestnuts roasting on the corner, of hot dogs turning on the spits. Even the steam rising from the subways didn't seem offensive. Toy glanced at it and thought of mist floating over a peaceful pond at dawn.

After walking a few more blocks and gawking at the buildings, Toy reached an intersection and saw a big yellow neon sign that read, Wolfe's. The name rang a bell and it wasn't much longer before she realized that Sylvia had mentioned the restaurant in the taxi the night before, indicating that it was only a short distance from their hotel. She stopped and looked in the window. In preparation for Halloween, the windows were decorated festively with huge orange pumpkins, red peppers, and arrangements made out of ears of corn. Toy's mouth was parched, and she was cold and wet. A slight drizzle had started to fall.

As the rain started coming down harder, Toy decided to go inside the restaurant and see if she could warm herself with a hot cup of coffee. Then she would ask for directions to the hotel.

Embarrassed that she was barefoot, she waited until a large group of businessmen entered and slipped in behind them, following closely as they headed to the rear section of the restaurant and ducking into the first open booth.

Stephen Johnson opened his eyes when the taxi pulled up in front of Roosevelt Hospital. His day had begun at three o'clock in Los Angeles when he'd been called out to perform an emergency appendectomy, and he'd just returned to the house to catch a few hours of sleep when Sylvia had called with the news about Toy.

Exhausted and irritable, he was beside himself with worry. And there was the guilt. He should have never refused to talk to Toy, let her run off to another city with that goofy Sylvia Goldstein. Although she had been Toy's friend for years, he'd never cared for Sylvia. For one thing, the woman was a slob, at least twenty or thirty pounds overweight, and he detested people who didn't take care of their bodies. She also had that nasal Brooklyn accent that he found annoying and distasteful, and she was always influencing Toy to do the wrong thing.

Handing some bills to the cabdriver, he got out of the taxi and decided that once he was certain his wife was receiving proper care, he was going to have a nice, firm chat with her best buddy, set her straight once and for all. He chastised himself for not doing it years ago. If he had, Toy might not have gotten herself in this mess.

Even now he couldn't figure it out, couldn't come up with a valid medical reason why his twenty-nine-year-old wife who appeared in every way to be in perfect health could have gone into cardiac arrest. He knew about her attack of pericarditis, but when they had been trying to have a child, Toy had undergone dozens of tests, including a full cardiac screening. Absolutely nothing was found to be amiss. In fact, none of the tests showed anything to be clinically wrong with her.

Checking in with the admitting office, he learned what floor Toy was on and headed to the elevators.

"I'm Dr. Johnson," he told the nurse at the nurses' station. "I'm here to see my wife, Toy Johnson."

The woman looked her name up on a list. "Room 746. It's to the right."

Stephen was mystified that Toy was not in intensive care, but he had to assume they had moved her to the regular medical wing because they thought she was in no immediate danger. That was a good sign. Finding the room, he opened the door and stepped inside. The bed was made and Toy was gone. They must have taken her down for more tests, he thought, taking a seat in the chair and picking up the phone to check in with his office.

"No, no, no," he yelled into the phone to his secretary, yanking off his tie and tossing it on the bed. "I don't want Henrik to handle that case. He's a pompous creep. The last person he sliced open died. Get Bill Grant to sub for me."

Hanging up the phone, he decided that Toy had picked the worst possible week to become ill and disrupt his schedule. He was completely booked every day. Most of the procedures were not elective, they were mandatory. Stephen had terminated his partnership last year. Now all he had to rely on was goodwill and friends to take over for him while he was away. Most of his friends in the profession had back-to-back surgical procedures scheduled every day just as he did. It wasn't going to be easy to get them to take over his cases. If Toy could travel, he decided, he would take her back on the plane this evening. He couldn't see any reason for her to remain in New York if her condition was stable.

After waiting a few minutes longer for her to return, he walked back to the nurses' station. "Excuse me," he said to the same nurse, now poring over a chart, "but my wife must be having tests now. Do you know when they're bringing her back or where her treating physician is? I'd like to speak to him."

"Oh," she said, "Dr. Esteban left several hours ago. And your wife—" She was flipping through Toy's chart. "I don't see anything scheduled for this morning. Dr. Esteban had penciled in an MRI and some other tests, but he cancelled them before he left the hospital."

"She's not in her room," Stephen said abruptly.

"You're certain. Did you go to the right room? Room 746?"

"Certainly," he said. "I can read numbers, you know."

She didn't react to his sarcasm. She worked with doctors all day. She was used to it. "Check again. Maybe she went for a walk."

Stephen glared at her and then shuffled off back down the hall. Still Toy was not in the room. When he walked up to the counter a few minutes later, he was hopping mad. "Look," he said, slapping the Formica counter with his palms, "she's not in her room. She's not walking in the hall. How could you lose my wife, you idiots? You must have moved her and no one made a note of it. Call the switchboard operator. Maybe they know what room she's in."

The woman hurriedly picked up the phone and called the hospital's main switchboard. A second later, she looked up at the handsome young doctor. "That's her room. Check again."

"Get Esteban down here. I want to speak with him. And try paging her. If she wandered off to another part of the hospital, she'll hear the page."

"No problem, Dr. Johnson," the woman said crisply.

Stephen was already headed back to the room. The page went out over the intercom. Surely that would work, he thought. After waiting another ten minutes, he was so exhausted that he climbed in his wife's hospital bed and promptly went to sleep.

"Dr. Johnson?" a male voice said. "Excuse me, but are you Dr. Stephen Johnson?"

Stephen bolted upright in the bed, rubbing his eyes. For a few moments, he didn't know where he was. "Who are you?"

"Ricardo Esteban. I'm one of the staff cardiologists."

"Where's my wife?"

"I don't know."

"What do you mean, you don't know? I was told my wife went into cardiac arrest. I took the first available flight out of Los Angeles. Now you're telling me you've misplaced her. Am I crazy? Is this a bad dream?"

"I'm sorry," Esteban said. "She was here, but we have no idea where she went. In my opinion, she walked out of the hospital and went back to her hotel room. The nurse said once her friend went in to see her, the monitors went crazy and she just disappeared."

Stephen's face flushed with contempt. "You're talking about Sylvia Goldstein, I presume. I should have known. That woman is a walking disaster."

"Well," Esteban said slowly, "according to the ICU nurses, Ms. Goldstein remained here at the hospital for some time after your wife left. Maybe she was waiting for you to arrive and then decided to return to the hotel as well."

"What hotel?" Stephen said, getting up and grabbing his jacket and tie from the chair.

"I have no idea," the doctor answered. "Why don't you check with the admitting office? Surely they have that information. As I understand it, your wife was in the hotel room when she went into cardiac arrest. This woman, Ms. Goldstein, administered CPR or your wife might be dead right now."

Stephen felt the first flutters of panic. This wasn't hysterical Sylvia telling him that his wife had been on the brink of death, this was a fellow physician. "What did you see on the EKG?" Stephen said frantically. "Did you do any other tests? What were the results?"

"Calm down," Dr. Esteban said, touching him lightly on the shoulder. "I'm sure she'll be fine. She was very adamant about wanting to leave, not undergoing the tests, so we haven't been able to complete them. With her history of pericarditis, however, the only way to proceed would be to admit her and submit her to a full battery of tests. I'd also like to hook her up to a portable cardiac monitor when she's released, so we can see what's going on over an extended period." He stopped. "Have you checked with the lobby? Maybe she left the name of her hotel at the front desk."

"This whole thing is insanity, you know?" Stephen said, pacing back and forth while Esteban checked with the lobby. Esteban slowly shook his head and quietly replaced the phone.

"What am I going to do? My practice is going to hell, and my wife is running around with some lunatic woman in this disgusting city when she should be in the hospital undergoing treatment."

"As I said before, your wife will surface. You're welcome to wait here in her room in case she returns, just in case the admitting office doesn't have the name of the hotel."

"Why did she go into cardiac arrest?" Stephen barked at the other physician. "What's wrong with her?"

"I have no idea. It's quite strange, really. Once they brought her in and we hooked her up to the EKG, there was no indication of tachycardia or anything along those lines, no irregularities at all. The only thing I can tell you right now is she spontaneously arrested. Could she have been using some type of drug that you weren't aware of? Possibly cocaine or some other stimulant? That's one of the tests I wanted to do this morning. I wanted to do a chemical screen."

"That's ridiculous," Stephen said, his face so pale he looked like he should be a patient. "My wife is dead-set against drugs. Even in college she never used drugs. Believe me, she wasn't on drugs."

Esteban shook his head. "I'm sorry. I don't know what to tell you."

Stephen stared at the other man's eyes a few more moments, then rushed out of the room to find his wife.

"Would you like to order now?" a male waiter said, eyeing Toy suspiciously. She was sitting in a red vinyl booth in the back of the diner staring straight in front of her, a glassy look in her eyes.

"Ah . . . I'm sorry," she said. "What did you say?"

"This is a restaurant, lady, not a shelter. You order or you leave."

"I'll take a cup of coffee."

"Humph," he said, wiping his big hands on the white apron wrapped around his waist. After clearing a few plates at the next table, he headed toward the counter and started whispering to the cashier. "Came in here about an hour ago. No shoes. Dressed real funny, almost like a bag lady."

The cashier had bright orange hair, obviously dyed to cover the gray, and was in her late fifties, perched on a tall bar stool behind the counter. "Want me to call the cops?" she asked, smacking a large wad of gum, craning her neck around so she could see the back booth. "No shoes, huh? Looks like a derelict to me."

"Should we wait to see if she has any cash? I didn't see a pocket-book."

"Get her outta here. Customers don't like to eat with these bums sitting next to them, smelling the place up. She ain't got no money." Street people were always wandering in, ordering food and then when the bill came, trying to sneak out without paying.

Toy heard dishes clattering and people talking, but she had no trouble shutting it all out. Images from the dream kept returning, and she was confused as to which memory was reality and which was the dream. Dr. Esteban, the hospital, and the night before seemed unreal, distant, vague, but the boy and the children in the field were as real as the table where her hands now rested. The waiter walked up, a scowl on his face, and slapped the coffee mug on the table. Right next to it was a check.

"Want me to take care of that for ya?" he said, standing with his hands on his hips.

"Oh," she said, patting the seat beside her, feeling like a complete moron. Of course, she didn't have her purse or any money. What had she been thinking? "No, thank you," she said politely. "I'll pay when I leave."

Grasping the coffee mug with both hands, she instantly released it and moaned in pain. Her hands felt like they were on fire. She'd have to wait for the coffee cup to cool before picking it up again.

"Hey, lady," a friendly male voice with a pronounced Brooklyn accent said about five minutes later. "I'm sorry, but you gotta come with me now."

Toy turned her head and saw a police officer standing there, his hat tipped back on his head. He was probably no taller than five eight or five nine, she decided, and his hair was dark and thick. Over his lip was a small, neatly trimmed mustache. Without it, Toy realized, he would have what her mother always referred to as a baby face. Although he was tan, his skin was smooth and soft in appearance. His eyes were the brightest of blue and completely mesmerizing.

"What did I do, Officer?" Toy said softly.

"Proprietors here complained about ya," he said. "No reason to make a scene, you know." He reached out and pulled Toy by the arm, trying to get her out of the booth.

"Please, wait," she pleaded as other diners turned to stare at her. "I'm not dressed appropriately, I know. I was in a hospital and that's why I don't have any shoes. I didn't realize I didn't have my purse when I came in here, but my hotel is right down the street and I can come back with the money." Toy stopped speaking and dropped her head, overwhelmed with embarrassment and frustration. Was he going to take her to jail over a simple cup of coffee? Suddenly New York didn't seem like a city bustling with vitality and humanity anymore. Toy felt a wave of negativity and contempt wash over her. It wasn't just the police officer or the nasty waiter, standing in the corner now and smirking at her. It was coming from every one of the patrons throughout the crowded restaurant. Toy realized they all thought she was a mental case. Either that or a homeless person who had wandered in off the streets.

"It's okay, lady," the officer said patiently, "just get outta the booth. I ain't gonna hurt you or nothing."

When she stood, Toy knew they would be able to see her dirty bare feet. She'd never felt so humiliated in her life. Stephen was right, she decided. He'd been right all along. It was her mind. Something was seriously wrong with her. "Could someone just tell me where the Gotham City Hotel is?" Toy asked. "You don't have to arrest me. I'll go and get the money. I promise. My hotel is only a few blocks from here. I just don't remember which direction."

The young officer leaned over close to Toy's face and whispered, "Let's get you on outta here, okay. I ain't gonna arrest you, lady. I already took care of your tab, see, but the management wants you to leave, so we got to oblige them."

Toy stood and let the officer take hold of her arm as he escorted her out of the restaurant, her head down in shame. When he passed the waiter, he tossed out, "You'se guys owe me one, Tony. Put me up a cheeseburger and fries. Be back in five."

Once they were outside the restaurant, the officer continued questioning Toy, shielding her body with his own as they talked while throngs of people moved past them on the sidewalk, everyone walking fast, few people even glancing in their direction. "What hospital were you in? Was it Bellevue?"

"I don't think so," Toy said. She felt like crying, but she didn't want him to see her that way. If one tear fell, she would erase what was left of her pride. "I'm almost positive it was Roosevelt, but I don't want to go back there. All you have to do is tell me where my hotel is."

"Okay," he said, eyeing her suspiciously, "if I get you a ride, you gotta promise me you won't wander off again." Then his face softened and he smiled warmly at her. "This ain't the safest place for a nice lady to be running around all by her lonesome. People a little different don't cut it here. Kinda know what I mean?"

"Yes," Toy said meekly, her head still down. She was looking at the sidewalk, at the concrete. With a hand still on her arm, the officer stepped a few feet away and blew in his whistle, holding his other hand in the air. Toy turned her head to see what he was doing just as a police car pulled to the curb and parked in the red zone. All around her she saw concrete, brick and steel. There were no tall fields of grass in Manhattan. No matter how real it had seemed, Toy knew she had imagined it, dreamed it, that she was losing her mind. Everything Stephen had always warned her about had happened. He always said she would get in trouble, do something awful, get hurt. Her hands were smarting and throbbing. She looked and saw the bandages on her left hand. On several of her fingers and the palm on her right hand, the skin was burned and charred, oozing and irritated. It must have been as Sylvia suggested, she decided, and she had sleepwalked out of the hotel and somehow injured herself. Maybe she had ended up in the basement of the building or something and touched the pipes for the heater by accident.

Without looking up, Toy let him lead her to the car at the curb. Then she felt his hand on her head, pushing her down into the backseat. All at once, her fear seemed to vanish. She was safe. She knew that wherever they were taking her was the place she was supposed to be. She didn't know why, but she simply felt it. It was as if she could read the young officer's mind and he was reassuring her.

The longer she looked at him, the more he reminded her of the young boy in the field.

"Drop her at Roosevelt," he said to the other officer, shutting the door to the backseat. "Take her inside, too. Don't just roll her out at the curb or she'll just walk off again, see?"

"She a mental?" the officer in the front seat said, eyeing Toy in the rearview mirror.

"Nah," the first officer said, smiling and winking at Toy in the backseat. "She's a special lady. We're buddies, her and me. Can't ya tell? What are ya, Bernie, an idiot? Woman's an angel, see. Says so right there on her shirt. Says she's a California Angel. Came to Manhattan to give us guys a hand."

"It's suppertime, Kramer," the other officer complained, not finding his friend's story very amusing. "I was just gonna clock off and get me something to eat."

"I can just walk," Toy said through the wire mesh that separated her from the front seat. "You don't have to waste your time, Officer. All you have to do is give me directions to my hotel."

The officer in the car ignored her as did the officer leaning in the window. "Hey, Bernie, take her over for me," he said. "I'll order you some supper. Whadya want anyways? Want Tony to put you up a burger?"

"No way," the officer said, running his tongue over his lips. "Get me a hot pastrami on rye, side of cole slaw, Dr. Brown's black cherry soda, and get me some new pickles, not those other pickles they put on the table."

As soon as he finished, he sped off, and Toy was slapped back against the seat on her way to Roosevelt Hospital for the second time that day. Despite her circumstances, she managed to chuckle at her predicament. She'd arrived in the city in a taxi. Next she'd ridden in an ambulance. Now she was riding in a police car. The only thing left to sample was the subway. With the kind of day she was having, she decided, she should be eligible for New Yorker of the week.

SIX

The restaurant was packed and noisy. Friday nights were one of their busiest nights, and Sarah was perspiring as she rushed back and forth to the hot kitchen and then back on the dining room floor, her arms laden with several heavy trays.

Her eyes kept turning to the door, and then to her watch. It was after five o'clock, and Raymond Gonzales had not shown up for work. The assistant manager was livid, as they relied heavily on busboys, and Sarah and the rest of the waitresses were having to bus the tables along with their other duties. That meant things were moving slower than usual, and New Yorkers wanted everything instantly. About thirty seconds after they sat down, they expected to see something on the table. Bread. Pickles. Water. Anything.

"Hey, you," a bear of a man in a brown leather jacket yelled out as Sarah rushed past him to another table, "I been here fifteen minutes already. When you'se gonna take my order? I got places to be, you know?"

"Sorry," Sarah said quickly. "Just let me deliver this order and I'll be right back. We're a little shorthanded tonight."

Raymond was going to lose his job. Sarah was certain of it. Even though he was only a busboy, jobs weren't that easy to come by, and she suspected that he had limited skills outside of his artistic abilities.

She chastised herself for leaving him as she had. She'd stomped out of his loft angry and annoyed, but her anger had quickly shifted to concern. Two years ago, her brother had committed suicide, and the entire family had been devastated. But unlike the rest of the family, Sarah had laid the blame squarely on her own shoulders. Why hadn't she seen the signs? They were so close, while her brother's relationship with their parents and other family members had been sporadic and strained. She remembered the look of hopelessness and despair she'd seen on his face the night before he hung himself, and suddenly recognized that same expression as one she had seen in Raymond's eyes earlier that day.

The next trip Sarah made to the kitchen, she pulled out a quarter and dropped it into the pay phone outside the rest rooms, having already jotted down Raymond's phone number earlier when he didn't appear for work. Quickly she dialed the number, glancing over her shoulder to make certain the assistant manager was not in sight. She let the phone ring at least ten or twelve times and then slapped the phone back in the cradle, more frightened than ever. If Raymond wasn't at work and he didn't answer the phone, he could easily be dead on the floor. Three days had passed before her brother's body was discovered in his filthy fifth-floor walk-up. Like Raymond, her brother fancied himself an artist, a poet specifically, but his dreams had fallen by the wayside and he'd slipped further and further into poverty and despair.

Sarah would never forget walking into that apartment after the funeral to remove her brother's meager possessions—the horrid stench of death. She might not have prevented him from taking his own life if he was determined to end it, like everyone had repeatedly told her, but she could have checked on him, made a simple phone call. At the very least, she could have found him immediately after he died.

Sarah pushed herself even harder to rush out the orders, to meet the demands of the customers, terrified that if she didn't do something about Raymond Gonzales, she would have once again looked the other way when someone was crying out for help. She wasn't a religious person per se, but she believed in a greater force, believed there was some pattern or grand design to the scheme of life. Possibly in a mysterious way, she told herself, she was being tested. She had failed her brother. Meeting someone like Raymond might be her chance to prove that she would not fail again.

As soon as she saw a lull in activity and a few empty booths, she approached the assistant manager.

"I'm sick," she said, inventing a pathetic expression. "I don't think I should stay for the rest of the shift."

The man went through the roof, ranting and raving at her like a madman. An enormous Greek, his hair was slick and oily and his stomach protruded over the front of his pants. "Don't look sick to me, doll. Get back on the floor. You'll be fine. Either that or go back to slinging hash at Bennie's Diner down the street."

Sarah narrowed her eyes at him. "What? You want me to barf on one of the customers?" She stepped closer to him and opened her mouth wide, holding her stomach. "I think I'm about to barf right now."

The manager jumped back several feet and glared at her. "Get the heck outta here, woman. Barf on me and you're fired. This is a brand-new shirt I got on."

Sarah immediately spun around, racing to get her purse and coat. She'd walk to Raymond's loft in TriBeCa. It shouldn't take her more than fifteen minutes.

Toy was in a hospital bed, her throbbing hands bandaged, an IV dripping into her arm. When the police officer had taken her to the emergency room, they had checked the burns and feared they were becoming infected. Since she was in pain, she decided to go along with the program this time and let them treat her. The scene in the restaurant had been enough for one day. She was no longer unhappy to be in a safe, warm place.

Just then she looked up and saw Sylvia and Stephen in the doorway.

"Jesus, Toy," Stephen said, his face twisted with concern. "Are you all right? We've both been frantic. Why did you leave the hospital to begin with?"

"I don't know," Toy said weakly, his presence in the room oppressive, particularly when she was prostrate in a hospital bed looking up at him. He seemed so big, so authoritative, the look out of his eyes so menacing. She tried to push herself to a sitting position, then realized she couldn't use her hands. She fell back on the pillow. Stephen leaned down and kissed her on the cheek.

Toy cut her eyes to Sylvia, but the woman was silent. The look on her face told Toy that Stephen had already jumped all over her, and was probably blaming her for enticing Toy to come on the trip.

Seeing them both standing there staring at her like she was someone from another planet, Toy turned to Sylvia. "Do you mind if Stephen and I have a word alone?" she said. "There's no reason to get you involved any more than you already are."

"No problem," Sylvia said, quickly leaving the room. Then she stuck her head back in and added, "I'll be right outside the door. Call me if you need me."

Toy couldn't stop herself and tears were soon streaming down her face. She was suddenly confused and miserable, whereas before she had been content and peaceful. Already they had taken her down for an MRI, and any time now, they would be coming to submit her to more tests. More needles, X rays, strange machines and chalky fluids she'd have to swallow. What were they ultimately going to tell her? That her heart was broken? That she was about to die? Noticing her husband's stern gaze, she only hoped her death would come quickly.

"It's okay," he said, his voice softening as he saw the tears on her face. Knowing she couldn't use her hands, Stephen removed a tissue from the nightstand and wiped her eyes. "Don't cry. We're going to figure this out now. I'm here. As soon as they say you're able, we'll fly home."

"There was this fire," she said, blubbering incoherently. "I was there. I was with a lot of kids in this field. One of the little boys . . ."

"What are you talking about, Toy?" Stephen said, tilting his head sideways. "Just a minute, okay? Let me check your chart."

Her husband darted down the hall, the door swinging behind him. A short time later he returned. "The burns on your hands are not that bad. Most of them are second- and third-degree. You have one first-degree burn on your left palm. They're giving you antibiotics to circumvent infection. The chart said they also gave you a shot for pain. Did it help?"

"Yes," Toy said groggily. The shot had made her feel dreamy and disconnected, but now that someone was in the room, she realized it also made her want to talk. "What's wrong with me? Why is all this happening to me?"

"I don't know," Stephen said. "Where was this field? How did you get those burns? Sylvia thought you were in the bed all night. Did you go out on the streets by yourself? If so, why?"

"I don't know where the field was," Toy said, blinking as she tried to make the dream crystallize again in her mind. "But I think it was a school that was burning. There were maybe fifteen or twenty children and no adults. A spark ignited the grass and this child's shirt caught fire. I had to reach into the fire to get him. That must be when I got burned."

"There are no fields anywhere near here," Stephen said, incredulous. "You're in Manhattan, Toy." Then he thought of something. "Were you in Central Park perhaps?"

Her eyes roamed around the room, droopy and drugged. "Maybe."

"There's no school in Central Park, not that I know of. There's the ice skating rink. There could be children there."

Toy just looked at him. She didn't know what to say, what to believe. Just then Dr. Esteban entered the room. Approaching the bed, he nodded at Stephen and proceeded to check Toy's pulse, the ice packs, the IV. Then he smiled down at her. "Did that shot ease the pain?"

"Yes," Toy said. "When can I go home? I want to go home."

"Soon," he said, glancing over at Stephen. "Perhaps we should step outside?"

Together they stepped outside the room, and Stephen fell back against the wall. Sylvia saw them from the bench where she was waiting and walked over to hear what they were saying.

"She just told me she was in a fire," Stephen told the doctor. "A fire in a field somewhere. She doesn't know where, but there were children. That's how she says she got burned."

"I know," Esteban said, his eyes on the floor. "She told me the same thing. I called the fire department, and the only fire they had this morning was in an apartment complex in the Bronx. It wasn't occupied. Do you think she somehow got all the way to the Bronx and was inside that building, maybe sleeping or something?"

"How would I know?" Stephen snapped. "This is all just insane. First her heart stops and then she suddenly turns up with burns. I have no idea what's going on." He gave Sylvia a harsh glance, as if to say, she knew but was holding back the information to spite him. He'd lost his cool with her in the hotel room, but he refused to apologize.

"I promise, Stephen," Sylvia said tensely. "I don't know any more than you do. All I know is we both went to bed, and when I woke up I heard her talking. I just thought she was talking in her sleep. She said something like, 'Hurry. Go faster.' I'm not certain of the exact words."

Dr. Esteban rubbed a long, tapered finger alongside his nose as he was thinking. "I have an idea. A lot of street people light fires in trash cans to stay warm. If your wife was in some kind of sleep state or trance state, possibly she held her hands over the flames and burned them this way. Or maybe she accidently touched a trash barrel that was hot, had been burning only a few minutes before."

Stephen thought Esteban's statement made sense. It made more sense than his wife's story about a burning school and children in a field, particularly since the fire department had no report of such an incident. But right now, figuring out how his wife had been burned wasn't as important as figuring out why she had gone into cardiac arrest. "When can I take her back to Los Angeles? I have a surgical practice, you know?" Stephen turned his head and looked at the door to the room. "At least I used to have a surgical practice."

"Not for a few days. It wouldn't be wise. The flight is over five hours. What if she suffered another cardiac incident on the plane? And she should have a full round of antibiotics for those burns."

"If you're so concerned about her heart," Stephen said to the doctor, his eyes hard and accusing, "then why isn't she hooked up to an EKG right now?"

"Look," Sylvia interjected, having had her fill of Dr. Stephen Johnson. "I'm going, okay? Toy doesn't need me now that you're here, and I'm just in your way."

"That's fine with me," Stephen said snootily, watching as Sylvia reentered Toy's room to tell her she was leaving.

Sylvia stepped up to Toy's bed and brushed her hair off her face. "Sweetie," she said softly, "I told Stephen I was going to leave, but if you want me to stay, I will."

"Where are you going?" Toy asked.

"Well, my nephew's Bar Mitzvah is tomorrow morning, so I guess I'll spend tonight in Brooklyn at my brother's house and check out of the hotel. I'll tell the hotel to lock up your suitcase and Stephen can pick it up later." She paused and then continued. "As soon as Dr. Esteban gives him the word, Stephen is going to take you back to California. From what he told me earlier, you might be able to leave by tomorrow morning."

"I ruined your trip, didn't I?" Toy said, sighing deeply. "I'm sorry, Sylvia."

"Hey," Sylvia said, giving Toy a weak smile, "don't worry about that. Just get well. We'll take another trip somewhere down the line."

"What am I going to do?" Toy asked. "You know, about Stephen? I don't know if I want to go back with him to California."

Sylvia shook her head. "I can't get involved in this, Toy," she told her. "I mean, I certainly didn't ask you to go on this trip so I could break up your marriage."

"But it isn't just Stephen," Toy said excitedly. "Something's going on, Sylvia. I'm certain I was in a fire. I remember trying to rescue this child . . . a little boy. It has to be true. If it isn't true, how did I get these burns?"

"I wish I knew, Toy," Sylvia said, leaning down to kiss her forehead. Then she removed a piece of paper and left it on the table by the bed. "This is my brother's number in Brooklyn. Call me if you need me, okay?"

Just as Sylvia was turning to leave, Stephen stepped into the room. She walked up to him and tapped him on the chest with her finger. "You better be good to her, buddy," she said forcefully. "Whether you realize it or not, this is one special lady you married." Then she glanced over her shoulder at Toy and walked out of the room.

Sarah rang the buzzer for Raymond's loft, but there was no answer. Stepping back to the sidewalk, she peered up at the windows and the metal fire escape. His window was open and she could see the curtains moving in the breeze, but at the same time it was raining and she was frightened that she would slip and fall on the fire escape. Finally she braced herself and started climbing.

When she got to the window, she stuck her head in and yelled, "Raymond, it's me. Sarah. I'm coming in, okay?"

As Sarah's eyes adjusted to the darkness of the loft, she could see a figure on the bed. Her stomach immediately rolled over and her heart started racing. She was certain he was dead. Quickly crawling through the window, she rushed to the bed. "Raymond, are you okay? Are you sick? Did something happen?"

He was perfectly still, his eyes open but unseeing, his head turned slightly to the side. She shook his shoulder, but still he refused to speak to her or acknowledge her presence. She could see his chest rising and falling, however, and was relieved that he was all right.

Shadows danced all around her, forbidding and ugly. Outside, the afternoon shower had suddenly turned into a torrential downpour. Rain splashed against the windows just as a loud crack of thunder rang out. A few seconds later, the entire loft was illuminated with a quick flash of lightning, revealing a poignant, surreal scene: the big bed in the center of the open space, the solitary figure of a man. He was emitting soft moaning sounds while the images on the canvases poised around the room watched, all bearing identical faces. One life-size painting from years ago was propped up against the wall right behind Raymond's bed like a headboard. An angel, its enormous wings were stretched wide, and the angel's head was thrust forward away from its shoulders as if she were trying to step from the canvas to comfort the man below. The hair was a brilliant yet delicate shade of reddish gold, and the angel was dressed in a navy blue

T-shirt, with the baseball team California Angels emblazoned on the front.

"You're mad at me, I realize," Sarah said softly, taking a seat at the foot of his bed. "When you didn't come to work, I got worried. I'm sorry we ended this morning on a sour note."

The body on the bed remained in the same position. Not a muscle in his body moved. Sarah waved her hands in front of his face, but still he didn't move or speak. "Raymond," she said, "please talk to me, let me be your friend. I want to help you. I might not have acted like it this morning, but I really do."

There was nothing.

Sarah looked around the room, uncertain what she should do next. Going to the sink, she soaked a dish towel in cold water from the tap and then returned and wiped his face with it. "There," she said, pleased with herself, "doesn't that feel better?"

When he still didn't respond, she got in the bed with him and put her arms around his waist from the back, holding him tightly, hoping it would make him feel secure. Then she just remained there, as still as he, waiting for him to speak to her. No matter how long it took, she decided, she was going to wait.

At ten o'clock that night, Sarah gave up. It was pitch-dark in the loft, and Raymond had not spoken, moved, or in any way communicated with her. He almost seemed to be in a coma, and Sarah wondered if she should call an ambulance or try to take him to a doctor. Quietly getting out of the bed, she found the yellow pages in the kitchen. She was flipping through them when she saw him slowly rise from the bed and walk casually to the bathroom as if nothing whatsoever was wrong. Sarah dropped the phone book and scurried down the hall after him.

He was urinating in the toilet, his back to her.

"Are you going to talk to me now?" she said. "God, I thought you were going to do something awful to yourself. I was scared to death. Why didn't you come to work?"

Zipping up his pants, Raymond turned and walked right past her out of the bathroom, a dazed look in his eyes. Then he squatted over his knees in a far corner of the room, his hands making small circles on the wood floor.

"Well," Sarah said, stamping her feet, deciding to try a different tactic, "you're not sick and you obviously don't want to talk to me, so I'll just leave." Spinning around, she started marching to the door, thinking Raymond would stop her. He didn't. At the door she looked back at him, unable to leave.

Sarah rushed over to him, getting on her hands and knees and embracing him. "I don't know what's wrong with you," she said gently, "but I'm not going to let you down, leave you here alone. Right now I'm going to go out and get you some food. Once you eat, you'll feel much better."

Sarah left the loft to get him something to eat, with a backward glance over her shoulder. There was something about this man that touched her heart. She suddenly had a terrifying feeling, more frightening than the fact that Raymond was possibly suicidal and might end up like her brother. At twenty-four, Sarah Mendleson was drifting. The year before she had been a junior at Long Island University, but a love affair turned sour and her guilt over her brother's suicide had pulled her down and caused her to drop out. She had sunk to the very bottom, working in a cheap diner, back living with her parents, all of them squabbling and miserable. But with her new job and new living environment in Queens, Sarah had hoped that she could get herself together and return to school the following fall. Right now, however, returning to school didn't seem as important as it had a few days ago. If she was reading her feelings correctly, which she was certain she was, she knew she had just developed a problem, one that could easily derail not only her college plans but all her plans.

Sarah was falling in love.

Toy was resting and Stephen was reading the newspaper, his chair pushed up next to her hospital bed. He had already made reservations on a flight back to Los Angeles the following day. He was going to take Toy home, then they would continue the testing. Stephen would personally research his medical books, all unusual and rare diseases, possibly even contact the American Medical Association and ask for their assistance. They couldn't take the chance that Toy's heart would spontaneously arrest again, particularly in a place where there would be no one to revive her.

"I'm thirsty," Toy said, opening her eyes.

Stephen got up and poured her some ice water from a pitcher by the bed. "How do you feel? You slept good. You've been out of it for two hours now."

"I feel fine," she said, gulping the water, trying to keep it from spilling down her chin. Both of her hands were still bandaged. "I just want to use my hands. I feel so helpless."

"I know, Toy. That's why I'm here. Are you hungry? They brought your dinner tray but I sent it away. I thought it was better to let you sleep. I can go to the coffee shop and get you a sandwich if you want."

"No," Toy said, shaking her head. She had no appetite at all. She just wanted to get out of the bed and go on with her life. All she could think of was the humiliating incident in the restaurant, everyone staring at her, laughing at her like she was a beggar off the streets. If everyone could spend just one day like that, she told herself, they might be more sympathetic to the plight of the homeless.

"Want to read the paper?" Stephen said. "I can prop you up on the pillows and turn the pages for you." Then he looked up at the television. "Maybe it would be easier to watch TV." He picked up the remote control attached to her bed and flicked on the set, immediately turning it to Cable News Network, hoping he could catch some local news from Los Angeles.

Stephen stroked Toy's arm gently, his eyes on the set. Toy was staring at the screen but not paying attention. The volume was low, but the image was one of a burning building, people in a field, rescue workers bending down over a small child. Stephen turned away from the set long enough to find the remote control and raise the volume. He'd seen something that perked his interest, something he couldn't quite put his finger on.

". . . as fire ravaged this wooden schoolhouse in rural Kansas, tragically claiming the lives of three teachers, a small boy was carried to safety after his clothes caught on fire by what officials are calling an unidentified woman. Arson investigators are on the scene and indicate the fire was possibly set by a youngster playing with matches. Nineteen children escaped without serious injury. Little Jason Cummings, who suffered severe burns on his back and chest, is listed in stable condition at Methodist Hospital in Topeka. His mother . . ."

Stephen was listening and now saw Toy. She was moving around in the bed, her eyes glued on the screen, her mouth open and gaping. "What's wrong? Are you in pain?"

"Look," Toy said. "The fire. The schoolhouse. The children. The boy."

Turning back to the television, Stephen listened and watched. There was a middle-aged woman on the screen talking to a reporter.

"Mrs. Cummings, who was the woman who saved your son? Have the police discovered her identity yet?"

"No," Mrs. Cummings said, wringing her hands as she spoke, "she

was there and then she just disappeared. She saved my boy's life."
She spoke directly to the camera. "If you are out there somewhere,"
she said, a tear escaping and making its way down her ruddy cheek,
"I want to thank you. Jason is asking for you. He keeps crying for his
angel. Please contact us here at the hospital. We'd really appreciate
it."

The woman's face disappeared, and the newscaster began another
story. Stephen turned the set off and faced his wife. "Toy, this was in
Kansas. Didn't you hear what they said? It couldn't be the same fire.
You're in Manhattan. Don't you know what city you are in?"

"I was there," Toy said flatly. "You don't believe me, do you?"

"No," he said, thinking there was no reason to let these delusions
get out of hand. "And no one else will believe you. Honey, if you
keep talking like this, they're going to think you have a mental problem for sure. Just reason with yourself. I know this has been hard on
you, but saying you were in Kansas when you're in New York is
nothing but insanity." He looked down at his hands. "Dr. Esteban
has a good theory about how you got burned. He thinks you were
standing over a trash barrel where some derelicts had a fire going.
You didn't realize it and burned your hands."

Toy slowly shook her head from side to side, her lips clamped shut
like a child who had been chastised by her mother.

Stephen suddenly exploded, standing and kicking the chair against
the bed. Toy jumped and the IV bottle on the stand almost toppled
to the ground. "Stop this idiotic talk, and stop it right this minute.
Do you hear me?" His face was flushed and a vein protruded in his
neck. "If you're sick, you're sick, but I'm not going to tolerate my
wife talking like a lunatic, saying she's been places she couldn't possibly have been. Do you hear me? Snap out of it. Get control of
yourself."

Toy turned her head to the opposite wall, trying to block out his
voice, the anger, the look of contempt in his eyes.

"I'm sorry," he said, his voice strained and cracking. "You know
I'm not good at situations like this." Then he walked out of the
room, letting the door swing shut behind him.

SEVEN

Toy's eyes remained on the door long after her husband left. She kept thinking he had just stepped outside to cool down, embarrassed by his temper tantrum and the things he had said to her. But after thirty minutes of staring at the door, Toy knew he wasn't coming back, might not return at all. In fact, her husband was probably changing his airline ticket, catching the next flight back to Los Angeles.

The young intern who had swept her off her feet with his rapid-fire banter and jokes had disappeared. Even the way he made love to her had changed. He was faster, rougher. It was as though he knew they were only turning pages, making the motions, both of them just waiting their turn to die. Little by little he had become more cynical, more critical, faster to fly off the handle and slower to apologize.

First you cry, Toy told herself, allowing herself to sink into self-pity, kicking her feet under the covers and sobbing like a child. Why was this happening to her? Her marriage was disintegrating in front of her eyes, and everything seemed crazy and distorted. What possible explanation could there be for what had occurred?

She didn't know where to turn, where to go, who to ask for help. Seeing the phone on the end table, she thought of calling her parents. Just hearing her mother's soothing voice would make her feel better. Possibly she could go and stay with them until she figured things out. But no, she decided. They were older now and set in their ways. Hearing that she was sick would make them worry, and there was nothing they could do.

The images from the television appeared in her mind. She knew she had been at the scene of that fire, knew she had pulled that child out of the flames. She even remembered his name: Jason Cummings. She searched her mind for the hospital he was in and it appeared. Methodist Hospital in Topeka. Toy reached for the phone, unconcerned with the pain and discomfort in her hands, desperate to verify what she knew was real. Once she had the number from the long distance operator, she had her dial it for her and then waited.

"I'm calling long-distance. Can you connect me to Jason Cummings's room?" she told the operator.

"Hold, please."

A few moments later, a woman answered. "Mrs. Cummings?" Toy said.

"Yes."

"Mrs. Cummings, you don't know me, but I was the woman in the field this morning with your son. How is he doing?"

"Jason," the woman said excitedly, speaking to the child. "It's her, Jason. It's the woman." Then she returned to Toy. "You saved my son's life. I can never repay you. Why did you leave?"

"I . . . ah . . . I had to catch a plane," Toy said. She didn't know what else to say. "How are Jason's burns?"

"The doctors say he's doing very well. We should be able to take him home next week if there's no infection. At first they were certain he would need skin grafts, but now they say he's going to be fine. He'll have some scars, but they won't be so terrible."

"Thank God," Toy said.

"Yes, we have God to thank," the woman said. Then her voice dropped lower. "And we have you to thank as well. Let me tell you, I was praying and praying. They wouldn't let us near the school, and I was certain Jason was inside there burning." She stopped short and Toy could hear her crying. "Talk to Jason," she said, sniffling. "He wants to talk to you. He's so sweet, bless his heart. He was certain you were his guardian angel."

The words made Toy bolt upright in the bed. "Does he remember what I was wearing?"

Toy waited while she spoke to the boy. "I'm sorry," the woman reported back. "I guess he was just too afraid. Why do you ask?"

"Forget it," Toy said quickly.

"God bless you," the woman continued. "We never met you, but you'll always be in our prayers. Oh," she said suddenly, "you didn't tell me your name."

"Toy Johnson."

"What a cute name. Here, I'll let you talk to Jason."

A small, frail voice came on the phone. "Hello."

"Jason," Toy said. "How are you doing there, guy? Your mom says you'll be going home next week. See, I told you everything would be okay."

"I hurt," he said. "They're giving me medicine, but I still hurt really bad."

"I know, Jason, but you're a big boy. You can handle it."

"Tell me the story, the one about the engine."

Toy's heart swelled with emotion. Yes, there was a God. Whatever had happened, however strange and unbelievable it had been, Toy was certain now that it was more than a dream.

As she recited the story from memory, she felt a gush of fresh air wash over her, like a gentle breeze on a chilly spring morning. Her hands were no longer throbbing, and she felt strong and capable, stronger than she had ever felt in her life. From somewhere far away she thought she could hear birds chirping in the trees, and the lyrical sounds of children's laughter, smell the fragrant aroma of spring flowers. She felt as she'd felt when she was seventeen—connected to every living thing, every object, every cell and molecule in the universe. The sun streaking through the window bathed her in warmth, and she felt secure and focused.

Yes, she told herself, her dry, cracked lips stretching in a smile of genuine pleasure and boundless joy. Miracles do happen. She had prayed for a miracle and received her request. She had died and brought something back, something that might have the power to change the world.

She had brought back the magic.

At ten o'clock that night, Stephen came waltzing through the door, a big bouquet of flowers in his hands and a smile planted on his face. Toy was propped up in the bed, eating a bowl of chocolate pudding. "First of all, are you still mad at me?" he said, stopping in the doorway, the smile falling from his face. "If you are, I won't come in."

Toy looked at him and then returned to her pudding.

"Okay, I see," Stephen said, about to toss the flowers on the floor. Then he collected himself and tried again. "Look, I rented a hotel room and got some sleep. I feel a lot better. Things have been tough. I think I was overtired."

"It's all right," Toy said between mouthfuls of pudding, "you can come in."

As her husband pulled up a chair, she continued eating as if he weren't in the room. "The silent treatment, huh?"

"No, I'm eating."

"I'm sorry, Toy, really. I was a jerk. You know me, though, some-times I just can't help it."

"Maybe you should see a psychologist," Toy said curtly. "Get control of your anger. You could be suffering from some type of mood disorder. Never know."

"Stop this, Toy. Either accept my apology or tell me to leave. It's your decision."

Shoving the tray away, Toy took a deep breath and turned to face him. "I was in Kansas at that fire, Stephen. I don't know how I got there, but I was there." Seeing the look on her husband's face, she held up her hands. After she had talked to Jason Cummings, she had removed both the bandages.

"Your hands. Why did you take the dressings off?"

"Because they're fine now," she exclaimed, smiling strangely at him. "Look."

He did, gently holding her hands in his own and turning them over carefully. There was a pale red outline where the burns had been, but, amazingly, they were almost completely healed. There were no blisters, no charred flesh. "Looks good," he said casually. Then his eyes expanded and he bent his head to get a better look. "Great, actually!" he said. "Boy, I don't know what they use around here to treat burns, but it must be fantastic." He dropped her hands and looked her in the eye. "Since you're doing so well, I guess we can leave tomorrow."

"I'm not going anywhere," Toy said. "At least not until you're willing to listen to what I have to say with an open mind. Are you ready to do that?"

Her husband shrugged his shoulders.

"Okay," Toy said, her speech rapid-fire and laced with excitement. "I called the hospital where the little boy was taken, the one on TV. His name is Jason Cummings. And guess what, Stephen? He remembers me." Toy paused for effect and then continued. "Don't you see, Stephen? He even called me an angel, probably because I was wearing that T-shirt."

"What T-shirt?" Stephen asked, thinking her story was getting stranger by the second.

Toy lifted up her hospital gown. She was wearing the T-shirt Margie Roberts had given her under the gown, too attached to it now to take it off. "See, he saw the halo and word angel on the shirt. That's why he thought I was an angel."

"That's ridiculous," he said.

"No, Stephen," Toy protested, "this isn't like my other dreams. This is different, more like the time my heart stopped when I was in high school. I have tangible proof that I was really there. I had the orange pumpkin ring the first time. Now I have the boy. This child remembers me. He even remembers the story I told him." She turned and smiled at him. "We're talking proof here, Stephen, real proof."

Unable to stop herself, Toy continued, revealing more to her husband than she had intended. "See, I've always thought these dreams meant something special, that they were more than just dreams. The children seemed so real, everything really. In the beginning I thought it was what they call a near-death experience, you know, because my heart stopped. Then I started reading stuff on astral projection and out-of-body experiences and thought it might be something like that. I always bypassed religion and God, because it seemed so far-fetched, but Stephen, can't you see, maybe angels and miracles do exist. Why not? What do we know? There could be angels everywhere. Some of them could even be perfectly normal people like myself. I could even be one of them. Isn't that a hoot?" She stopped and laughed. "I don't know about you, but I think the whole concept is marvelous."

Her husband leaned over his knees and placed his head in his hands, appalled at what his wife was saying. Peering at Toy through his fingers, he tried once more to reason with her. "There's no physical way for you to have been in the state of New York and the state of Kansas at the same time. If I remember correctly, they said on the news that the fire occurred at eight o'clock in the morning. That means it was ten o'clock here in New York. I looked at your chart, Toy, and it was almost exactly ten o'clock when you went into cardiac arrest, so there was no way you could have been in Kansas." Then another thought came to mind. "I could have made a mistake on the time. I think they said eight o'clock, but I'm not completely certain. If the fire was later, I guess you could have managed to get on a plane to Kansas when you disappeared from the hospital, since you were gone a number of hours. Then after the fire you got on another plane and flew back." He stopped and slapped back in his seat, realizing that even this scenario didn't work. Toy might have been unaccounted for for a number of hours, but with the traffic he doubted if she could have even managed to get to the airport, much less fly to Kansas and back again. He wanted to believe her, appease her, but the premise was just too insane.

"You can tell me anything you want," Toy said, "but I was still there. I didn't imagine the boy or the fire. They're real." She stopped and made a sweeping motion with her arms. "Hey, maybe I flew on gossamer wings, just soared through the air to Kansas."

Toy started giggling. It felt good, natural. All the stress of the past few days seemed to melt away, and she couldn't stop laughing. Stephen was glaring at her. "I know," she said, emitting another burst of laughter. "I got to Kansas like Dorothy in *The Wizard of Oz.* See, there was this tornado and . . ."

"It's not funny, Toy," Stephen said, his face grim. "This whole thing isn't funny."

"But it is, Stephen," she said emphatically. "Maybe it's not funny, but it's fun. It's exciting. It's a mystery. I've never felt so alive. When I spoke to that kid on the phone and he remembered me, I can't begin to tell you how overjoyed I was."

His head was tilted to the side and resting in his hand. "It was a mistake, Toy. You burned your hands by holding them over a trash can. This child you keep talking about has been injured. He's on narcotics for the pain. Whatever he said to you was just drug-induced drivel."

Toy wouldn't let it go. "No, you're wrong. It's something spectacular, something magnificent. Something about me is different from everyone else. I'm being dispatched on missions, like missions of mercy. What else could it be? All these dreams I've had. In every one there are children in some kind of grave danger. And I make a difference," she said proudly, a fanatical fire burning in her eyes. "I feel great. It's like my whole existence on earth has finally been validated, like I've been searching for this all my life."

Stephen was looking at his wife as though he had just seen her for the first time, as if she were a complete stranger. The feverish look in her eyes, the crazy way she was talking. "You're a rational, intelligent person, Toy, a teacher for God's sake," he said. "How can you accept something you can't explain?"

Toy leaned back on the pillows and then slowly turned her head to look at him. The longer he argued, the longer he stayed in the room, the more she felt her energy and joy ebbing. "How can I not accept it? I don't really have a choice."

"Why did you go into cardiac arrest, then? How could that possibly fit into your ridiculous hypothesis?"

Toy sighed. "I don't really know. I haven't thought about it. How do you know I don't go into cardiac arrest every time I have one of these dreams? That would be great, you see? That would mean all the dreams I've ever had are real." She arched her eyebrows. "I've had a lot of dreams, Stephen, more than you'll ever know. That means I may have helped tons of kids already, and if I can find a way to have more of these dreams, then I could help even more."

Stephen tossed his hands in the air. "Right. Sure. Like your heart stops beating and you fly through space and pull people out of burning buildings. Then what happens? Do you come back to life and return to your body? Hey, Toy, maybe you're a vampire. Ever think of that one?"

He was never going to accept her, Toy thought, never accept something he couldn't see in black and white. All she had done was compound the problem by speaking her mind, make him even more convinced that she was a delusional hysteric.

As Toy figured it, she was standing at a crossroads. She could completely fall apart and let Stephen shuffle her from one clinic to another where they would dissect her body and mind systematically until they either forced a square peg through a round hole or found some absolutely dreadful disease that they could attach to her symptoms. Or, she could stand up for herself.

She analyzed her options. She could believe she was dying or crazy, or she could elect to believe something divine and miraculous had taken control of her life. Toy being an optimist and a dreamer, opted for the latter. "Tell you what," she said, pushing herself back up in the bed, "you go back to California and your medical practice and your neat and tidy life. I'll stay here in New York."

His mouth fell open and all the blood drained from his face. "Are you saying you want a divorce?"

"Sort of," Toy said, her eyes roaming around the room as her heart raced. She felt like she couldn't catch her breath, like she had stepped over the line now and there was no way back. The words rushed out in a thin stream of breath. "I think we should live apart awhile. Not a divorce. A trial separation."

"You're going to throw everything we have away simply because I won't feed into your stupid fantasies? What about your teaching post at the school? Are you going to just walk away from that, too?"

"Not exactly," Toy said, realizing that he had a point. "I could take a few weeks off, though. I might even find a school that needs me more here. How do I know? I have to go where I'm needed. Maybe I came here because this is where I'm supposed to be. You know, like a sign?"

Toy thought of Margie Roberts and how the child depended on her. She'd have to keep sending the family money, she decided. Then if she decided to stay on the East Coast, she'd fly back and see her parents and Margie every month or so.

Stephen stood, angry and frustrated. "I thought you loved me, Toy. Evidently I was wrong."

His back was turned and he was leaving. Toy held her breath. She wanted to call him back, have him hold her, believe her, love her. He should feel what she felt: the wonder and awe, the blissful feeling of peace and contentment. The world was expanding in her hands, the boundaries of everyday existence no longer in place.

But then he was gone and it was just as well, she thought. During the six years of their marriage, Toy had been a nonentity, her own desires and opinions sinking under the weight of her husband's. It was his career that was important, that had to be constantly nurtured. It was his desires they fed with the expensive cars and houses. And it was his ego that was so swollen that it was about to burst like a balloon filled with water. He would never understand something he could not cut open and inspect, examine, and dissect. He was the omniscient, all-powerful healer. For Stephen, the buck stopped right there.

Toy hugged the covers to her chest and smiled coyly. Whatever was happening to her obviously did not include her husband. She knew it was wrong, but she couldn't deny that she felt a sense of satisfaction. People had choices, and her husband had clung to his cynicism with the same tenacity as he did his money. Toy had always thought her husband was a brilliant man, but she now had her doubts. How brilliant could he be? After all the sacrifices he had made to become a surgeon, a healer, all the years of hard work and stress, he had just turned his back on a miracle.

Sarah's concern for Raymond grew with each passing second. She'd made pasta and a salad, but the only way she could get him to eat was to feed him. He wouldn't look at her. He wouldn't speak to her, but he seemed to know she was there. After she fed him, she led him like a child to the bed, where he just sat there staring off into space.

Sarah decided that the time had come. It was late and she needed to go home, but she couldn't leave him alone and find out later that he had committed suicide. For all she knew, he might have a medical condition, even a brain tumor. He had allowed her to feed him and lead him back and forth to the bed. She decided to get him dressed and make him get into the elevator. Once she got him downstairs, she'd catch a cab out front and take him to the hospital. She knew just where to go, too, the same hospital where she had gone when she'd been hit by a car a few years back. Some of the hospitals in New York were far from good but at this one, Sarah had received excellent care. She'd decided to take Raymond to Roosevelt Hospital.

Toy was tossing and turning in her hospital bed, unable to sleep. She couldn't get the events of the day out of her mind, and she was restless and anxious.

The night nurse came in and took her vital signs. "Do you need a sleeping pill?" she asked Toy. "I can check your chart, see if Dr. Esteban prescribed one."

"No," Toy said. "I'll be fine."

As soon as the nurse cleared the door, Toy again tried to close her eyes and sleep. She wanted it to happen, wanted to be transported somewhere else. But she had a definite feeling that it wouldn't happen as long as she was in the hospital. The scientific community, she thought, had to be at war with the community of the unknown. How could it not be? As long as she was sequestered in an enemy camp, nothing miraculous could happen. Her eyes sprang open and her body stiffened. Not only that, she decided, but she was wasting time. There were things to do, places to go, lives to save.

Making the decision, she got up and ripped the hospital gown off her body. Stephen had brought over her luggage and Toy found a comfortable pair of clean pants and a white baggy sweater, pulling it on over her T-shirt. Once she was dressed, she went into the bathroom and brushed her hair, sprayed on some cologne, and then smiled at her reflection. She didn't look sick, she thought, she looked good. A little pale maybe, but that she could fix. Digging in her makeup bag, she found an old lipstick she seldom used, and in seconds her lips were a bright, moist red. She turned off the light, dusted off her hands, and checked the room to make certain she had all her belongings. Then she walked out the door and headed to the lobby, carrying her suitcase in one hand and her overnight bag slung over her other shoulder.

"Where are you going?" the same nurse said, standing up behind the counter. She was a petite blonde with large, expressive blue eyes and a soft face.

"I'm checking out."

"You can't do that, not without the doctor's approval."

"I don't think so," Toy said, giving the girl a harsh look. "This isn't a prison."

"But . . . you have to pay your bill."

Toy recalled seeing her checkbook in her purse. "I'll stop by admitting and take care of it. Tell Dr. Esteban I said thanks for his help."

The elevator opened and Toy stepped in, hoping her insurance had covered most of the bill. She didn't know how much money was left in their joint checking account. Without Stephen, she needed money to live. Tonight she could stay in a hotel, but tomorrow she would have to find an apartment. Stephen might be cooperative and wire her some money or he could be obstinate and do what every attorney advised their clients to do when facing a possible divorce situation: tie up all their assets, close the bank accounts, cancel the credit cards. The elevator opened, and Toy stepped out into the lobby, still deep in thought. Knowing Stephen, she had to think he would be a difficult adversary. First thing Monday morning, she'd have to find a local branch of their bank and make a withdrawal. She might be living in the Twilight Zone, but a portion of her had to be firmly rooted in reality to deal with her husband.

Following the signs to the admitting office, Toy's heels clanked down corridor after corridor, first this way, then that. She felt lost in a maze and ended up in an emergency room. "I'm sorry," she said, kicking her suitcase up to the counter, "I'm looking for the admitting office."

A pretty dark-haired girl came up beside her, her face knitted with worry. "I'm going there now," she told Toy. "Want to follow me?"

"Sure," Toy said.

The girl turned and smiled weakly. "My name's Sarah Mendleson. What's your name?"

"Oh," Toy said, "Toy Johnson."

"Are you checking in?"

"No," Toy answered, "out, thank goodness."

"Lucky you. What were you in for?"

"I accidentally burned my hands," Toy answered, thinking it was easier than telling her the truth.

"That's too bad." Sarah looked up and saw the placard on the door. She stepped inside, Toy right behind her. There was a long wall of partitioned cubicles, all of them occupied. "I guess we have to wait. You wouldn't think they would be so busy this late at night."

"Well, this is New York," Toy said to the young woman. "Do you live here?"

"Yeah," she said, taking a seat in the waiting room. "Well, not in Manhattan. I live in Queens. And you?"

"California, but I'm thinking of relocating to New York."

"Why? I'd love to live in California. Do you live near the beach?"

"Yes, we do."

"Sounds so glamorous."

"It isn't," Toy said. Then she laughed. Everyone always thought that, thought the streets were paved with gold, that movie stars hung out on every corner, that beautiful tanned women and men decorated all the beaches.

Sarah wasn't listening. She had slid all the way down in her seat and had her arm up over her eyes. Her thin legs were stretched out in front of her and spread apart in an undignified pose. Toy suddenly realized the girl was crying. "What's wrong? I didn't even ask you why you were here. Are you sick? Do you want me to get a nurse?"

"No," Sarah said, sniffing back tears, looking in her purse for a tissue and then blowing her nose. "It's not me. It's my friend. He's . . . he's not right."

"Do they know what's wrong with him?"

"No, but they're checking. The doctor in emergency seems to think it's a mental problem, and he's probably right, but they're going to check him for a brain tumor just to be certain." Sarah stopped and wiped her face with the back of her hand. "I'm so scared. I'm afraid I shouldn't have brought him here. If they put him in a mental institution, I'll never forgive myself."

Toy leaned back in her chair, thinking Sarah Mendleson might be right. If she'd let Stephen continue, Toy thought, she might be headed to the insane asylum herself. Just then a woman walked out of the admitting office, a piece of paper in her hand, walking rapidly down the corridor. "I think you can go in now," she told Sarah. "That woman just left, so they must have a clerk available."

"Oh, you can go first."

"No," Toy said. "Go on."

"Well," Sarah said, staring at Toy's face, "it was nice to meet you. I hope everything turns out for you." She started to walk away and then froze, her eyes glued on Toy's face. "You . . . you look so familiar now. When I look at you straight on. I . . . have we met? Are you on television or something?"

"God, no," Toy said, giggling. People thought if you lived in California, you had to be involved in the entertainment industry. "I hear that a lot, though. I guess I have one of those faces. People are always thinking they've seen me somewhere before."

Still the girl didn't move. Her eyes were riveted on Toy. "I know I've seen you. You're just so familiar. Your red hair, your eyes, even your mouth." She sort of shook her head as if to clear it, like she was seeing things that weren't really present. Then her eyes lit up. "You're the model. Of course. God, I can't believe it. You're Raymond's model."

"Who's Raymond?" Toy asked. The girl was so excited now, she was jumping up and down like a pogo stick.

"My friend. He's an artist. Your face is in dozens of his paintings. It has to be you. It just has to be."

"I'm sorry," Toy said. "I've never posed for a painting in my life. Like I said, I have an ordinary face. People are always mistaking me for someone else. You better go in now, or you're going to lose your place."

"Wait," Sarah said, full of enthusiasm, undaunted by Toy's words. For one thing, the woman she was blatantly staring at was certainly not ordinary. She had a distinctive look, a rare delicacy and beauty to her face, and it was natural and unaffected. Her eyes were huge and seemed to glow with a light radiating from somewhere inside her. Her colorful hair almost floated around her face, weightless and free, strands fluttering here and there as if she were standing in front of a window fan. "Raymond said you were an angel. I guess you left a big impression on him because he's been painting you ever since." Then she remembered why she was here and her face fell, thinking of the silent, sad man she had brought to the emergency room.

"You have to see him. If he sees you," Sarah pleaded, even going so far as to drop down on her knees in front of Toy, "he might snap out of it. I mean, he obviously cares about you in some way. He's been painting you all these years. His family isn't here. He's so alone. Please, I'll take you to him right now."

"No," Toy said, shaking her head. "I can't. Really. I don't know your boyfriend."

"Please, please, please," Sarah pleaded. "He's not even really my boyfriend. He works with me in a restaurant, but he's special, very talented. And he's in terrible trouble."

Toy's face flushed with embarrassment as several other people exited the admitting office. She had enough problems right now. She couldn't deal with everyone else's problems. It was like the old adage, physician heal thyself. Suddenly her zeal for her newfound celestial mission seemed silly and unreal. All she could think about was Stephen, where he was right now, if he had already left for Los Angeles, how she should have never said all those stupid things to him. Everyone had odd thoughts now and then, but they didn't regurgitate them and submit themselves to ridicule.

If the young girl wasn't going to go inside, Toy decided, standing, she was. "I have to go now. Everything will be okay. Keep the faith, you know."

Toy entered the admitting office and took a seat in a booth, waiting while the clerk punched in numbers on her computer and called up her account. "The national debt, huh?" Toy said once the woman had activated the printer and the invoice started spilling out. Toy thought it would never stop. When the woman finally ripped it off, she had what looked like five or six pages in her hand.

"Not too bad," the clerk said. "Your insurance covered most of it. We need five hundred dollars, the amount of your deductible."

Toy opened her checkbook and starting making out the check. Once she had done so, she flipped to the register and glanced at the balance. It read eleven hundred dollars, but she had no way to know if all that money was still there. Stephen could have written checks while she was gone. And the six hundred dollars that would be left after this check cleared would hardly be enough for her to get an apartment if she decided to stay. She'd have to get more, call the bank that held their savings accounts and try to make a withdrawal or a wire transfer.

"All right," Toy said, handing the check to the clerk and then sticking her arm out so the woman could cut the plastic identification band off her wrist, "set me free."

Toy shoved the receipt in her purse and headed for the exit. Sarah was in another booth and grabbed her arm as she walked by.

"Here," she said, pressing a piece of paper into Toy's hand, "this is the phone number and address to Raymond's loft, and I also put down my home phone. Once you get a place here and everything, please call. If nothing else, you can come to see the paintings. Then you can see for yourself how much you resemble his model."

"That would be nice," Toy said, accepting the paper and placing it in her purse with the receipt. "Good luck."

"Yeah," Sarah said under her breath, "I'm going to need all the luck I can get."

EIGHT

Toy checked into the first hotel she saw, the Montrose, the same hotel Stephen had mentioned staying at the day before. In the room, she removed her clothes and tossed on a robe, calling room service to bring up a bucket of ice and a ham sandwich. By the time it arrived, however, she was too tired to eat.

Saturday morning she woke up fresh and alert. She started to call Sylvia in Brooklyn and tell her what she had learned about the fire in Kansas, but found herself hesitating. Like Stephen, Sylvia was firmly rooted in reality, a nice person but a hardened cynic. But then on the other hand, she told herself, both Sylvia and Stephen were probably no more closed-minded than the majority of people. No one was going to believe her story without proof, and a young child's fuzzy recollections would not suffice. Stephen had already proved that theory. The kid was injured and frightened, they would say. He didn't know what he had been really seeing that day. It was all just a case of mistaken identity.

Just as she had when she was preparing a paper in college, Toy realized that she had to write and document her findings. Then she had to back them up with solid evidence, evidence that even the most hardened cynic could not dispute.

Taking out a pad of paper, she jotted down the events as they had occurred, trying to determine how to proceed. The first thing she had to do was dispel Stephen's theory that she might have taken a plane to Kansas, and the only way to do that was to come up with a witness, someone who had seen her during the time she was absent from the hospital. Once she had eliminated that problem, she would move on to the next.

Picking up the phone, she called the restaurant and described the waiter over the phone, thinking she could get a written statement from him.

"Sounds like Tony Hildago," a woman told her in a gravelly voice. "Tony ain't here. His shift starts at lunchtime."

"I see," Toy said quickly, afraid the woman was going to hang up on her. "What about the police officer that you called when I was there? I was the woman without shoes. You know, the one who couldn't pay for her coffee? Remember?"

"Hey, lady, we got dozens of people can't pay for their food."

"What about the police officer?" Toy persisted. "I'm certain he was a regular there. I think his last name was Kramer. Do you know who I mean?"

"Joey?" the woman cackled. "You mean Joey Kramer. He ain't no real cop. Not NYPD, anyway. He works for the Transit Authority."

"No," Toy said, "that can't be true. He was wearing a uniform and he put me in a police car. He had to be a real police officer."

"Joey Kramer's a righteous nut case," the woman said. "Thinks he's some kind of Good Samaritan or something. See, when we get a derelict in here that's got nowhere to go, we call Joey. Says he don't mind. Even distributes little cards to all the businesses around this part of town. All we do is call him up, and he comes right over and takes care of the problem. The regular cops, well, they don't spend too much time worrying about that kinda stuff."

"Do you know how I can reach him?" Toy asked, hearing the cash register ring in the background and a cacophony of voices.

"Look, lady," the woman said curtly, "I got a business to run here." With that, she promptly hung up.

Toy was confused. She'd been so certain the man was a regular police officer, but then she realized a lot of people wore uniforms. She looked up the number for the Transit Authority and was transferred to the only office open on Saturday, the supervisors' office where they kept track of the scheduling. "I'm looking for a man named Joey Kramer," she said. "He's one of your transit officers. It's extremely urgent that I contact him. I'm a relative of his from California."

"Hold on," the man said. A few minutes later, he came back on the line. "Let's see here. We got Kornwell, Kramacy, Kayman, Kidwell. We got a Charles Kramer. Is that who you mean?"

"No," Toy said, "his first name is Joey."

"Well," the man said, "I been in this job for ten years, and the only Joey Kramer I ever heard of is dead. Real swell fellow too, let me tell you."

"He's dead?" Toy said, mystified. "There must be some mistake. I saw him just the other day. Everyone knows about him. He helps the homeless people in his spare time. You know, things like that."

The man started laughing. "Funny, but it sure sounds like old Joey, may he rest in peace. He was always giving people money and stuff. Like I said, the man was a pretty decent guy. But listen up, lady. I guarantee it ain't the same Joey Kramer. See, some lunatic went berserk on one of our trains and shot up a bunch of people. Joey took him down, but the man shot and killed him. Didn't you hear about it? It was in all the papers."

"No," Toy said. "How long ago did this happen?"

"You know, couple years ago or something. I don't remember the exact date."

Toy thanked the man and disconnected, more bewildered than ever. But New York was a big city, she reminded herself, and it was entirely possible that the cashier in the restaurant had made a mistake about the officer's first name.

Toy took a shower and dressed, deciding she would go out and get some fresh air. When twelve o'clock rolled around, she would go back to the delicatessen and see if she could get a statement from the waiter.

Stepping out into the crisp morning air a few minutes later, Toy started walking down the street when she felt someone touch her shoulder. "I thought that was you," a man's voice said. "Hey, how you doing there?"

Toy spun around and gasped. Standing right in front of her, only a few feet from her hotel, was the mysterious Joey Kramer. He looked exactly the same as he had the day she saw him in the restaurant. He was wearing a uniform, his hat tipped back on his head, a broad, friendly smile on his handsome face. Only now Toy could see the patches on the sleeves and the words Transit Authority. "I can't believe it's you," she said. "How did you find me?"

"What makes you think I found you?" he said. "You found me."

"No," Toy said, shaking her head. "You don't understand. I just called the Transit Authority looking for you, and they claim they've never heard of you. The only Joey Kramer they know is dead."

He burst out laughing. "Whadya think, do I look dead to you?"

"Of course not," Toy said, dropping her eyes in embarrassment.

"Look," he said, "my full name is Charles Joseph Kramer, but I go by Joey. That old fart who does the scheduling is always getting me confused with my cousin."

"The one that got killed?" Toy asked.

"Yeah," Joey said. "Real sad, huh? Guy had a family and every-thing."

He studied Toy's face and then said, "What did you need? Why were you looking for me?"

How could she explain it? "Can you spare a few minutes?" she said. "You were so nice to me, I'd like to buy you lunch."

"Well, I sure can't turn down an offer like that," he said, winking at her. Then he stepped closer and linked his arm in Toy's, and together they continued on down the street.

The waitress was standing by the table, her notebook in her hand. She removed her pencil from behind her ear and stared at Toy. "What can I get you, sweetie?"

"A side of revenge," Toy said, exchanging knowing looks with Joey and then giggling. "But if you're out of that, I guess you can give me a roast beef sandwich."

On the walk to the restaurant, Toy had tried to tell her new friend why she'd wanted to find him. Thinking originally that she would make up a fictitious story, she was surprised to find herself rattling on about everything. He was such a pleasant person to talk to, so kind, so understanding, so warm. Before she knew it, she had told him about her heart and how it had stopped beating, the fire in Kansas, the boy, her problems with Stephen and how he refused to believe what was happening to her. Then she backtracked and told him about the first episode and the dark boy she had seen in the classroom. She even told him about the pumpkin ring he had given her, and how she had awakened in the emergency room with it on her finger.

"What you're saying don't sound so crazy to me," he said. "I mean, it's pretty far-out there, but I believe in things like that." His face flushed, as if he were suddenly embarrassed. "Miracles and them kinds of thing. Hey, what about that place in France? What's it called? Lourdes or something. Well, there you go. There's miracles in that place all the time."

"This is a little different, though," Toy said, sighing deeply. "I don't think anyone's ever going to believe me."

Joey leaned back in the seat, removing his hat and running his fingers through his thick, dark hair. "Say, I got a plan," he said. "Why don't you call those TV people? Those guys that filmed that fire. If you was really there, bet they got a picture of you somewheres. You get that, then I'd say you got yourself some real proof. Am I sharp or what? Told you Joey ain't no dummy."

"You're right," Toy said, leaning forward excitedly. "That's a great idea. Brilliant, actually. If they were shooting footage of the fire, they may have some film with me on it. The only problem is, how am I going to get them to give it to me?"

"Lie," Joey shot out without a second thought, a mischievous look in his eyes. "Now, don't get a guy wrong. I don't think telling lies is kosher, but hey, don't they say everything is given to us for a reason? Way I see it, there really ain't no bad things, just bad people. Now, if you told a lie just to hurt someone, well, we're talking wrong here. But this is different, okay. Just tell them that you're in the business, that you're with a television station here in the city, and you need that film to do a follow-up story on the fire."

Just then the waitress returned and slapped their food down on the table. Toy took a dainty bite of her roast beef sandwich, while Joey dug into his meal, an open-faced turkey sandwich with stuffing and cranberries. Toy stopped eating and reached across the table to touch his hand. "You've really helped me," she told him. "I don't know how to thank you."

With a mouthful of food he said, "Hey, you're my angel, remember? Where's that T-shirt you had on the other day?"

"Oh," Toy said, "I still have it. It's in my hotel room."

"Then why you wearing that?" he said, pointing at her green pantsuit and shaking his head. "You looked real pretty in that T-shirt."

"Oh, I did, huh?" she said playfully.

"Yeah," he said, giving her a rakish smile.

"You sure?" she said. "You don't like this outfit better than a cheap baseball T-shirt? This is one of the nicest outfits I own."

"Nah," he said, "I like that T-shirt. Wouldn't mind having one of those shirts myself, to tell you the truth."

"I tell you what," Toy said, "you give me that statement I need, and I promise I'll get you one. How about that?"

Joey picked a toothpick off the table and stuck it between his teeth, moving it to one side and then the other. "That would be real swell," he said slowly. "You got yourself a deal."

Parting company with Joey in front of the restaurant, his handwritten statement in her purse, Toy headed back to the hotel to call the television station as he had suggested. She knew just what she was going to do when she had all her testimonials down in black and white, and she felt like jumping up and down and screaming it at the top of her lungs. It wasn't exactly what an angel should probably pursue, but if she was an actual angel, Toy knew she was different from all the others who had gone before her. If there ever was such a thing as a contemporary angel, Toy was going to be one. She decided to bring this angel business right into the twenty-first century. And Joey Kramer had been the one to show her how to do it.

The media.

If people thought UFO's had attracted the fancy of the American public, Toy decided, just wait until they got wind of this story.

Sarah had slept in a cot next to Raymond's bed. Waking when they brought in the breakfast tray, she tried to talk to him and get him to eat, but he just stared at her as if she weren't there.

Deciding there was nothing else she could do, she started feeding him, just as she had the day before in his loft. Every once in a while he would mumble something, but she couldn't figure out what he was saying. After half the breakfast was gone and Raymond kept turning his head away, Sarah ate the rest herself. They had told her last night that the doctor would see them this morning. She kept watching the door. Finally it opened.

With short blond hair and a thin mustache, Dr. Robert Evanston didn't look much older than Raymond and Sarah. The young physician was bursting with energy or flying on caffeine; his speech was so rapid, Sarah had to ask him constantly to repeat what he had said.

"I understand exactly what you're saying, Dr. Evanston," she said, once he had finished his dissertation on autism. "But how do you know that's what's wrong with him?"

"We found his next of kin listed in his wallet and made a call to Texas. His mother thought he was doing well. She was quite distraught that he'd suffered a relapse."

"Is she going to come out here?" Sarah asked, knowing she couldn't stay with him forever.

"Not right now she isn't," the doctor replied. "Seems her husband just suffered a heart attack and they're pretty strapped for cash."

The young doctor shifted his eyes between the vibrant young girl before him to the dark, brooding face of his patient. For some reason the two images didn't mesh. "You can take him home if you want," he finally said.

"What do you mean?" Sarah said, her mouth open. "Like this? You have to do something, get him to snap out of this."

"There's nothing I can do. I can give him some pills. They may make a difference, but I seriously doubt it. He's physically fine. He's simply autistic, exhibiting pronounced symptoms of autism."

"But he can't even feed himself, dress himself, speak," Sarah argued. "How can he survive?"

The young doctor had a puzzled look on his face. "Aren't you his wife?"

"No," Sarah said, wrapping her arms around herself. "I'm his girlfriend."

Quickly the doctor opened Raymond's chart and started thumbing through the pages. "Lives alone, huh?"

"Yes," Sarah said. "He's an artist. He has a loft in TriBeCa."

Approaching Raymond, the doctor positioned himself directly in front of him. "How you doing today, Raymond? Are you ready to get out of here? Talk to us, fellow. Tell us what's going on inside that head of yours?"

Just then they turned around. Raymond had said something. They both fell silent and listened. He was muttering again, his lips barely moving. Sarah leaned her ear close to his face and listened.

"My angel," he whispered. "I need my angel."

"I'm here, baby," Sarah said. "I'm right here."

The doctor slapped Raymond's chart against his thigh, eager to get on with his rounds. "We've got two choices," he said. "We can have him transferred to a mental institution until he improves enough to take care of himself, or you can assume full responsibility for him. As to the mental institution, he doesn't have any insurance, so it will have to be a state facility. Private ones are extremely costly." He paused, letting his words sink in. "It's your decision. If you want, I can write up a release and you can take him home this morning."

"Do it," Sarah said without turning around, her arms locked around Raymond's head, his head pressed to her chest. He had called her his angel. How could she walk away now?

"You're certain?" the doctor asked. "I don't want you to take the guy out of here and then find out a few days from now that he walked out in the street and got run over by a truck or something. Until he improves, someone will have to be with him twenty-four hours a day. Are you absolutely certain you can handle something as extensive as this?"

Sarah stared hard at the doctor. Then she turned back to gaze at Raymond's face, and her expression instantly softened. He was like a baby, so helpless, so lost. How could she allow them to put him in a terrible place like a state mental hospital? She knew she was being rash, that she was taking on more than she could handle. She was simply powerless to do anything else.

"So," the doctor said, "what's it going to be? You want me to start processing the paperwork for his release?"

"Yes," Sarah said firmly. "I'll take care of him. I don't know how exactly, but as long as he needs me, I promise I'll be there."

Toy had her shoes off and was stretched out on her bed in the hotel talking on the phone. She'd stopped off at a stationery store and bought some spiral notebooks, and they were now scattered all over the bed. Suddenly the caller said something, and Toy let out a whoop and a holler. "Great," she said, "you've got the footage. The boy with the redheaded woman, right? You've really got it."

"Yeah, we got it. What television station did you say you were with?"

"WKRP in New York." Toy hoped there really wasn't such a station. The letters just popped into her mind. "Listen, Federal Express the tape to me. Send it overnight mail. I'm on location. Let me give you the address of the hotel."

"Hey, CNN owns that tape. You guys want it, you buy it."

"How much?"

"Hell, I don't know. What's it worth to you?"

My life, Toy thought. "I'll give you two hundred dollars for it."

He laughed. "That's an insult. How do I know that you don't have a bigger story? Maybe something happened out there that day that we missed and you're going to scoop us."

"Please," Toy pleaded, "I'm new on the job. This is just a little human-interest story on acts of heroism. You're not going to run this again. Be a sport. Sneak me a copy and I'll make the check payable to you. No one will know the difference."

He mulled it over for a while and then bit. "Jeff McDonald. Put it in the mail today. If you don't, I'll come looking for you."

"No problem," Toy said, rattling off the address of the hotel. "Federal Express, remember?" she added. "Make sure you ask for overnight delivery." Then she thought about what she was saying. The following day was Sunday, and Federal Express didn't deliver on Sunday. "Look, I changed my mind. Send it air freight or I won't get it tomorrow. I'm on a deadline. I have to have it by tomorrow."

"Yeah, yeah, yeah," he said, slamming down the phone.

*   *   *

Due to her shrinking wallet, there was very little Toy could do to occupy herself. Saturday evening she remained in her room watching television, ordering her supper from room service. Several times she tried reaching Sylvia at her brother's house in Brooklyn, but no one was there, so she left a message on the machine.

Sunday morning she slept late, then went out window shopping until late afternoon.

As soon as she entered the hotel, she rushed to the counter to see if the videotape from Kansas had arrived, but the clerk told her that it had not. Rather than go upstairs and sit in the small room, she took a seat on a sofa and flipped through a magazine. Every few minutes she would look at her watch. Around five o'clock, she saw a uniformed man enter the lobby with Emerson Air Freight written on his shirt and hat. She jumped up and almost assaulted him. "Toy Johnson. You should have a package for me."

"Just a minute," he said, looking at his list. "Yep, sure do. Sign right here and it's all yours."

Toy quickly scribbled her signature and clutched the package to her chest, almost running to the elevator. Once she was in the room, she ripped it open and shoved the tape into the VCR. This was it, she told herself. This was the moment of truth. If she was on this tape, she was on her way to glory.

Instead of sitting down, she simply stood right in front of the television set, her eyes glued to the screen. Evidently when the fire broke out, the teachers had evacuated the children, telling them to wait on the front lawn. Then they had seriously misjudged the extent of the fire, and all three teachers had reentered the building, probably to get belongings, try to save equipment, or simply to make certain there were no children they had missed. While they were inside, a gas stove had exploded and they had been killed.

There it was: the group of children moving across the field. The camera was so far away, however, that all Toy could see were dark shadows. But one of the people moving across the field was taller than the others, and Toy held her breath. Suddenly the cameraman zoomed in for a close-up, and Toy knew without a doubt that she was watching her own image.

Her heart started racing in her chest. There she was in living color, running across that field, little Jason Cummings in her arms, flames nipping at her feet. She watched as she handed the child to the fireman, watched as she ran along beside him and then kneeled down next to him. The camera zoomed in for another close-up of her face, and she read her own lips. "I know I can. I know I can. I know I can." Then she ran around the hotel room chugging like a train, completely out of her mind with joy.

Hearing the announcer's voice, her image no longer on the screen, Toy stopped and listened. "The woman you just saw with Jason Cummings suddenly vanished right after this film was shot. The boy's family is eager to find her to offer their appreciation. If she had not pulled him out of the flames, risking her life, the child would more than likely have perished in this tragedy."

Hitting the rewind button, Toy jumped onto the bed and watched the tape again from start to finish. How had she and Stephen missed this portion of the broadcast? It must have been aired right before they turned on the television. When she started to play it back a third time, she became fearful that the tape would break in the VCR and hit the stop button. Ejecting it from the VCR, she held it in her hands. It was so light, so small, but in her hands was her own private Shroud of Turin, her personal Dead Sea Scrolls.

Clutching the cassette tape to her bosom, she raced out of the room and took the elevator down to the lobby, rushing to the counter. "I'd like a safety-deposit box please," she told the clerk.

"Certainly," he said. "Just fill out this card and I'll be right back."

Toy scribbled her name, address, phone number on the card and then looked around her at the people waiting at the counter. What if someone stole it right out of her hands? Then she would be right back where she started from. But of course, she told herself, no one knew what was on this tape, what it meant, not just to her but to the entire world.

"Follow me," the clerk said, leading her to a small locked room behind the counter. "What size box do you need?"

"Big," Toy said, her eyes on fire.

"Is this big enough?" he pulled out a large metal box.

"Anything bigger?" Toy asked.

This time he pulled out an enormous safety-deposit box. Toy glowed. "This will be fine." As soon as he had left, Toy reverently placed the black cassette tape in the box. It looked lost in there, she thought, but not for long. This was her first piece of evidence. Hopefully there would be much more.

Slamming the box into the wall, she removed the key and secured it inside the zippered compartment of her purse. Then she headed out the front door of the hotel and asked the doorman to get her a cab.

"Where will it be?" the cabbie said, already pulling away from the curb, chomping at the bit like a racehorse about to come out of the gate.

"Wolfe's Delicatessen," she said, having jotted down the cross streets. "Fifty-seventh and Sixth."

The cab lurched forward, darted around three cars and then the driver floored it, roaring up the street and skidding to a stop at the first signal. "Boy," Toy said, "where did you learn how to drive? The Indianapolis five hundred?"

The cabdriver laughed. "You ain't that far away, lady. You could have walked. Where you from anyway?"

"Everywhere and anywhere," Toy quipped. "You know, wherever I lay my hat is home."

"Here we go," he said, pulling to the curb a few minutes later.

Once he had sped off, Toy looked through the glass windows into the restaurant. Then she stepped to the storefront next door and pulled out her compact, checking her lipstick, fluffing up her hair. This was more than just verifying her story, she thought. It was a matter of dignity.

Glancing to her right, Toy saw a homeless person sleeping under a piece of cardboard in the alcove. At least it wasn't snowing yet, she thought. In another month or so, these poor people would freeze.

"You want a booth or a table?" the woman with the orange hair said from her stool.

"Neither," Toy said crisply. "I'd like to speak to one of your employees. He's tall, ugly, and has pockmarks on his face."

"Hey, Tony," she yelled, "someone's looking for ya."

Tony was heading to a table with a whole tray full of plates. Seeing Toy, he blinked but kept on walking. Toy waited by the register. She didn't think he recognized her. That wasn't too hard to figure out. She was standing there in one of her best outfits, her finest leather shoes, her one and only decent handbag. Obviously she didn't look the same as she had before.

"Whadya want?" Tony said on his way back to the kitchen. "Hey, don't I know you? You're Sam's wife, aren't you?"

"No," she said, looking him squarely in the eye, "I was here Friday, right back there in the booth. I was wearing a blue T-shirt and no shoes. Remember me now?"

"Yeah," he said, looking her up and down. "Now that you mentioned it, I do."

Toy said, "Look, I'm sorry about what happened the other day. I was in the hospital with a medical condition, and I guess I just wandered off. I'm glad you called that handsome officer to assist me. That was kind of you." As the words rolled off her tongue like butter, Toy felt an incredible urge to stomp on his foot, just dig her heel right into his instep. The man was a megaton jerk. If his mother was lying in the middle of the road, he'd run right over her. "So," she said, fluttering her eyelashes, "I wanted to give you a nice tip." The money was already in her palm, a crisp hundred-dollar bill. Toy had used her credit card the day before to get a cash advance of two hundred dollars. She reached out and handed it to him.

"Hey, thanks," he said, sticking it in his pocket and turning to walk off.

Toy grabbed his sleeve. "I need a little favor."

He gave her a dirty look. "Oh, yeah? What?"

"Well, while I was here in your restaurant, something incredible happened. I won the lottery. Ssssh," she said. "Don't spread it around. You know, someone might rob me or try to follow me home."

He just kept staring at her. New Yorkers were astute people. You had to get up awfully early in the morning to pull one over on them. "Won the lottery, huh?" he said, smacking his lips and popping his knuckles. "How much you win?"

"Plenty," Toy said, stepping closer and lowering her voice even more. "What I need from you is a little like an absentee note from school. If you could, I'd like you to write down what I look like, what I was wearing that day, where I was sitting, and how you called that officer to take me away. Of course, the time is the main thing. You do remember what time it was?" When he just gave her a blank look, she pushed ahead. "It was a little after five, right?"

"Yeah, that sounds about right. How much do I get for this and why do you need a note?"

Greedy creep, Toy thought. She'd just given him a hundred big ones for tossing her out on the street. Now the jerk wanted more. "I need it because I didn't turn in my winning ticket in time. Thank goodness, no one else came forward and I explained my circumstances. But since I wasn't in the hospital that entire day, as you of course know, I need something to prove I was a little out of it. Know what I mean?"

All he did was rub his fingers together. He didn't care about the story. All he cared about was the cash.

"Another hundred," Toy said. "But you have to do it right now. That's part of the deal. I'm not coming back to get it."

"No problem, sugar," he said. "I can write with the best of them. Just got to get me a piece of paper."

"Here we go," Toy said, removing a notebook from her purse. "I'll just have a cup of coffee while you get it ready."

Once she had the waiter's written statement in her purse, Toy stepped outside into the chilly, evening air. She started to cross the street and ask for directions back to her hotel, but instead she just stood there on the corner, lost in her thoughts. Did she have enough? Could she really approach a newspaper or television station with what she had? She had done what she'd set out to do. She had accounted for her whereabouts almost every second of the day the fire had occurred in Kansas, and she had the tape to prove that she had been the one to save the boy. She even had the child itself to back up her story, but still she wasn't certain what she should do next. She weighed the merits of simply taking her prearranged flight with Sylvia back to Los Angeles on Tuesday and setting everything that had happened aside. She was concerned about little Margie Roberts, as well as all the other students who counted on her at school. How would they feel when they walked into the classroom and found out she wasn't coming back?

Glancing down the street, Toy saw the greenery of Central Park, and decided to walk awhile and enjoy the evening before returning to the hotel. Once she entered the park itself, she marveled at the sheer size of it. Right here in the middle of this massive city was a sprawling, spectacular piece of real estate: trees, ponds, paths, benches, an ice skating rink. She heard the tapping of horse hooves and looked behind her as a horse-drawn carriage passed. Then the driver pulled up on the reins and stopped.

"Want to go for a ride?" the man said.

"How much?" Toy asked, inhaling the wonderful odor of the horse's body. The horse seemed to know she was sniffing him, enjoying him. He stamped his hooves and tossed his head.

"Well, since it's quiet tonight and I'm about to head home, I'll give you a deal. Sixty-five dollars for a ride around the park."

The man looked quaint in his top hat and tails, but his eyes were the same eyes she saw in the street hustlers. "Sorry," Toy said, turning and walking away. She certainly couldn't squander sixty-five dollars to ride in a horse-drawn carriage.

The horse hooves caught up to her. "All right, let's make it fifty, but only for you, and only because it's late."

"Thirty and not a penny more," Toy said firmly. "Really, it's not that I don't want you to have the money. I just don't have it to spare."

"Cash?" he asked.

"No," Toy said, "I'll have to give you a check."

The driver stared at her for a long time, trying to make up his mind. Then he seemed to be taken by her. "Climb on, you got a deal."

Toy got into the carriage and quickly slid back in time. She imagined what the city had been like in the early days. All the horses and carriages, the ladies in their beautiful hats. Cleaning up manure was a lot easier than cleaning up the ozone, she decided, wishing they could magically turn back the hands of time.

But all that didn't matter. Toy was alone. And being alone in a horse-drawn carriage simply wasn't that much fun. She thought of Stephen and wondered what he was doing, suddenly wishing he was beside her and she could rest her head against his shoulder. She thought of all the long talks they had enjoyed when they were first married, and the way Stephen had always made her laugh. How had he lost his sense of humor, his enthusiasm for life? Toy remembered his passion for medicine and his overwhelming desire to become a surgeon. "It's like being God," he'd told her one night after completing his first procedure. "When you cut into someone's body, it's like you're an extension of God. You become His hands, His eyes. It's awesome, Toy. It's opened my eyes to the wonder of life, and made me feel like I'm an intricate part of the overall process."

Well, Toy thought, she hadn't heard any speeches from Stephen lately about God and the wonder of life. These days her husband seemed to view his patients as mere commodities, his surgical procedures evaluated on how much he would earn instead of how many lives he could save. Was it possible for a person to change so drastically? She decided her husband had misplaced more than his sense of humor. Somewhere along the way he had lost his heart as well.

As the horse hooves tapped on the asphalt and the carriage gently rocked, Toy pulled the woolen shawl the driver had given her over her body and closed her eyes. In no time she felt herself drifting and floating, a strange constrictive feeling in her chest. But she didn't feel pain or fear. She felt completely at peace. Then she heard the soft whimpers of what sounded like a child crying, seemingly calling to her from somewhere inside the darkness.

NINE

Toy was walking in the park, walking through damp grass. It was dark and she was frightened. Somehow she had managed to get turned around and couldn't find her way back to the main thoroughfare leading out. As she passed a bank of trees, she saw a large, looming shadow off in the distance and headed in that direction, thinking it was a building or some type of structure. When she got up closer, though, she saw that it was a carousel for children and stopped, mesmerized by the colorful horses and the way they looked in the moonlight. Then she heard the rustling of leaves and another strange sound, but she couldn't figure out where it was coming from. Holding her breath in order to hear better, Toy thought it sounded like a child crying. She raced around the circumference of the carousel, but found the sounds becoming even less pronounced. She simply couldn't tell where they were coming from. Finally Toy stood perfectly still and just listened.

There it was again, a faint, muffled sound that distinctively sounded like a child sobbing. Taking one step at a time and then stopping to listen for the sounds, Toy walked in circles around the carousel, each time enlarging the size of the circle. On the far right, about eight or nine feet from the carousel, she found the sounds were much louder. Dropping to the ground, Toy crawled on her hands and knees, having no idea what she was looking for. Suddenly she froze, hearing the sound clearly, the voice echoing strangely as if it were coming from a well.

Then she saw it—a hole in the ground that appeared to be about eighteen inches in diameter. Next to it was a metal cover, and Toy quickly assumed the hole led to a drainage ditch for the sewer system. Sticking her face inside the hole, she distinctly heard what sounded like a growl, a low, almost inhuman noise.

She again froze, thinking it was a dog that had accidentally become trapped in the shaft. The dog could even be rabid, she thought, a one-time house pet dumped loose in the city by owners who no longer wanted to care for it. That would tend to make a dog vicious, she decided, with or without rabies. She certainly didn't want to reach her hand in there and draw back a stump.

Then she heard the noise again. It wasn't so much a growl as a moaning, raspy sound. She lifted her head out of the hole and glanced around her at all the trees and greenery. There had to be all kinds of animals in Central Park, she told herself. It could be a raccoon, a squirrel, even an owl. There were more strange sounds, and then Toy heard what sounded like a choking, gurgling sound, followed by a violent fit of coughing.

"Is anyone there?" she yelled down into the shaft, her curiosity outweighing her fear.

"Help me," a small, strained voice said.

Had she really heard what she thought she had, Toy asked herself, or were her ears deceiving her? There was a strong easterly wind now. Far off in the distance, she could hear horns honking and the sounds of traffic. Overhead, a jet streaked by. Maybe she was just imagining that the voice was coming from the hole.

"Hello down there," she yelled again. "If you can hear me, yell out."

"Help me," the tiny voice cried. "Please, I want my mommy."

Toy felt inside the shaft with her hands, touching something metal that seemed to be attached to the interior walls. Turning her body around, she held onto the sides and dropped her lower body down inside the shaft, feeling along the side walls with her feet. If she was right, she decided, what she was feeling were metal footholds for a person to climb down.

Toy positioned her foot on one of the metal bars and dropped even farther into the shaft. She could hear the person inside now clearly, and was certain it was a child. "I'm coming down, honey," she said. "Just hold on until I get to you."

The farther she went down the shaft, the more Toy had to compress her body. Even though the opening appeared to be approximately eighteen inches in size, the railing made the interior of the shaft several inches smaller. If Toy hadn't been so slender, she knew she would never have been able to fit inside. The walls of the shaft were tight against her body and she felt claustrophobic and panicky. But the child was sobbing again, and her respiration was so labored it sounded like someone sawing each time she took a breath. As Toy got closer to the bottom, she could hear what sounded like rushing water, and became fearful that the child was going to drown.

"Are you in water?" she called out.

"Yes," the voice said. "Help me. I can't get out. I need my medicine."

"Okay, relax. I'm coming," Toy said, unable to see anything in the dark shaft. But she knew she was close. The child's voice seemed to be right below her. "I'm going to reach out my hand to you," she said. "When you see it, try to grab it."

Toy leaned sideways, but it was so tight that she couldn't get her arm free to reach out for the child. Sucking in all her breath, she finally managed to squeeze herself into a tight ball, dropping her hand into the darkness. "It's there," she said. "Can you see it?"

"No," the voice said.

Toy swung her hand back and forth like a pendulum, hoping the movement would catch the child's attention. Finally she felt a small, slippery hand brush across her palm and clasped her fingers tightly around it. "Don't pull away or I'll lose you," Toy said. "What's your name?"

"Lucy," she said weakly.

"Okay, Lucy," Toy said calmly, "I'm going to move up the ladder and pull you with me. Use your feet to find the rings on the ladder."

"I . . . going to fall," the child pleaded, her breathing more tortured and raspy than ever. "Please . . . get me out. I can't breathe. I'm . . . having an asthma attack."

"Hold on," Toy said, jerking on the child's hand as she pulled herself up with her free hand. The muscles in her side were smarting from trying to hold her entire body weight up with only one hand, but Toy was oblivious to any discomfort. The child was sick, asthmatic. She had to get her to a hospital. "Did you find the place to put your feet?" she asked.

"Yes, I think so."

"Okay, here we go again," Toy said, giving her another firm yank and stepping onto the next ring on the ladder.

"I . . . can't," the child said, her body weight collapsing, pulling Toy's hand.

Toy struggled to hang on. Even though the child wasn't that heavy, Toy was extremely light herself and the force of gravity was making the child seem like a stone. She wanted to get beneath her and place her on her shoulders, but the shaft was so tight that she didn't think she could. "Lucy," she said, "you have to help me. Are you ready to try again?"

There was no reply.

Toy's heart started pounding in her chest, more from fear than exertion. The child had passed out, she decided, probably from lack of oxygen. Of course, she had no idea how long the poor thing had been trapped in the storm drain. She could be suffering from starvation and dehydration as well.

Moving more slowly and making every attempt not to scrape the unconscious child's body against the metal railings as she pulled her out of the shaft, Toy struggled up the ladder, one foothold at a time. Her muscles were so overtaxed by this time that her arm was trembling, and she was terrified she was going to let the child fall back to the bottom of the hole. There must be a water main that ran down there, either that or the sewer, maybe an underground well. If she let the child fall now that she was unconscious, Toy knew there was a good possibility that she could drown.

Finally Toy saw a dot of light and realized that she had made it. Pulling herself out first, she then carefully pulled the child out. Her face was covered in mud and filthy, but Toy estimated her age at eight or nine. She had been certain she was older, since her words had been so perfectly enunciated. Just then a beam of moonlight streaked through an opening in the trees, and Toy could see her more clearly. She saw a dirty and disheveled little girl wearing what looked like a jumper and a long-sleeved white blouse. On her feet were patent leather shoes and white ankle socks with lace. Her head was a mass of tangled curls, and Toy could see leaves and twigs among the curls. Around her mouth was a tinge of blue.

She wasn't getting enough oxygen to her brain, Toy realized, immediately standing and sweeping up the limp child. Toy then took off running, the child in her arms, tripping on a gnarled tree branch stemming from the base of a tree trunk. Quickly scurrying to her feet, Toy lost her balance again and landed on her buttocks on a thick bed of leaves. Her weight combined with the child's, as well as the force of gravity, caused Toy to slide down the hill as though she was riding on a sled.

Reaching the bottom, she immediately scrambled back to her feet and started hiking up the hill, carrying the child again, panting and on the verge of collapse. Just then the little girl's eyes opened. "Hold on, Lucy," Toy told her. "We're almost there."

"I want my mommy," she blubbered.

Toy's side was cramping, and she knew she had to stop and rest before continuing. "Baby, can you tell me how you fell down that drain? Where're your parents?"

"You're not my mommy," the child said, wheezing and coughing. "I want my mommy. I don't talk to strangers."

"That's right," Toy said patiently, "but I want to help you. Can you tell me what happened?"

"They brought me here. They made me come. They took me from my Sunday school."

"Who took you?" Toy asked.

"The bad men," the child said. Terror leaped into her eyes, and her small body trembled violently.

Toy cradled the child's body in her arms, rocking her gently as she spoke. "Oh, honey," she said, stroking her head and back, "we're going to get you to a doctor and get you all fixed up. Everything's okay now. Everything's going to be fine now."

Suddenly the child started flailing her arms around and kicking, her breathing more strained and raspy than before. Toy kept a gentle but firm hold on her small body as she struggled to free herself. "I'm here. No one's going to hurt you. I won't let them."

"No," the child screamed. "Let me go. You're going to hurt me just like those bad men."

"Look," Toy said forcefully, trying to pick her up again in her arms, "I'm a schoolteacher. You know a teacher would never hurt you. I'm going to take you home, help you find your parents." When the girl persisted in thrashing about, Toy came up with something else. "I'm your guardian angel, okay? Have you ever heard of a guardian angel, sweetheart? They're angels sent by God to help you when you get in trouble. That means I have special powers and can make everything safe again. All you have to do is believe in me. Can you do that, huh?"

The little girl's eyes found Toy's, and she silently nodded. Toy then swept her up in her arms again and began walking. She cooed to her and sang to her until she was once again out on the grassy knoll, but the child couldn't relax. Her body kept stiffening in Toy's arms as she struggled to breathe.

Toy had no idea how to get out of the park and the child was heavy, heavier than she had thought. She couldn't just keep walking and walking. They could end up deep inside the park.

Gently she set the child down on the grass. They needed to formulate a plan. Toy had to get her bearings. "Please," she said to the little girl, "tell me about the bad men."

"The men . . . they came . . . they took me from my Sunday school where I go to church with my mommy. But Mommy wasn't there, and I was swinging on the playground. They . . . they held me around and took me away so I can't find my mommy."

"Did they hurt you?" Toy felt a stab of fear. The child had been kidnapped, snatched right out of a churchyard. She could have been raped, abused. There was no telling what atrocities had been inflicted on her.

"They . . . stole my underpants . . . and I peed. I couldn't help it," she cried. "Then they hit me and . . . kicked me . . . and put me in that hole."

"After they stole your panties," Toy said slowly, "did they touch you down there, put anything inside you, do anything else to hurt you?"

The child shook her head, as her chest expanded and contracted.

Suddenly the little girl's body fell backward on the grass and her stomach bowed upward, her entire body becoming stiff and rigid. She started screaming again at the top of her lungs.

"Please," Toy said, "don't scream. You're all right. I'm here." Scooping her up in her arms again, Toy took off, trying to see the buildings over the trees and figure out which way to go. Finally she reached a clearing and thought she heard the sounds of cars zipping by. A few seconds later, she saw the street and was overcome with relief.

Several yellow cabs sped by, already occupied with fares. Toy stepped off the curb and tried to flag down a passing motorist, but no one would stop. A few minutes later, a long black limousine appeared, and Toy stepped right in front of it, waving her free hand in the air.

The driver rolled down his window and stuck his head out. "What's wrong? Has there been an accident?"

"Yes," Toy said, almost falling against the car door in relief, the child still in her arms. "We have to get her to a hospital. She was kidnapped from a church playground, and the kidnappers left her in a drainage ditch."

"Put her in the backseat," the man said, reaching back to open the door for her. "Are you her mother?"

"No," Toy said, leaning down and gently placing the little girl on the plush velvet seat. "We're going to take you to a doctor now, honey," she told her. "You're going to be okay. I promise you."

Toy looked over the child's head and suddenly saw an older man sitting in the far corner. He leaned forward and started to say something, but Lucy interrupted him.

"You're so pretty," she said to Toy, her arms still wrapped tightly around Toy's neck. "Is being a guardian angel like being a fairy princess? Are you really an angel?"

"I try to be," Toy said, smiling as she kissed her on the forehead. Then she quickly turned to the driver, ignoring the man in the shadows. "Take us to the closest hospital."

Toy reached for the handle to close the door when everything suddenly went black, and she felt herself falling and falling, as if she were being sucked through space.

What Toy remembered next were white, blazing lights. They were so bright and harsh that she opened her eyes and then quickly closed them. She heard beeping and ticking, and she was cold, terribly cold. Sharp pains pricked her arms. Forcing her eyes open again, she saw bars and for a brief moment thought she was in jail.

"Welcome back," a woman in a starched white nurse's uniform said.

"Where am I?" Toy said, her eyes darting around the room frantically. "What happened?"

"You're in Roosevelt Hospital. You were brought here by ambulance from Central Park. You've been unconscious for some time now."

"Where's the little girl? Is she okay? Did you find her parents?"

"What little girl?" the nurse said, her eyes wide with interest now. "No one was with you when they brought you in. What are you talking about?"

"What happened to me?"

"The charge nurse called your physician, Dr. Esteban," the woman said. "I'll see if he's arrived yet. You were just here the other day, weren't you? I remember you."

The nurse disappeared, but Toy could see her through the glass. She could also see a counter and several nurses sitting behind it talking while they monitored a wall of blinking, flashing screens. Needles attached to tubes were running from both Toy's arms into bottles on stems. She brought a hand to her chest and touched the electrodes for the EKG. She was in intensive care again. She wanted to scream. She was hooked up to these awful machines, and she had to find the child, find out what had happened to her, find out if she was okay.

The door to the room banged open, and Dr. Esteban entered. "Mrs. Johnson," he said, peering down at her, his dark eyes full of compassion, "I'm glad to see you're awake. How are you feeling?"

"I'm cold," Toy said. "And I need to get out of here."

"I'll get the nurse to bring a blanket. Your blood pressure is still quite low." He paused and then continued, his voice serious and concerned. "Your heart arrested again. I'm sorry. From what we were told, you were in a carriage in Central Park and passed out. When the driver noticed, he tried to revive you. When he couldn't, he called the paramedics. Just as they began CPR, your heart spontaneously started beating again. Luckily, you had the receipt from admitting in your purse, so they returned you here, and the staff called me at home."

"There was a little girl with me. She had been kidnapped. Can you please try to find out what happened to her?"

Dr. Esteban looked deep in Toy's eyes. Then he let down the bed rail and sat on the edge of the bed. "Mrs. Johnson, listen to me, there was no little girl. You were riding alone in a carriage. The police were fearful something criminal had occurred and interrogated the driver quite carefully. He said he saw you walking alone in the park and solicited you for a ride in his carriage. You got in and after a few moments he heard a noise. When he looked back, your head had fallen forward and at first he thought you were asleep. He continued on since apparently this isn't unusual. Many people fall asleep. Then he heard another loud noise and looked back again. This time you had slipped out of the seat and were unconscious on the floorboard of the carriage."

Toy shook her head from side to side. She recalled being in the carriage, but she also knew she had been with the child. It had to be the same as before. When her heart stopped, she had been somehow dispatched to help the child. "I have to leave. I have to see if the girl is all right. I promised her."

"Please," he said, "don't do this again. I've already called your husband. He's deeply concerned."

Sure, Toy thought bitterly. He probably had a room reserved for her in a mental institution. "I'm fine, Dr. Esteban," Toy said. "And I'm checking out, so you can get these tubes out of my arm and these electrodes off my chest. If you don't, I'll remove them myself."

Toy tried to sit up. Dr. Esteban gently tried to push her back. "We could keep you here," he said, a veiled threat in his eyes. "Please don't make us go to court and obtain legal sanction just to save your life."

Toy was livid. She knew what he was talking about. With Stephen's cooperation they could drag her into court and declare her mentally incompetent. Then they could do anything to her they wanted. They could use her like a laboratory rat, poking, probing, examining her to their hearts' content.

Esteban saw her distress. He also saw the fierce look of determination in her eyes. "We're getting close to the answers," he told her. "If you leave now and don't allow us to treat you, you'll most certainly die. It's only a matter of time."

"You said you were close to the answers," Toy said sharply. "How close?"

"I think it's a combination of several problems," he said. "This is one of the reasons your condition has been so hard to identify. When you suffered the attack of pericarditis, the muscle in your heart was more than likely weakened. It wasn't enough to be detectible right after the incident, but as time went on, this weakness became more and more pronounced." He stopped and stared at Toy. "Are you following me? It's important that you understand the severity of your condition."

"Go on," Toy said.

"I'm almost positive you have a rare neurological disorder. It falls somewhere between sleep apnea and narcolepsy. Have you ever heard of sleep apnea?"

Toy shook her head.

"Well," Esteban explained, "it's an illness that causes a person's respiration to stop spontaneously while they are sleeping. The incidents last only seconds, but the condition can be quite dangerous. Now, in narcolepsy a person does not stop breathing. Instead they fall asleep inappropriately, sometimes many, many times during the course of a day. In most instances they have no advance warning and when they awaken, they are seldom aware that they have been sleeping. Meaning, they nod off in the middle of conversations, meetings, whatever."

"What does this have to do with me?"

"I was just going to explain that," he said. "Somehow your brain is sending electrical impulses to your heart that cause it to abruptly shut down. Then a short time later, these same electrical impulses spark your heart into beating again. But the part we are still uncertain of is with what kind of frequency these episodes occur and whether or not these episodes always follow the same exact pattern. Even though your heart apparently resumed beating on its own this evening, we have no idea if this will continue to happen. If we don't intervene, the next time this occurs . . ." He looked away. "Need I say more?"

"You're saying I could die."

"Yes, Mrs. Johnson, that's exactly what I'm saying. But I've been conferring with other specialists, and I think we have arrived at a solution. What we would like to do is to install a pacemaker. It's a fairly simple procedure, and I'm almost positive it will circumvent the problem."

"Then my heart won't stop again, right?" Toy asked.

"Exactly," Esteban said, smiling at her.

Without hesitation Toy said, "I don't want it."

Esteban tensed. "Please, Mrs. Johnson, I just tried to explain to you how serious this condition is. Why would you want to risk your life over a simple, surgical procedure?"

"I can't explain it," she said. "Besides, you wouldn't believe me. Just tell me one thing. Is Stephen coming?"

He skirted her question. "Would you like me to get him on the phone for you, speak to him yourself?"

"No," Toy said, certain now that her husband was on his way. She had to get out of the hospital before he got here. He would insist that she undergo the procedure and then the dreams would stop. She couldn't let it happen. She knew it had to be this way. If it meant she was risking her life to save just one more child, then she had to think it was well worth the risk. "I'd like to leave now."

Esteban scowled, his patience growing thin. "I've already scheduled you for surgery tomorrow. In addition, I assured your husband—"

Toy sat up in the bed and promptly ripped the electrodes off her chest. Then she faced the doctor. "Dr. Esteban, my husband and I are separated, and I'm a mature adult, able to make my own decisions. I'll never sign a consent for surgery, so you're just wasting your time."

Dr. Esteban was both frustrated and determined to reason with her. "Your husband is a physician. I'm sure you know how a pacemaker works. It will regulate your heartbeat. Once it's in place, you should never encounter this problem again. You can lead a normal life. And it's a very simple procedure. You'll be out of here in less than a week."

Toy let his words run through her mind and then turned to him again. "No," she said loudly, almost shouting. She felt a driving, urgent need to get out of the hospital, out of this room, out of the reach of her husband and Dr. Esteban. Whatever had happened in the park, she had to know, had to find the child, had to verify that she was safe as she had promised. The last thing Toy remembered was placing her in the back of the long black car. She had no idea who the driver was, where he had taken the child. He could have even been one of the kidnappers and Toy had merely handed him the child like a fool.

"If this is your final decision," Dr. Esteban said, "then I have no choice but to honor it. But I'm telling you you're making a mistake, the worst mistake of your life. You're a beautiful young woman with many productive years ahead, turning your back on a simple surgical procedure for absolutely no valid reason."

Once he had made his speech, he turned to leave the room. At the door, he glanced back at Toy. "The next time I see you, Mrs. Johnson, you may not be able to leave."

"Why? Because my husband will have me locked up?"

"No, because you will be dead." With that, he quietly slipped through the door.

Toy watched him step up to the nurses' station, shake his head, and wait until the nurse handed him her chart. After scribbling a few lines in it, he slapped it on the counter and disappeared down the corridor.

It was an unseasonably warm fall in Atlanta, but inside the air-conditioned newsroom, it was actually quite chilly. Thirty-five-year-old Jeff McDonald, a recent recruit of CNN's from the *Los Angeles Times,* was pulling an evening shift in the newsroom when his supervisor, Stan Fielder, stopped at his desk. Stan was a seasoned journalist in his fifties. An African American, he was short and balding. He favored suspenders with his white dress shirts, and frequently rolled up his sleeves when working. McDonald had left the *Times* because he wanted to shift gears, move into television.

"Take a look at this, Mac," Fielder said. "Am I crazy, or have we seen this lady? And I mean, recently, maybe in the past few days."

McDonald slipped on his glasses and glanced at the papers. "Where'd this come from, the New York bureau?"

"You got it. Looks like she stepped right out of a Botticelli, huh? Can't simply look at the drawing and get the full impact. Got to read the description. Red hair, green eyes, skin like milk."

McDonald realized he was looking at a composite drawing of a woman. The face was eerily haunting, the delicate features, the fine bone structure, the perfectly shaped lips. "You know what," McDonald said, "I think you might be right, Stan. She does look familiar. Has sort of a startled look about her, don't you think?" He was intrigued by the hair, the way it seemed to move back from her face. It was almost as if she was moving too fast to be captured, stepping right out of the drawing. "What else do you have?"

"Eight-year-old girl kidnapped from a church playground by two men in Manhattan early this morning, but located a short time ago. They evidently tried to rape her and then left her in a drainage ditch. State Senator Robert Weisbarth and his driver stopped when they saw this woman running out of Central Park carrying the kid. The girl suffers from chronic asthma." Fielder paused. His son was asthmatic. At twelve, he was finally coming out of it, but it had been a long, hard haul. More nights than he wanted to remember, he had awakened to the sound of labored, raspy breathing. "The trauma caused her to have a severe asthma attack. Little one already had a cold, so she was in pretty bad shape. Guess if this woman hadn't found her, she could have easily died." Fielder knew all about it. Every time his son caught a cold, it would escalate to pneumonia. Asthma caused the bronchial tubes to become inflamed and swollen, dangerously trapping fluids in the lungs.

Fielder continued, "After this lady placed the kid in the limo, she disappeared. Makes it kind of a mystery. Good story, don't you think? Good Samaritan. Doesn't want any credit. Does the deed and then splits. I like the feel of it."

"Wait," McDonald said, holding up his hand and rummaging through all the papers on his desk like a madman. "Kid. Pretty lady hero that vanished. There was another story just like that a few days ago. Came out of Kansas. We ran a clip." Finally he found what he was looking for: the UPI story on the schoolhouse fire. "Got it," he said, waving the copy in the air.

"What you got?" Fielder said, peering down over McDonald's shoulder.

"Nope," McDonald said jokingly, covering the paper with his hands. "If I put this together, it's mine, right? You have to promise you won't take it and give it to someone else. All I've been getting lately is the dregs."

Fielder issued a belly laugh, slapping the other man on the back. "You skinny little white boys think you can come down here to Atlanta and move right on in. You got to *earn* your way here, boy."

McDonald really liked Fielder. Not only did he like him, he respected him. He was one hell of a journalist. "Don't call me boy," he said, trying to keep a serious face. "Don't you ever call a white person boy. I'll report you, man. That's discrimination."

Again Fielder's deep laughter rang out. Then it suddenly stopped. "You got five seconds, McDonald."

The younger journalist spun around in his chair and promptly handed the article to Fielder. Then he sat back again with a smug expression on his face and placed his arms behind his neck. "Sound like your Botticelli?"

"Well, yes, it does," Fielder said, licking his lips. "There's no photograph, huh?"

"*Nada,* my man. But like I said, I think we have some footage of her." McDonald felt acid churning and popping in his stomach. He had duped the tape and sold it to a New York station. Right now he felt like he'd shot off his own foot. If the two people were the same and Fielder felt inclined to put together a half-hour news special on this vanishing hero, Jeff might get his first chance at producing. But he wouldn't get anything if the New York station had somehow managed to scoop them.

"Good," Fielder said calmly. Even though he didn't show it, Stan Fielder was excited. And he was a man who seldom got excited. Too many years had gone by and too many stories had passed his desk to do more than raise an eyebrow. But a lady hero as pretty as this one who suddenly appeared and rescued children and then vanished into thin air. Well, he told himself, that might just be something worth getting excited about. "Pull it out and let's run it," he told McDonald, turning to head back to his office. "What are we waiting for?"

TEN

"Voilà," Sarah said, jumping out from the kitchen, twirling around in the middle of the floor and then stopping to stare at Raymond. "What do you think?"

Sarah's lovely black hair was now a bright artificial shade of red. She looked almost identical to the image on the canvases. Stepping closer, she touched Raymond's face, tilting it so he was looking directly at her. "Don't you see? Now I'm the woman you always paint, the woman you love so much. But I'm here, Raymond, and she's not."

Like a disembodied portrait, Raymond could see only her hair, her face, her eyes. But what he saw set him on fire. She was here. His angel had finally found him. Tears streamed down his cheeks. He was safe now. Joy and elation coursed through his body, fueling his muscles, sending flashing signals to his brain. He spun around and rushed to the corner of the room, returning with a sketch book and what looked like a box of pastels. Dropping to the floor, he clasped Sarah's hand and brought her down next to him. Then he carefully selected a chalk pastel out of the box and handed it to her. "Here," he said in a small, childish voice, "you can have the green."

As Sarah watched, he spread out on the wood floor on his stomach and started drawing on a sheet of paper. He looked up at her and then tore off a sheet for her to use, sliding it across the floor.

Sarah followed his lead and positioned herself on her stomach facing him. Like two kindergarten children, they drew and colored. Raymond was drawing circles within circles. Sarah didn't know what to draw so she copied Raymond. After a few moments he looked up at her and smiled.

Sarah beamed back, thinking he was on the verge of a breakthrough. He had to be, she thought, trying not to let her concern show on her face and spoil the moment. The day before, that awful

Francis Hillburn had suddenly appeared at the loft with another artist in tow, insisting that Raymond had to vacate the premises within a matter of days or he would legally evict him. Sarah pleaded with him to no avail. Already she had begun packing up Raymond's things to move them to her house in Queens, but she was doubtful that her female roommates would tolerate her bringing a man to live in the house. Especially a man as troubled and strange as this one.

But she had no choice. Sarah had fallen hopelessly in love with Raymond Gonzales, so much so that she had already sacrificed her job and was living on her meager savings, money she had diligently set aside in order to return to school in the fall. She didn't care. Being alone with him in the loft since they had walked out of the hospital, surrounded by his visions of winged angels, she had found something in herself that she had never known existed. While Raymond had slept or stared blankly into space, Sarah had prayed for the first time since she was a child. And she had prayed reverently and passionately, begging God to save this man, to restore him to normalcy so he could continue to paint and one day be her husband.

As he pathetically reached across with another color, Sarah tenderly stroked his hand and felt an instant jolt of electricity. "One day you're going to be the most famous artist in the world," she said prophetically, the words appearing in her mind the second before they were spoken. "Your paintings will hang in all the museums, and everyone will want to meet you."

Raymond raised his head and mumbled a word under his breath, "Michelangelo."

"Yes, Raymond," Sarah said, smiling over at him, "just like Michelangelo."

The newsroom at CNN headquarters in Atlanta was buzzing with activity. Banks of color monitors decorated an entire wall while printers spilled out copy and telephones jangled. They had a remote crew down in Wyoming, where a religious cult had been holed up for over a month; someone had called in a bomb threat for the Empire State Building; and there was some maniac in Los Angeles cutting up young women and leaving their body parts on people's lawns.

Business as usual.

Jeff McDonald was poring over his notes, trying to decide which way he wanted to proceed with the Good Samaritan story. The story had tremendous potential, but only if they struck the right nerve. Jeff knew true-crime shows were extremely popular, but Fielder wanted to make it strictly human interest.

New developments on the Kansas case had given Jeff two distinct options. Arson investigators had determined that the fire was purposely set and not by a kid playing with matches. Someone had soaked a rag in gasoline and tossed it into the basement where other flammable liquids had been stored by the janitor. Now they had to consider that the mysterious woman was their arsonist. Why would she save the boy and then vanish if she didn't have something to hide? Everyone liked to be a hero, get that big pat on the back. And arsonists frequently loitered around at the crime scene, watching their own handiwork. Just because she saved the boy meant nothing. Most arsonists didn't want people to die. They were nut cases. They got high on the flames themselves, the excitement.

The Topeka Fire Department and their arson investigators wanted to have a few words with this mystery woman, and they weren't contemplating a medal.

But the Manhattan situation was slightly different. They didn't have all the details yet, since it had just occurred and the authorities in Manhattan moved painfully slow, but the victim, an eight-year-old apple-cheeked girl with a mind like a steel trap, had insisted that it was two men who kidnapped her from the playground at the church and two men who dumped her in the drainage ditch after trying to rape her. She had discouraged them by urinating all over one man's hand. She was an investigator's dream: smart, precocious, willing to talk at the drop of a hat, excellent memory. No, she told them again and again, the woman had not been working with the men or involved in any way. She was a guardian angel sent from heaven to rescue her.

But the NYPD and the FBI were not as convinced as the child. Although they were not actively seeking the mystery woman as a suspect, as they were in Kansas, they had not ruled it out. The premise was the woman wanted a child, hired the men to kidnap the little girl, and then instructed them to leave her in the drainage ditch, where she would later retrieve her. When the child suffered the asthma attack and almost stopped breathing, the woman had panicked and decided to get rid of her, handing her off to the first person she saw and then fleeing the scene.

Jeff leaned back in his chair and sighed. It made sense. Childless woman wants baby but can't have one. Sees a beautiful little girl one day in a playground and decides she has to have her. Hires a few goons to snatch her, thinking she can take the kid away somewhere and make her forget her old life. It wasn't as if it had never happened before.

Did he have a hero, a saint, a Good Samaritan? Or did he have a dangerous baby snatcher? He looked down at the still photo of the woman taken from the film clip. He just didn't know. It was the same woman. He was almost certain of it. In both cases children had been involved. The arsonist in Kansas may have fully planned to snatch a child after setting the fire, knowing that there would be chaos. When she saw the banks of reporters and cameras, she realized her plan had failed. Then she got on a flight to New York and somehow put plan two into effect.

Jeff brought his chair to an upright position and rubbed his eyes. He was supposed to get out of here by midnight. But he had a serious problem. Trying to track down the woman he had sold the copy of the tape to, he had learned that there was no WKRP in New York. One of the programmers had even laughed at him. "Have you ever heard of WKRP in Cincinnati?" they taunted. "It was a television series not long ago, you fool. It isn't real. Someone's playing a joke on you." Not only that, in the show, the fictitious station was radio not television. Jeff had sold the tape that could change his entire career to an entity that did not exist.

He fingered a piece of paper on his desk: the Emerson Air Freight shipping order to Toy Johnson at the Montrose Hotel, Manhattan. Then he reached under his desk blotter and pulled out the check. He had yet to deposit it in his bank. If there was anything else to feel good about tonight, it was the fact that he had not got around to cashing it. Right in the left-hand corner was all he needed to get the tape back: Dr. and Mrs. Stephen Johnson, their address, and their phone number. It went even further than that. Evidently not wanting to produce their ID each time they wrote a check, the couple's driver's license numbers were printed right on the check.

"How convenient," he said, picking up the phone to call the FBI.

"Look," he told Stan Fielder about thirty minutes later, "this mystery hero story is getting bigger and better by the minute. I need to do some fieldwork, however, if we want to get this aired in a timely fashion. We sit around on our behinds too long and the woman will step forward or be apprehended and the story shifts to the mundane." McDonald was standing in front of Fielder's cluttered desk.

Behind the glass, the entire newsroom was visible, a whirl of frantic activity. "Worse yet is the fact that someone could scoop us."

"I see," Fielder said thoughtfully. "How much time you need?"

"Only a few days, and I think I can set up a production schedule. I need to fly to New York and make a plea for some related footage so we'll have enough to stretch to a half-hour slot."

Fielder narrowed his eyes. "What footage?"

Fielder had street smarts, McDonald thought. The man could smell a lie from five miles away. But McDonald had grown up not far from South Central Los Angeles. He was ready. He wanted to make sure that CNN paid for his expenses when he went on his house-cleaning mission. "See, I have it all mapped out in my mind. We'll glorify this whole thing like you won't believe. Get interviews with the kids she saved, interviews with the grateful family, the senator and his driver. Then I thought we could interject other similar stories of heroism, sort of make the whole program a story about remark-able heroes in history. I even thought if I got enough, we could shoot for a full hour slot, prime time. I've been thinking of titles like *Reluc-tant Hero,* or something along those lines. You know, the angel of mercy approach."

Fielder had his chin down almost on his chest and was staring up at the younger man. McDonald always favored brevity when making his pitches. Fielder had never seen him so loose-lipped. "I thought you wanted to play this the opposite direction. Isn't that what you told me the other day?"

"Oh," McDonald said, "if you want to play her as a suspect, some deranged diabolical baby snatcher, you've certainly got the muscle to do it. Kansas state police and the NYPD would be more than willing to give us the goods. They're hurting for leads right now. Taking this public . . ."

"No," Fielder said thoughtfully, "we've got enough bad actors out there to populate a continent. Don't you think people need some-thing to make them feel good now and then? Not only that, but I think the media has an obligation to provide it."

McDonald smiled. He'd pegged Fielder right: an aging news jockey who'd somehow lost his taste for blood. "Glad we agree," McDonald said, nodding. "So, what do you say? Do I get my travel papers?"

Fielder stared over his head, gazing at the newsroom through the glass. After several moments he looked Jeff in the eye. "You got three days. Bring it in, kid. And watch that expense account. No three-hundred-dollar hotel suites."

"Thanks," McDonald gushed. "You won't be sorry, Stan. This is going to be big. We're talking Emmy time."

Fielder laughed, a big, booming sound that came from somewhere in his gut. McDonald leaned over the desk and pumped his hand. Then he did a fancy pivot turn and left.

What Fielder didn't know wouldn't hurt him. As soon as McDonald had the tape back in his hands and verified that it had never been aired, he was going to paint this mystery hero as the most heinous criminal on the block. Fielder might have lost his taste for blood, but Jeff McDonald sure hadn't. When you were in the business of news and you developed a soft spot, you might as well pack your bags and move on.

Walking fast through the newsroom to his desk, McDonald looked around him and smiled. Someday he might be the one sitting behind the glass at a big desk, in a comfortable chair, with an actual door, all this bustling activity his own little empire. "Yes," he said, shoving a fist in the air as he flopped down in his chair. Jeff McDonald was sitting on top of the very vehicle he needed to take him straight to the top.

There was just one little problem, but nothing he couldn't handle. Grabbing his phone, he called the airlines. "What you got going to New York in the next hour? I'll take anything you got. Prop jet, cargo plane, you name it. Just get me there and get me there fast."

Toy was walking back to the hotel from Roosevelt Hospital. She was tired and confused, more confused than she had ever been. Having been fueled by religious zeal for days, she felt like someone had forgotten to charge her battery. Her body ached all over and she missed her home, her rosebushes, her little car. She missed the ocean, the sound of the waves, the smell of salt water. She missed her students. But of everyone she missed Margie Roberts. In the past two years she had become like a mother to the girl, even though her own mother adored her and did everything she possibly could. But when a child was terribly ill, Toy knew there could never be enough love, enough encouragement. It also worked in reverse, as Margie had become the daughter Toy had always wanted.

But she couldn't think of that now, she told herself. She couldn't help Margie without her health.

Science had once again triumphed over the spirit, she thought bitterly. Dr. Esteban and his colleagues had managed to turn a handful of miracles into a hodgepodge of awful diseases. They'd slice her open, pop in a pacemaker, and Toy Johnson's heart would keep on beating like a Timex watch. Right now she wasn't certain she wanted her heart to keep beating. It was only a spare part. There was no such thing as a real heart, not the heart of poets, lovers, hopeless romantics. Just as that thought crossed her mind, Toy reached up to touch her necklace, the one Stephen had given her with the little locket shaped like a heart. It was one of Toy's prized possessions, and she had placed both hers and Stephen's pictures in it, taken on their wedding day. At first she thought it was inside her shirt, and then she realized it was no longer on her neck. She knew she didn't take it off. She never took it off. She decided to call the hospital and see if they had taken it off when she was brought into the emergency room.

Reaching her hotel, the doorman nodded at her. Toy nodded back, dropping her head and hurrying into the lobby. Just as she passed the reception counter, one of the clerks called her over.

"Excuse me, Mrs. Johnson," the man said politely, "but the manager requested that you take care of your bill."

"I gave you my credit card," Toy said. "Just put it on my credit card."

"Your credit card isn't any good. We ran it yesterday and it's been canceled. The manager would like you to clear up your balance and then give us a cash deposit if you'll be continuing your stay here."

Toy's face blanched. She'd been right about Stephen. "How . . . how much do I owe?"

"Let me check," he said, punching her account up on the computer terminal. "Did you order room service this morning or remove anything from your mini bar?"

"No," Toy said, shaking her head.

"Then your current balance is five hundred and fifty-three dollars."

"How could that be?" Toy protested. "I've only had the room two nights."

"Well," he said, "the room rate is one hundred and fifty dollars per day, and your husband charged a room with us as well. Of course, with the cancellation of your credit card, we can't collect that amount either." He studied the bill before handing it to Toy. "There's also a number of room-service charges."

She felt like an idiot. She had sized up the situation from the beginning, knowing Stephen would cancel the credit cards, clean out the bank accounts, but then she had failed to follow through. In her purse, she had maybe twenty or thirty dollars and no more. "I can give you a check," she said, opening her purse to retrieve her checkbook.

"Under the circumstances," the clerk said apologetically, "I'm afraid the manager insists on cash."

Toy dropped the checkbook in the bottom of her purse and pulled out her wallet instead, plucking all the mangled and twisted bills out of the small change pocket and placing them on the counter. Then she dumped the wallet upside down and counted out all the change. "I have almost forty dollars. I promise this is all a mistake," Toy said quickly. "Keep the forty, and first thing in the morning, I'll get some money wired from my bank."

Before the clerk could say anything else, Toy spun around and headed for the bank of elevators. Would they lock her out of her room tomorrow? she wondered. But at the moment her financial straits seemed to pale in light of more serious concerns. Stephen was probably on a plane right now heading to the city to force her to undergo the surgery. Toy was face to face with reality, and the supernatural seemed far removed. She had run out of money, was about to go through a divorce, and had suddenly found herself staring down an operation.

Her New York adventure was about to come to a screeching halt, along with her brief career as a purveyor of miracles.

Seeing the door to her room, she stepped inside and just stood there, lost in her thoughts. At only twenty-nine, she needed a machine to make her heart beat, keep her from dying. If she let them perform the operation, an alien object would take up permanent residence in her body. They might as well give her an artificial heart, an artificial soul. Then they could connect her to a computer and she could spill out data using artificial intelligence.

Touching her neck again, she took a seat at the small writing desk and called the emergency room. After identifying herself, she said, "Do you have my necklace?"

"No," the nurse said. "We gave you back all your property when you left."

"But I had a gold heart locket on," Toy persisted. "You have to have it."

"I'm sorry, but we're very careful about things like that. Perhaps you're mistaken and you weren't wearing it."

Toy thanked the woman and hung up. Normally she didn't care

about her possessions, but this was the one thing that meant something to her. Stephen had given her the locket as an engagement gift. They had been so happy then. Going through her cosmetic case and her luggage without finding it, Toy suddenly had a mental image of the little girl in the park reaching for her neck just before she blacked out. All she could figure out was the child had managed to get her hand on the necklace and accidentally pulled it off. Well, she thought, so much for Stephen and so much for the locket. She couldn't seem to hold onto anything anymore—not her jewelry, her husband, even her sanity. Collapsing on the bed, she prayed for it all to be over. She would remain this way, never leaving the hotel. Eventually her heart would stop again and there would be no one to revive her. She heard the phone ringing and tried to ignore it, pushing the pillow up on both sides over her ears. No one else would be calling but Stephen or possibly Sylvia, and she had nothing to say to either of them. Sylvia would only try to talk her into the operation.

Finally Toy couldn't stand it anymore and picked up the phone and listened.

"Hey, this Toy Johnson?" a man's voice said. "This is Joey. You know, your pal, Joey Kramer?"

"Oh," Toy said, "how are you?"

"I'm great," he said. "What's up?"

"Nothing," Toy said, not knowing what else to say.

"Well, then, why don't you'se come down to the lobby? You got yourself a visitor."

"You're here?" she said, surprised. It was late, after twelve o'clock.

"Yeah," he said. "You coming down or what?"

"I don't know," Toy said. "Maybe I shouldn't."

"Why not? You ain't got nothing else to do."

"It's too late," Toy said. "And I wasn't feeling well earlier. I guess I should stay in bed, but thanks anyway." She started to hang up the phone when she heard him say something else.

"Ah, come on," he urged, "you ain't sick. You just been hanging out with the wrong people. Joey's gonna buy you a nice cup of coffee, maybe get you some chicken soup or something. Then you'se gonna feel great."

Toy laughed in spite of herself. "You're on," she said. "But it'll take me a few minutes to put my clothes back on. I was already in bed."

"Heck," he said, "just put on that T-shirt I like so much."

Joey disconnected and Toy did as he said, pulling on her baseball T-shirt and a pair of Levis, then heading to the lobby to meet him.

Joey Kramer was wearing jeans, a plaid short-sleeve shirt, and a brightly colored nylon parka. He wasn't a tall man, but to Toy he looked as cuddly and appealing as any man she had ever seen. He was telling some kind of story to the night clerks and had them all in stitches. As soon as he spotted Toy, he walked over and threw his arm around her shoulder, pulling her close to his body. "This is my angel," he said to the clerks, smiling with pride. "Ain't she something?"

"I don't know if the hotel restaurant is still open," Toy said once they had stepped away from the counter. "But we can go into the bar. It's right over there."

Joey looked behind him and then shook his head. "I know a joint down the street," he said. "This joint's gonna charge us five bucks for a glass of water."

"Oh," Toy said, "it's awfully late. I thought we were just going to have our coffee here."

"Whadya worried about?" Joey said, tilting his head to the side and grinning at her. "Getting mugged or something? When you hang with Joey here, you don't gotta worry about nothing."

They stepped out into the evening air, Joey linking his arm through Toy's. The temperature had dropped to the low fifties and it was very brisk, but Toy didn't find it unpleasant. She found it invigorating. Lights were twinkling in all the buildings, and the city was still bustling with activity. From a nearby club they could hear the smooth, clear notes of a tenor saxophone filtering into the atmosphere.

"This is it," Joey said, opening the door to a dimly lit bar and standing back while Toy stepped inside.

Making their way to the back was like passing through a receiving line at a wedding. Joey knew almost everyone perched on the bar stools, but then Joey knew almost everyone in the bar. "Hey, Joey" rang out again and again, and each time he stopped, smiled, engaged in a round of back slapping, hand pumping, and "How's the wife and kids?" always adding his new line, "Meet my pretty angel. Ain't she something?"

Picking up their two mugs of coffee from the bartender, Joey carried them to a back table. "Is it too loud in here?" he asked Toy. "We could go somewhere else. Didn't figure it would be so crowded to-night. Lotta guys from the job."

Toy was intrigued. "Are you saying all of those men are police officers or transit officers?" To her, they looked so ordinary, so com-mon. They reminded her of relatives on her father's side of the family. Most of them were many years older than Joey, had bulging bellies, cigarettes dangling from their lips, and looked like they might have a heart attack if they ever tried to wrestle anyone to the ground. But they smiled at her and shook her hand, making her feel wel-come. In Los Angeles, she thought the police officers looked like Roman gladiators, their muscles barely contained inside the fabric of their uniforms, their tanned skin glistening in the ever present sun-light. And they never smiled, absolutely never. Here in New York things were evidently a little different.

"That's the Murph Man over there," Joey said, pointing. "Captain Paul Murphy. Retiring next week. Sitting next to him is his son-in-law, Harry Maitland, and next to him is Murph's son, Billy. Been on the job two years." There was another man also at the bar, bent over a glass of Jack Daniels. "Oh, and that there is Snoop. He's the best darn dick in the country. They ain't no crime too tough for old Snoop to solve."

Toy's eyes fell to the table. "I probably shouldn't have come. I'm on a downer right now."

"Me, too," Joey said, his face shifting into a strained expression. "My mom died on this day last year."

"Oh," Toy said, "I'm sorry. You must have loved her very much."

"Yeah," he said, dwelling a moment on his grief, peering down into his coffee mug. Then he lifted it and took another sip, setting it back down on the table. "My girl dumped me last month, too. That can make a guy feel pretty rotten."

Toy felt obligated to drink her coffee, even though she was fearful that the caffeine would keep her from sleeping. "Why did she dump you?"

"You know, the job. Not around enough evenings. She liked to go out all the time. Besides, she thinks I don't manage my money."

"I'm married," Toy blurted out.

"Married, huh?" Joey said. "Right. Yeah, I remember now. But your husband don't treat you right. Don't know what he has, does he?"

"Actually, we're separated," Toy said. As soon as she said it, she regretted it. She didn't want to give him the wrong impression, make him think she was interested in him romantically. But Joey Kramer had a way about him. He was good-looking in a working class way: dark hair, nice eyes, long lashes, good clear skin, a mustache that tickled his upper lip. Even though he wasn't a gladiator, he had as yet to develop a potbelly, and he had the face of men who always appeared when you need them: plumbers, electricians, paramedics, firemen.

"Where's your old man now?" he asked Toy.

"He went back to Los Angeles, but I think he's coming back to get me."

"How long you staying?"

"I don't know," Toy said. "I may have to have an operation. If I decide to let them do it, I'll probably have it done in Los Angeles."

Joey arched his eyebrows. "What kind of operation?"

"No big deal," Toy said, shoving her hair out of her face and taking another sip of her coffee. "Where do you live?"

"Brooklyn. Ever been to Brooklyn?"

"No."

"Ain't missed anything. Tell me about this operation."

"I'd rather not," Toy said. "Like I said, it's not serious."

Joey's face became animated. It was the first time she had seen him grimace. Now she saw the potential for anger. It was sparking all around him. His shoulder twitched as he spoke. "Oh, no, well that's what they told my mom. Just a little operation. Come in that morning, we put you to sleep, go home that afternoon. No big deal, right? Know what my mom died from? A lousy cataract operation." Joey paused and shook his head. "They put her to sleep, all right. They put her to sleep permanently."

Toy was staring at him, but she couldn't see his face. All she could see was a gaping mouth, rows of not so straight teeth, the back of his throat, his pink tongue moving in and out of his mouth as he spoke. Would they put her to sleep permanently? "What happened? Did she have a negative reaction to the anesthesia?"

"I guess you could call it that. She died." Now Joey's other shoulder started twitching. "When I think about what happened to my mother, I get a little crazy."

Toy felt a sense of camaraderie now. "Believe me, I don't want to have this operation, Joey, but they're telling me I'm going to die if I don't. So I'll probably end up giving in."

Joey hunkered down at the table, moving his elbows out and shoving his chest forward. "You look okay to me," he said. "Don't let them make you do something if you don't want to do it. Just 'cause they're a doctor don't mean they always know what they're doing. Believe me, if someone puts a bullet in old Joey, I'll just get a pair of tweezers and pull the sucker out myself. Ain't getting me in no hospital."

Toy finished the last of her coffee, never taking her eyes off Joey Kramer. Then she gave him a big lopsided smile. "I like your attitude," she told him. "I like it a lot."

"Oh, yeah?" he said, smiling. "Anyone ever tell you how cute that dimple is in your chin?"

"Yeah," Toy said, tossing her head and laughing. "Anyone ever tell you that you're a pretty swell fellow?"

"All the time," he said. "Hey, Murph," he yelled out. "Tell my angel I'm a great guy. She ain't sure yet."

"Shut up, Kramer," the other man said jokingly. "Always picking up those bums on the street. Man, you're gonna catch a disease someday. Got some kind of screw loose in that pointy little head. You're a crazy do-gooder is what you are."

"I can live with that," Toy said quickly. Then she added, "By the way, I wanted to ask you something. What exactly do you do for the homeless people? At Wolfe's they told me you give out cards to local businesses, offering to come in and handle the situation if a homeless person or derelict wanders in off the street."

"Oh, that," Joey said. "Ain't nothing. All I do is get them a room, give them some money for food and things, a little extra maybe to hold them over until they can get themselves together." He stopped speaking and stared in Toy's eyes. "Have you ever seen a person with frostbite?"

"No," she said, "I don't believe so."

"Well, you come down in the tunnels with me when it gets cold and you'll see plenty. Don't look so bad at first. Whatever it touches, though, they got to chop off. I pulled this guy out one night, carried him to the hospital, and next time I see him, both his legs are gone."

"How do you afford it?" Toy asked, thinking of her own problems in trying to assist needy families. Then she remembered that Joey Kramer wasn't married, which made things a lot easier.

He was flushing and fidgeting. "I don't need much, see," he finally said. "I don't keep my own place. I sleep on the sofa at my uncle's house. Pay them a little money every month." The shoulder started twitching again. "Way I see it, somebody's got to do it. Can't let people starve and freeze out there."

"Sounds like we have a lot in common," Toy said. "I try to do what I can. It isn't much, but it makes me feel good."

"Homeless?" Joey asked. "You better be careful," he cautioned. "It's not the thing for a lady like you to be messing with. See, some of these people ain't right in the head, and they can get kinda nasty. Other night, well, an old fart kicked me in the gut. Didn't mean nuthin', though. Just crazy."

"Oh, I don't work with the homeless," she told him. "I just try to help some of the needy families and kids at the school where I teach."

"That's better," he said with relief. "So, you work with kids? Bet you're really something." He thought for a few moments and then continued. "Yeah, I can see it, you know. Can't imagine a kid wouldn't take a shine to you. Not with those eyes you got, and that pretty red hair."

Toy gazed at him warmly. They were alike, she thought. Two kindred souls trying to swim upstream in a river of despair. But her new friend was right. Working with kids was her forte. It took a man like Joey to deal with the problems of the mentally ill and the homeless, particularly in a city as tough as New York.

"Let's get outta here," Joey said finally, tossing some bills down on the table. On the way out, he stopped in front of the bar and pointed at Toy's chest. "See that right there on her shirt?"

"Yeah, I see it," the detective they called Snoop said, his shoulders slumped forward over the bar, so intoxicated that he could barely keep his eyes open. "What about it?"

"This ain't just any angel, Snoop. She's my California Angel. Wanna make sure you get it right."

As Toy and Joey made their way out of the bar, Snoop snorted, "Well, whadya know, Kramer found himself an angel. Think I'm gonna go out and find me an angel, too." Then he pushed himself to his feet and staggered out of the bar.

Jeff McDonald stepped up to the counter at the Montrose Hotel and asked for Toy Johnson's room number. "Mrs. Johnson isn't in now," the clerk said. "Would you like to leave a message?"

"No," McDonald said. "Do you have any idea when she'll be back?"

The man narrowed his eyes at the reporter. "We don't keep track of our guests."

"Oh, yeah," McDonald said, reaching in his jacket for his press pass. "I'm with CNN, Cable Network News. Can you describe Mrs. Johnson? It's urgent."

"Oh," he said, "Mrs. Johnson is quite pretty. She has long red hair. Her eyes are green, I think, and . . ." The clerk leaned over the counter. The reporter had suddenly sprinted toward the bank of pay phones on the wall on the other side of the lobby.

As soon as he heard red hair, McDonald knew. It all made sense. The call signs for a television station that didn't exist. The woman's burning desire to have the tape. Dropping some change in the pay phone, McDonald dialed information and then quickly hung up. A second later, he was speaking to the New York bureau of the FBI.

"You fellows are working with the state police on a case out of Kansas, a woman suspect in a school fire." McDonald stopped and looked behind him, then continued. "Well, if you can get some men over to the Montrose Hotel right away, I think you'll have your suspect in custody."

ELEVEN

About a block from the hotel, Joey stopped in front of the entrance to the subway, eager to jump on a train and head back to Brooklyn. "You sure you'll be okay walking back alone? Hey, maybe I should go, too."

"No, I'll be fine," Toy insisted. "It's only a block and it's well lit. Go on home. It's really late. If we wait any longer, the sun will be coming up."

"Yeah," he said, stretching his arms over his head and yawning. "When am I gonna see you again?"

"I don't know," Toy said.

"I'll see ya," he said. "Don't you worry. When Joey takes a shine to someone, he's always around. All you gotta do is snap your fingers," he said, laughing and snapping his own, "and the next thing you knows, I'll be there."

Toy was sad to see him go, fearful she would never see him again. Even though they had known each other only a short time, she had grown very fond of him. He possessed a goodness of heart that was extremely rare. "Take care of yourself," she said. "Be careful on your job and when you're trying to help people. Don't let anyone else kick you."

"Same to you," he replied. "And don't let those docs give you any trouble. You got my card, right? Anyone hassles you—"

"I'll be fine," Toy said, reaching over and pecking him gently on the cheek. "Go on," she whispered in his ear. "Extended farewells always make me cry."

Once Joey had disappeared down the subway, Toy started walking back to the hotel. Entering the lobby, she saw several men standing around in black raincoats with somber looks on their faces.

"Toy Johnson?" one man said.

"Yes," Toy said.

"FBI," he said, flipping a badge in her face. "We have a warrant for your arrest."

His partner quickly reached out and grabbed Toy's hand, pulling it behind her back.

"What? What's going on?" Toy said frantically. Then she heard it. A sound like no other. The sound of stainless steel handcuffs snapping into place.

"No, God," she said, panicked now, "I didn't do anything. I swear." It must be bad checks, Toy tried to tell herself. Stephen had cleaned out the bank account and all her checks had bounced. But the FBI? And this quick?

Suddenly a flash of light exploded in her face. Toy was temporarily blinded by it, and then she heard the click, click, click of a camera shutter.

The FBI men were pulling Toy, trying to lead her away. She started kicking out and yelling, all while the camera lens continued to snap in her face. "What are the charges? Tell me the charges. This is insanity."

"You're under arrest for three counts of first-degree murder, as well as arson. You have the right to remain silent," the agent continued. "You have the right to have an attorney present during questioning. If you don't have an attorney . . ."

Toy wasn't listening. She stared straight ahead while he continued reading her rights, while the camera's relentless clicking continued. She was completely paralyzed by fear. Murder, the man had said. Her heart was pounding out a staccato beat; she was certain she was going to faint and fall right on the ground.

She was walking now, her hands cuffed behind her back, her head down, still wearing the navy blue baseball shirt and her jeans. She felt fresh air on her face, saw the brown car at the curb, felt the coarse fabric of the agents' suits against her arms as they almost carried her along, her feet dragging on the ground.

"Toy," a voice called to her. "Look over here."

She looked up, thinking it was someone she knew, someone here to rescue her and explain what was happening, explain how she could be arrested for murder. But when she looked up, she just saw a man leaning on one knee with a camera, shooting away. "That's good. Stay right there," he said. "That's great."

Behind him was another man with an enormous camera strapped on his shoulders. Toy knew instantly it was a television camera. The other man was directing him now, yelling at him. "Get her getting into the car. Make sure you get a close-up of her face."

Toy tried to bring her hands up to shield herself, but they were handcuffed behind her back. Instead she dropped her chin to her chest. Then the FBI agent opened the car door and pushed her head down, shoving her into the backseat.

As the car took off, Toy turned around and looked out at the people on the sidewalk, the reporters, photographers, onlookers. They had all come to see her. She had fantasized about this moment, the press all gathered around while she told her incredible tale, the oohs and ahs, the sensational headlines. In her fantasy she was a person sent here to provide people with hope, restore their belief in miracles. She had been behind the veil of death and discovered another world. Her dream, however, was a far cry from being arrested for murder.

Toy continued watching the people until they slowly receded and then disappeared.

"So what do you think?" Special Agent Reggie Briggs said, staring at the woman through the one-way glass.

"Guilty," Paul Davidson said.

Briggs rubbed his fingers back and forth over his chin, scratchy from day-old stubble. He and his partner had started their day at five in the morning, participating in a large narcotics raid. It was now after four, and they were both exhausted. "I don't know. It's all pretty far-fetched. She would have had to set the fire in Kansas, save the kid, and somehow catch a flight back to the city the same day. Then she had to select the kid she wanted to snatch here and hire some thugs to snatch her. Pretty wild, if you ask me, particularly when you look at how fast this all went down."

"Hey," Davidson said, "I didn't tell you I knew how she did it. I just think she's guilty."

"What did her husband say?"

"Righteous creep if you ask me. Said we were out of our minds. He's flying in tonight. Got some hot-shot attorney he says is going to represent her."

Briggs moved up close to the glass, his breath smoking a circle. Toy was sitting at a long table, staring out into space. She looked small, delicate, distraught. For a second Briggs felt a flurry of sympathy. She had the kind of face that pulled you in, disarmed you. He shrugged his shoulders. Why would an attractive woman like this one, married to a prominent doctor, want to commit such awful crimes? To get a child, of course, but it still defied description. Three schoolteachers had lost their lives in that fire, and that wasn't considering the ordeal Lucy Pendergrass had been through in Central Park.

Davidson came up beside him. "The attorney isn't here now, but he'll be here tomorrow."

Briggs looked over at him. "Exactly my thoughts. Want to try and crack her?"

"You bet," Davidson said.

The door opened and two men entered the room, the same two FBI agents who had arrested her. Toy tried to swallow, but her mouth was too dry. What were they going to do to her now? she wondered. Lock her in solitary confinement? String her up from the rafters?

"Mrs. Johnson, I don't think we were formally introduced. This is Special Agent Davidson, and I'm Special Agent Briggs. Is there anything we can get you: a soda, cigarettes, something to eat?"

"Soda," Toy managed to say.

Briggs got up and left the room to get the soda. Davidson faced Toy with a pleasant, relaxed expression on his face that said we're just having a talk, you and me; it's nothing to get upset about. "Do you know what's going on? Do you understand the charges?"

"No," Toy said.

"Would you like me to tell you?"

"Yes."

"The warrant we arrested you on was issued by the Topeka County Superior Court. Does Topeka ring a bell?"

"Yes," Toy said. "The fire, right?"

Davidson felt his stomach do a little cartwheel. Admission number one was down. Now he had to move on to the good stuff. "You were there at that fire, weren't you?"

"Yes," Toy answered, never taking her eyes off the FBI agent.

"So," he said, taking it slow, not wanting to make mistakes, "you left your hotel here in Manhattan, flew to Kansas, and went to that schoolhouse. Right?"

"No."

Briggs was back and handed Toy the soda. "I hope Coke is all right?" he said politely.

In his late twenties, Reggie Briggs had a boyish, wet-behind-the-ears look. His hair was blond and neatly cut, his eyes a nondescript gray, and he was a small, compact man. Davidson, on the other hand, was over six foot five, an ex-lineman for Notre Dame, with hair almost the same shade as Toy's. Last week he had celebrated his fortieth birthday.

Toy lifted the can of soda and drank it almost in one swallow. Then she set it back down on the table.

Davidson continued, exchanging knowing glances with Briggs. "So you were in Kansas, but you didn't go to the school? Is that what you're saying?"

"No," Toy said. "I went to the school. You know that. I was the woman who saved the boy. It's on film. I saw it on television."

Briggs stepped into the conversation. "We don't want to have a misunderstanding here, Mrs. Johnson. As you can see, we're not recording this interview. So we want to get everything straight."

"Okay," Toy said. "So do I."

"You saved that little boy?"

"Yes."

Briggs had the ball now. Davidson sat back and let the younger man run with it.

"How did you get to Kansas?"

"I don't know."

Briggs was silent, just watching her face, her body language. She was perfectly still except for one corner of her mouth that was trembling.

Briggs continued, "Where were you before you went to Kansas? Here in New York, you said?"

"First, I was in the Gotham City Hotel with my friend, Sylvia Goldstein. I have her number if you want to verify it. Then I was taken to Roosevelt Hospital in an ambulance."

"The day of the fire, right? That was Friday morning, right?"

"Yes."

"Are you trying to say you have an alibi for the entire day?"

"Exactly," Toy said eagerly. "If you let me go back to the hotel, I've even got statements from several people who saw me."

"What people?" Briggs asked.

"Well," Toy said slowly, "I left the hospital in the afternoon and went to a restaurant. I didn't have my purse and couldn't pay for my coffee, so they called a transit officer and he had another officer give me a ride back to the hospital."

"Back up a minute," he said. "The fire was in the morning, not in the afternoon."

"I know," Toy said, "but I wanted to cover the whole day. Just think about it. If I went to Kansas on a plane, I'd have to fly back. I wanted to show everyone that I didn't do it that way."

"I see. And did the hospital discharge you?"

"Not really," Toy said. Then she drank the rest of the Coke and slammed it down on the table. "I was in cardiac arrest at the time of the Kansas fire. All you have to do is check with the hospital."

Both Briggs and Davidson snapped to attention. "You mean your heart stopped?" Davidson said.

"Yes," Toy said. "But they revived me. I have a medical condition that makes my heart stop every now and then. It's hard to explain."

"I bet." Davidson smirked. "Look, I don't know what you're trying to tell us, but you can't be in Kansas at this fire, admit it, and then tell us you have an alibi in Manhattan."

Toy looked up defiantly. "I just did."

"You just did what?" Briggs snapped.

"That's what I just told you."

The two men exchanged glances, as if to say they had seriously misjudged their suspect. She was leading them in a circle, wasting their time. She had to be off her rocker or an egomaniac, Briggs thought. She apparently not only believed she could do anything she wanted and get away with it, she thought she could hand them this silly story as well. "Have you ever been in a mental hospital?" he asked. If that didn't cut her down to size, he didn't know what would.

"Never," Toy said, cutting her eyes first to one man and then the other.

Davidson was getting annoyed and restless. "Let me tell you something, Mrs. Johnson—or Toy. Do you mind me calling you Toy?"

"Yes, I do."

Things were getting more hostile by the minute, Davidson thought. Whereas she had been frightened and disoriented earlier, the woman sitting in front of them was now fully alert and in control. She knew exactly what she was saying, exactly what she was doing.

"Let me tell you something, Toy," he said, putting emphasis on her name, "three schoolteachers died in that fire. The authorities have classified it as arson. They believe you set that fire, that you used that fire to force the children out of the building. Once you accomplished that, they contend, your intent was to kidnap one of those children."

Toy's hand flew to her chest. "Kidnap a child? Why would I do that? I would never hurt a child."

"Do you have children?" Briggs asked, knowing she didn't. Dr. Johnson had already informed them of that fact.

"No, I don't," Toy said, still reeling from the last statement.

"But you'd like to have a child, wouldn't you?"

"Of course," Toy said, "but you'd have to be insane to kidnap a child just because you couldn't have one."

"And you can't have one? You're incapable of having one? Isn't that right?"

Toy didn't answer. She considered these questions personal and inappropriate.

"Did you hear me?" Davidson said, getting right up in Toy's face.

"Yes, I heard you. There's no medical reason why I can't conceive. I'm not sterile."

"But you have gone to fertility doctors?"

"Yes," Toy said, wondering how they had acquired all this information. Surely, she told herself, Stephen wouldn't have told them anything, not if they were about to charge her with a crime. He was too smart. Toy thought they were bluffing, just making wild guesses that happened to be correct.

"I see," Briggs said. "Your husband says you've been having some pretty strange delusions. Is that correct?"

Toy's eyes fell to her hands. So, Stephen had told them everything. She should have known. She'd never felt so small, so despised in her life. There was no use to lie. Eventually it would all come out. "Yes," she said, without looking up, feeling a stab of bitterness. "I mean, I don't consider them delusions, but my husband does."

"Mrs. Johnson, there's another serious problem we'd like to discuss with you. Yesterday a little girl was kidnapped from a playground and left in a drainage ditch. Did you see this girl? Were you involved in this crime as well as the crime in Kansas? Was this another child you tried to steal?"

Toy leaned forward excitedly. "Is she okay? Is Lucy okay?"

Briggs arched his eyebrows. "So, you do know about this child?"

Toy suddenly stiffened. Her husband might be a fool and play into their hands, but she knew better. These were serious allegations. "I'd rather you don't question me anymore without my attorney."

The men stood. The interview was over.

Toy was booked at the Women's House of Detention at nine o'clock Monday morning. She had not slept the night before and was so exhausted that she was certain she was going to collapse.

The night before she had remained in the interview room, just sitting there as the minutes clicked off on the wall clock. Once the agents had finished interviewing her, around four o'clock in the morning, they left and did not return. At one point Toy had rushed the one-way glass, knowing they were in there, knowing they were watching her, but no one had come to take her out. Finally she had resigned herself. It was some type of police tactic, she decided. They wanted her to sit in there alone until she went crazy and confessed. But she couldn't confess to something she hadn't done.

At the pretrial detention facility, Toy was searched, ordered to undergo a delousing shower, given a stack of clothes and a bath towel, and marched down a corridor of cells in front of a female deputy. The bars rattled and women stood up close, checking out the new inmate. One of them let out a wolf whistle, and Toy turned around.

The deputy seized her arm and pulled her along at a faster pace. "There's some pretty tough bulls in here, Johnson. Better watch your back and stay to yourself. These women could make mincemeat of a tasty little toy like you." She laughed, liking the pun on Toy's name. The poor woman was going to have it tough, no doubt about it.

Toy looked up at the older woman. She was tall, at least five ten, and looked like she could handle anything that came her way. Her short-sleeve uniform shirt showed wiry arms laced with muscles as developed as most men, and the skin on her face was leathery and worn. Sandy Hawkings had been working in jails for over fifteen years. She was beginning to look like one of the prisoners.

"Here's your house," she said, stopping and speaking into her portable radio. "Open sixty-three west," she said. A few seconds later, the metal door opened automatically.

Toy walked in. There was a woman on the bunk reading a paperback book. Toy was about to say something to her when she heard the metal doors clanking shut with a distinctive ring of finality. Dropping her clothes and towel on the floor, Toy went to the bars and peered out, lacing her fingers through them and holding on for dear life. If she stood like this, she thought, her claustrophobia and panic raging, she could see down the hall, see open spaces.

"Pick up your stuff," a loud voice said. "They're gonna do a cell inspection in fifteen minutes. You'll get reported."

Toy couldn't move. She couldn't force herself to turn around and see the back wall of the cell only a few feet away, to face the fact that she was confined in this tiny, tight space, locked in here with a complete stranger. Her face was small. She tried to press it through the bars, managing to get her chin and nose through but not far enough to see all the way to the end of the hall. If she could just see out, Toy thought, she could make it. All she had to see was the door leading out. Then she could keep that image in her mind, just stand here until someone came to get her out.

"Get away from the bars," her cell mate said, standing right next to Toy now. She yanked on Toy's shirt and Toy moved back a few inches. "If Hawkings or one of the other correctional officers comes around, they'll knock your nose off with their nightstick."

"Oh," Toy said, her eyes down, her stomach in knots. Slowly she raised her eyes and looked at the woman. She wasn't much older than Toy. Her shoulder-length dark hair was beautifully styled, her nails painted, and she was wearing carefully applied makeup, as if she were about to go out on the town. Although she was ten or fifteen pounds overweight, the woman was quite attractive. She looked of Latin descent, but it was hard to tell.

"Name's Bonnie Mendoza," she said, shaking Toy's limp hand. "What's your name?"

"Tony," Toy said quickly, knowing they would make fun of her if she used her real name. "Tony Johnson."

"Okay, Tony Johnson. Pick up your gear and put it away."

Toy did what she said, finding a little open shelf next to her bunk. She glanced over at Bonnie's side of the room and saw that she had her clothing neatly folded and stacked on an identical shelf. The woman also had pictures in plastic frames, at least a dozen different nail polishes, and a whole box full of cosmetics. Toy wondered why she wanted to look good in a place like this.

"What are you in for?" Bonnie asked, sitting on her bunk now, filing her nails.

"Murder," Toy said, swallowing, expecting to see shock on the other woman's face.

"Me, too," she said. "Have you been arraigned?"

"No," Toy said. "The FBI arrested me on a warrant from Kansas." Then she added, "I think they're going to charge me with kidnapping as well."

The other woman's face lit up with recognition. "Damn, you're the baby snatcher. I should have recognized you. You were on the news this morning."

Toy felt the room spinning. She was about to pass out. She had been on the news? They were calling her a baby snatcher? Grabbing the bed rail, she tried to steady herself. "I didn't do anything wrong. I didn't take anyone's baby."

"Oh, right," Bonnie said sarcastically, "you just tried to snatch them after you burned up the school and three teachers. That's not nearly as bad. And what about that little girl down the well or something in Central Park? They said you tried to snatch her, too."

Toy blanched. "I didn't set fire to that school. I just saved the little boy. I swear. And the little girl was trapped down there all alone. I only got her out. I didn't kidnap her."

"Hey, girl," Bonnie said, "you don't have to convince me. Save it for the judge."

"What are they going to do to me?" Toy said, a hand over her chest now.

"How the heck do I know?" Bonnie said, tossing the nail file back in the box. "I know you'll be going to Kansas, though. They're probably processing extradition orders right now."

"To Kansas? Why?"

Bonnie looked at her as if she was crazy. "Where have you been? How can they try you in New York State for a crime that occurred in Kansas? That's called jurisdiction, babe."

Toy dropped onto the bunk, staring off into space. If they transferred her to Kansas, she would have no one. Here, at least, she had Joey Kramer. She would call him. He was her strongest witness. He could testify that she had been in Manhattan, nowhere near the scene of the crime. Then she thought of her parents. Had they seen it on the news? Seen their only daughter being led away in handcuffs? Her mother had a heart condition. Toy felt tears on her cheeks.

"Don't cry," Bonnie said curtly. "It doesn't do any good."

Toy walked over and picked up one of the small framed pictures. "Is this your little girl?"

"Give me that," Bonnie said, snatching the frame out of Toy's hands, almost ready to cry herself. "Don't touch that. Don't ever touch that."

"How old is she?"

"She would have been seven next week."

Toy felt all the blood drain from her face. The child was dead; Bonnie was in here for murder. Could she have killed her own child? "What happened?"

"He killed her," Bonnie said, bitter tears streaking down her face. "He killed my precious baby."

Toy took a few tentative steps toward the dark-haired woman. When she didn't balk, Toy sat down next to her on the bunk. "Who killed her, Bonnie?"

"My ex-husband."

"And this is the man you killed?"

Bonnie wiped her face with the back of her arm. "Who do you think I killed? The Easter Bunny?"

Two hours later, Sandy Hawkings appeared in front of the cell. "Got a visitor, Johnson," she said, waiting for the doors to open. "Let's go."

Toy had been resting on the bunk. She stood and walked out of the cell, taking a deep breath of freedom. "Do you know who it is? Is it my husband? My attorney?"

"Move it, Johnson," Sandy said gruffly.

They passed through one locking gate to another section of the jail. Finally Sandy stopped at a room, found a key on her large metal key ring and unlocked the door, shoving Toy inside.

A man in uniform stood. "I'm Officer Hill with the United States Marshal's Office. Are you Toy Johnson?"

"Yes," she said. "Don't you know that? You're the one who came to see me."

"I have to be certain, miss."

Toy took a seat at the table. The marshal remained standing and removed a rolled-up paper from his hip pocket. "Toy Johnson, by the powers vested in me by the United States government, I'm placing you under arrest at the request of the Topeka County Superior Court. You have been charged with three counts of homicide, felony arson, and felony child endangerment. Do you understand?"

"No," Toy said, her whole body shaking with fear. This was a nightmare that just wouldn't stop. How long could it go on? What else could they do to her?

The marshal had a pained expression on his face. "I'm not asking you if you understand why you have been charged, and I'm not asking you if you're guilty or innocent. All you have to do, Mrs. Johnson, is verbally acknowledge that you have been formally arrested on these particular charges, that you are aware of what just transpired inside this room."

"But what does this mean?" Toy said. "Does it mean they're going to take me to Kansas now?"

"You're here on a warrant, Mrs. Johnson. The New York authorities are planning to charge you tomorrow with conspiracy in a kidnapping. Since you're physically in the state of New York, they will try you on these charges first, and then Kansas will initiate extradition proceedings. All this means is that if for some reason the New York authorities decide to drop the charges and release you, you will be held for the authorities in Kansas."

Toy was so frightened that she couldn't think. "You mean, even if the New York people say I can go, I'll still be locked up?"

"Exactly."

"And then what will happen?"

"I'm not an attorney," the marshal said. "And we're restricted from giving any legal advice." He looked at her and then softened. She had such a kind face, such pretty red hair. Other than being a few years older, she resembled his kid sister.

Toy's heart was thumping, thumping, thumping against her breastbone. She was certain if she looked, she could actually see her heart pulsating right through her skin. Her hands were clasped so tightly in her lap, her knuckles were turning white. What she understood was that no one would be coming to release her, that she would never get out of this place. And if she did, there would just be another prison, another set of bars. Even if she was eventually exonerated of all criminal charges, it could take weeks, months, even years to wade through the red tape and bureaucracy of two different states.

"That's it," the marshal said, banging on the door. Someone came and let him out, then left Toy to wait in the room.

TWELVE

Miles Spencer's law offices were located at Madison and Fifty-ninth and took up the entire tenth floor of the skyscraper. Although it was Miles's practice, he had fifteen other attorneys working under him, most of them fresh out of law school, all of them with dreams of one day becoming a partner. But Miles didn't like partners. Once the young recruits got their sea legs, learned how to put together a case, learned how to look and act like an attorney, they drifted off to other positions. Those that remained were the type that always remained.

Working with Miles Spencer was like being in the eye of the hurricane. He would represent anyone: Mafia members, cop killers, rapists, child molesters, drug dealers, anyone who could pay. And he would stop at nothing to win a case. The word *victim* had no place in his vocabulary. Instead he perceived all victims as losers, people who were not strong enough to protect themselves, who by their very weakness deserved whatever punishment came their way.

By not having partners, he could also keep most of the profits for himself, paying his young lawyers a pittance compared to the huge sums he sent to his overseas bank accounts. As Miles saw it, they should actually pay him for the honor of learning from the best.

But money was no longer the primary issue for the fifty-eight-year-old dapper attorney. What he liked was to bask in glory. He loved to see himself on the evening news, loved to open the morning paper, sit down with a cup of coffee and see his face staring back at him.

The face that stared back at him lately, however, was not a young face, and Miles had lost his wife last year to cancer. Lately he had been thinking about death a lot, wondering where his wife was now, asking himself if there was such a thing as an afterlife. He had prohibited his wife from ever having children, for he had felt there was no place for them in his hectic life. His wife had never forgiven him for the emptiness she felt as she grew older, and lately Miles had finally come to understand what he had sacrificed. He had no one now. No one to come home to, no one to care when he didn't feel well or had experienced a particularly grueling day. While many in the legal community respected his expertise, they also secretly considered him cruel and mercenary. He had taken advantage of untold numbers of innocent souls in his battle to rise to the top, and he knew he was forever tainted with their suffering and sorrow. When he died, he asked himself now on a daily basis, would he face retribution, would there really be a final judgment? Would he be condemned for all of eternity?

Miles Spencer was facing his own mortality. Defending himself in the court of all courts would be his grandest challenge, but the renowned attorney felt he didn't have a case. There was no defense against charges of ruthlessness and greed. He hadn't suffered a tragic childhood. He carried no buried secrets. If he could only approach it like every case, he told himself, approach it logically and realistically, then he could possibly win as always. His confidence in himself was paramount, but he needed a break, an edge, a star witness who would testify to his worth. It was all just a matter of finding what he needed before it was too late. He had stood on the backs of others his entire life. Why couldn't he continue into eternity?

Striding into the conference room, Miles slapped a file down on the table and gazed out over the faces assembled in front of him. "Are we ready? Have you all reviewed the materials?"

"Ah, yes we have," Philip Connors said. He'd been with Miles for five years.

"So," Miles said, leaning back in his leather chair at the head of the table, "should we take on this case or not?"

"It's a crazy case, Miles," Connors said, arching his eyebrows. "I mean, really crazy. Whoever takes this is going to be in for a long, long haul."

"I realize that," Miles said. "But can we win? What do they have? What are we looking at here?"

Connors opened the file folder on his desk. It was identical to Miles's folder and all the others on the table. "Toy Johnson claims she was in New York in cardiac arrest when the fire broke out in Kansas. She also claims she was experiencing another cardiac arrest in the emergency room of Roosevelt Hospital when the child was rescued from Central Park. I spoke with her husband this morning. He called from the airport. He indicated that she had been in the hospital the day of the Kansas fire, but she had vanished for several hours during the afternoon. The hospital verified that she'd been a patient, and they insist that Toy Johnson was returned to the hospital later that same afternoon. She was returned by an NYPD officer."

"Fabulous," Miles said. "If that isn't an air-tight alibi, what is?"

Connors looked up and rubbed his eyes. He'd been up all night studying this, trying to figure all the angles, identify all the traps. "The NYPD has no record of ever picking up a Toy Johnson or anyone else, for that matter, and delivering them to Roosevelt. In checking with the hospital, all they know is Mrs. Johnson was escorted into the emergency room by a man in a uniform."

"I see," Miles said. "But they did confirm she was in the hospital and her heart stopped. If she was in the hospital, how could she be in Kansas?"

"Well," Connors said, a look of exasperation on his face, "she even admits she was in Kansas. She told her husband she was in Kansas. She told Dr. Esteban she was in Kansas. I'll bet you anything she told the arresting officers she was in Kansas as well. All she has to do is get up on that stand and say she was at the scene of the crime, and the rest won't matter. We can't impeach our own witness."

"We can if she's mentally incompetent," Miles said with authority. "We can get the criminal proceedings suspended on the grounds of incompetency, ship her to a mental hospital, and let them set her memory straight. Then we'll bring her back to court and get her acquitted. Either that, or we won't allow her to take the stand at all."

"Let me tell you something, Miles," Connors said, "this woman fits the profile of a body snatcher to a tee. She's childless and wants a child desperately. According to her husband, they've gone through all the tests, saw a fertility doctor, the whole ball of wax. She's been exhibiting bizarre behavior. It's Mrs. Johnson's image on that video-tape out of Kansas, right there at the scene of the crime. How can we possibly win this case?"

"Have you seen the film?" Miles said. As they had as yet to accept the case, most of the evidence was off limits.

"Everyone has seen it," Connors said, looking at Miles as if to say, where have you been for the past twelve hours? "They ran a thirty-minute news program on CNN this morning. I thought you watched it. They had the clippings from the fire. Close-ups, too, Miles. Then they had the footage of her arrest. It's the same woman. Anyone could tell it's the same woman."

Miles had not caught the news that morning. "Did you tape it?"

"Of course," Connors said.

"I'll look at it later." He looked out over the room, "So, did all of you see the tape?"

Sixty percent of the people nodded; the rest shook their heads. Miles asked them, "Should we take the case?"

"I vote no," Connors said, placing his hands on top of the closed file, a symbolic gesture that he felt their involvement belonged right where it was. Closed. "These are nasty charges, Miles. And this is the most muddled and difficult case I've ever seen. We're talking three counts of first-degree homicide. We might also be looking at the death penalty. With the kidnapping charges as well, you could tie us up for years on this case."

"Hmmmm," Miles said, thinking, "but is it sensational?"

Connors grimaced and looked away. A chorus of other voices rang out, expressing their opinions. They all knew it was sensational, particularly those among them who had seen the tape of Toy Johnson in her California Angels T-shirt getting into the back of the police car.

Ann Rubinsky spoke up, and everyone turned to listen. She was in her middle thirties, had gone to law school only after she had started her family, and was Spencer's newest rising star. Brilliant and articulate, Ann wore her straight brown hair in a tight French twist and was dressed in a navy blue two-piece suit with a lace collar. "This is a tremendous opportunity, Miles," she said, leaning forward in order to see him. "I completely disagree with Phil on this one. This is the kind of case that the public adores. And I think you will have no problem getting the woman cleared. Obviously there's a mistake here. She must have a dead ringer in Kansas. And think how good you'll look when you save this poor, innocent woman from a prison sentence. She's pretty, charming, theatrical. My God, they arrested her in a T-shirt with a halo. She's so innocent-looking, she looks like she could spread wings and take flight."

"Did you see this?" Miles said, pushing a copy of the New York *Post* across the table. On the front page was a picture of Toy and the headline ANGEL OR KIDNAPPER?

A flurry of commotion rang out around the table. Connors glared at Rubinsky. Miles pushed his chair to an upright position. "I've decided to take the case. Whatever we can throw in the fire to keep them from transferring her to Kansas, we have to set in motion. She was in a hospital," he said, his glasses on his nose now, everything about him cranked and turning. "Get someone over to the jail and have them get her to sign a consent for her medical records. Find out what they were treating her for, if there's any risk if she travels. Also, see if we can't use this to get her moved to a medical facility. Her health might be one reason we can keep her in the state. And send someone over to the hospital, find out if anyone knows where the cops picked her up. We've got to find the police officer who brought her back to the hospital." Miles stopped, took a slug of coffee, set the file aside, and began making a list on a yellow pad of paper. "Ann, line up an expert to study that tape . . ."

"Oh," she said excitedly, "I forgot to tell you who picked her up when she ran out of Central Park with that kid in her arms."

"Who?"

"None other than our own state senator, Robert Weisbarth."

"Has anyone talked to him?" Miles said, thrilled at this development. "What did he think?"

Ann Rubinsky tossed her head back and laughed. "He didn't think anything. His chauffeur told the police that the good senator was drunk as a skunk that night. After the woman vanished from the car, he started babbling like an idiot and had to be sedated."

"When you say vanished," Miles asked nervously, "exactly what do you mean?"

"Just that," Rubinsky said. "She was in the car, and then she simply wasn't. I interviewed the chauffeur this morning and he says the same thing. He looked in his rearview mirror and the woman was there, and then she just vanished into thin air."

"So, she opened the car door and got out. Right?" Miles said, his eyes narrowed to slits, his fingers playing with an edge of the newspaper with Toy's photo on the front page. "What's so mysterious about that?"

"She vanished, Miles," Rubinsky repeated. "Both Weisbarth and his driver insist she didn't open the car door and get out. As they tell it, the car door was already open. She was bending over the child and talking to her, and then suddenly she disappeared. I can't explain it more simply than that. I mean, let's face it, people don't vanish, so it's obvious the woman just ducked down and slipped out of the car without them seeing her."

Miles Spencer had one hand pressed firmly on top of the newspaper now. He dropped his eyes, seeing only Toy's image and the word Angel, his hand covering the rest of the headline. The muscles in his face became rigid, and he stared at the photo for some time in complete silence, every eye in the room watching him intently. Then he simply stood, picked the newspaper clipping off the table, and with no explanation walked out of the conference room.

"Help, get help," Bonnie Mendoza screamed through the bars. "She's not breathing." Then she ran back to the body on the floor, pressing her head to the chest, trying to see if there was a heartbeat. "Oh, God," Bonnie yelled, "she's dead. Her heart isn't beating. Get help, get help fast."

Toy's eyes were wide open; she was on her back on the dirty linoleum floor, Bonnie bending over her, uncertain what she should do. One minute they had been sitting on the edges of their bunks talking about Toy's case, and the next, Toy just froze and then fell to the ground, the same exact expression on her face as before she passed out.

Feet were pounding in the hall. The other prisoners were making a racket, sticking their heads up close to the bars, trying to see what was going on. One woman had a small mirror and slid it through the bars to see down the hall.

Sandy Hawkings was panting and out of breath. As soon as the door to the cell opened, she shoved Bonnie Mendoza away and placed a finger on Toy's neck. "Starting CPR," she yelled into the portable radio. "Get an ambulance rolling and a gurney up here. And get me some backup. Quick."

As soon as she tossed the radio on the bunk, she bent down and ran her fingers up Toy's midsection, trying to locate her sternum. Once she had, she began pressing on her chest. "What happened?"

"She was fine," Bonnie said, "and then she just fell on the floor."

Sandy leaned over and forced oxygen into Toy's mouth. Out of the corner of her eye, she saw another female correctional officer in the cell.

"Ambulance is en route," the woman told her, holding Bonnie at bay with an outstretched arm. "Want me to spot you?"

"No," Sandy said, pressing again on Toy's chest, determined to bring the woman back. Sandy had given many people CPR in her long career. When she pressed her mouth to theirs and blew her breath into them, they were no longer prisoners, no longer strangers. They were Sandy's responsibility. "Are they bringing a gurney from the medical wing?" she shot out just before bending down to Toy's open mouth again.

The answer came rushing into the cell. Two men with a stretcher.

The other officer took Bonnie outside to give them room, then they both stood and watched.

"We can't stop CPR," Sandy said quickly, depressing Toy's chest. "Just lift her on the gurney. I'm going with you."

The men did as she said, Sandy standing with them and continuing mouth-to-mouth as they rushed down the hall. Every few seconds they would stop, drop to the floor, and Sandy would complete the compressions. Then she would continue ventilating Toy as they moved down the hall. They passed through the gate into the cell block, moved through another long corridor and were finally outside in the open air.

An ambulance was parked at the curb, the rear doors open. They had a hospital inside the detention center, but they were not equipped to handle such a serious problem. And if the prisoner did die, they wanted her to die outside the walls. It didn't look good on the stats.

Sandy Hawkings dropped to the curb and placed her head in her hands as the ambulance carrying Toy Johnson screamed down the road, lights flashing, siren squealing. Several other members of the correctional staff joined her, and one officer put her arm around Sandy. "I didn't save her," Sandy said, her voice cracking. "I tried. I tried. God, how I tried."

"You were great," the other woman consoled.

"Yeah," Sandy said, looking up, "but was I great enough?"

Toy was walking down a long, narrow path lined with cobblestones. On either side of the path were vibrant fields of spring flowers, their fragrant scent meshing into one wonderful odor, so sweet, so delicate that Toy could feel tears of joy in her eyes. Somewhere in the distance she saw Margie Roberts in a beautiful peach dress. The dress was of the richest satin, trimmed with intricate white lace. Around her waist was a broad satin sash, and her hair was tied with white satin bows. Toy shielded her eyes, for Margie appeared to be standing right beneath an enormous sun, its warm yellow glow bathing her in blazing light. She was laughing and happy, and as Toy got closer, she could see a large white tent, its canvas tarp billowing in the gentle breezes. Carried on the wind were the lyrical sounds of laughter and people's voices. It sounded like a birthday party or a wedding.

Just as Toy got close enough to see her face, she saw that Margie was beckoning and waving to her, encouraging her to join the celebration. Then as suddenly as the dream had begun, it abruptly ended. The last thing Toy recalled was Margie extending her hand to her just as she reached out to accept it.

Instead of Margie Roberts, Toy opened her eyes to Dr. Esteban, a man in a police uniform, a number of white-uniformed nurses, and surprisingly, the time-ravaged faces of her mother and father. She shut her eyes and let the darkness take her again. The man in the uniform was there to take her back to jail. She couldn't bear it.

Then she heard her name over and over again. "Toy, wake up. Toy, it's Stephen. Can you hear me? Your parents are here."

She heard his voice, but she couldn't respond. Something was holding her down, trapping her inside her body.

"Toy, darling," her mother's voice said in the darkness. "Oh, my baby, my beautiful baby. Talk to me, Toy. Squeeze my hand if you can hear me."

Toy felt the presence of herself, her identity, but she couldn't answer, couldn't squeeze her mother's hand. She didn't have hands. She didn't have a voice. Her body seemed to be a mass of swirling particles that had been stirred into a frothing, boiling mess and then allowed to disperse into the universe.

"Toy, doll," her father's deep, scratchy voice said, "come on, sugar. Where's my little fighter, where's my little Toy?"

A stab of pain entered her chest and Toy groaned. Then she opened her eyes and saw Dr. Esteban's face. "She's conscious," he turned and said to the group, then quickly looked back down at Toy. "How do you feel?"

Why do they always ask that? Toy thought, closing her eyes again as she mumbled bitterly under her breath, "Sameness, sameness, sameness." The same hospital, the same doctor, the same concerned expressions on the same unknowing faces. Didn't they realize they were on a merry-go-round, that they had been through all this before?

"Mrs. Johnson," Dr. Esteban continued, "I know you can hear me now. If you can't speak, just listen. You underwent surgery. You're in the recovery room at Roosevelt. We inserted a pacemaker. Everything went very well."

Toy opened her eyes a few moments later and looked up at her mother and father. Right behind them she saw Stephen. "They put in a pacemaker?"

"Yes, honey, they did," her mother said. "And now you're going to be just fine. All these problems will soon be behind you."

Toy gazed lovingly at her mother's face. She'd once been so pretty. But now she was old, her face a mass of lines and crinkled flesh. Toy focused on her hazel eyes, on the kindness and understanding there. "Why did you let them do it, Momma?"

"Well, Toy, we had no choice. You almost died. Why didn't you call us before and tell us you were sick?" Suddenly her mother put her hand over her mouth, and tears pooled in her already watery eyes. "We had to see it on television . . . that our precious Toy had been arrested."

Her father leaned down and kissed her face. His breath smelled like tobacco. "You've been smoking again, Daddy," Toy said.

"Yeah," he said.

Now it was Stephen's large, looming face staring down at her. Toy turned her head to avoid it. "Go away. You had no right to let them butcher me, put some machine inside my body."

"I had no choice, Toy," he snapped. "Either you had the operation or you died. What did you want me to do?"

"Let me die," she said.

A few minutes later, she heard him in a far corner of the room speaking in whispers to her parents. "I just can't reason with her," he said. "This is the way it's been for the past three or four months."

Toy had meant what she had said. She wanted to die, was ready to die. As soon as she was well, the man in the uniform would take her back to the jail. Everyone despised her, thought she was a baby snatcher and a lunatic. She couldn't save anyone, she thought bitterly. She couldn't even save herself.

Sylvia had tried calling Toy at the hotel for days, but had repeatedly missed her. Concerned, she had called Roosevelt a few times and was pleased to learn that Toy was no longer at the hospital. That was a good sign, she told herself.

Tuesday morning she got up after her brother had already left for work, wondering if her friend was still in Manhattan and if so, was she going to return with her today on their prearranged flight? She poured a cup of coffee in the kitchen and sat down at the table to read the morning paper. "Thanks, Abe," she said, grabbing a donut out of the box on the counter and taking an enormous bite out of it.

When she saw the headline and Toy's face staring back at her, she spat the food out of her mouth.

"Good Lord," she exclaimed. "Arrested? Toy was arrested for murder." Sylvia's head was spinning. How could it be? What in the world were they talking about? She quickly scanned the text and thought it was the most bizarre thing she had ever seen. But there was Toy, in that silly baseball T-shirt, looking radiant and gorgeous.

Rushing to the phone, she started making phone calls. She had to find out where they had taken her.

Sarah was tired and bedraggled. It wasn't from overwork, since she had hardly left the loft in days. She was emotionally exhausted. Sadly she realized she was reaching some kind of milestone in her relationship with the tortured young artist. If Raymond didn't improve soon, they would have to vacate the loft, and Sarah didn't know what would happen to them in the future. If she didn't work, they would have no money, and with Raymond the way he was, she simply could not leave him alone for longer than a few minutes while she ran out to get food. In his disconnected state he could wander off and be seriously hurt.

Sarah knew she would have to let them admit him to a hospital. She simply could not accept such a grave and time-consuming responsibility.

Raymond's condition had improved but only slightly. He was still uncommunicative, and when he did become alert, his behavior was childish and strange. He seemed to be locked in a repetitive fantasy of that one day in his life, the day he had seen the mysterious red-headed woman. One night when he had been particularly lucid, he had told her the story of what had occurred that day in rambling, disjointed sentences that didn't make much sense to Sarah. But she was thrilled each time he spoke. Every word that came from his mouth was like a morsel from heaven.

Opening the New York *Times,* she thumbed through the pages absentmindedly and then suddenly gasped. "It's her," she screamed at Raymond. He was sitting at the table, his head dangling loose on his neck, dressed in his pajamas. Sarah shoved the paper right in front of his face and then leaped to her feet and circled the table until she was standing beside him. "Look, Raymond," she said excitedly, "it's your angel. Don't you recognize her? God, she even has on the same T-shirt that's in the paintings. Look, Raymond. Look!"

When he didn't respond, Sarah moved his head so it was positioned over the paper. Then she lifted it right under his nose. "You have to see it," she cried. "Can't you see? It's her, Raymond, it's the woman I met at the hospital. It's your angel."

His arms were limp at his side, but Sarah saw his right hand open and close. Then she heard his feet moving under the table.

"She's in trouble, Raymond," she said loudly, wanting him to hear and praying that this was the miracle they had been waiting for. "Your angel is in trouble and she needs you. Are you going to let them send her to jail? Aren't you going to try to help her? Didn't she help you?"

The *Times* had run the same photo of Toy, but the text was considerably different. Far less sensational than the *Post,* they reported merely that Toy had been accused of trying to steal a child. Even though Sarah didn't really know the woman, she felt in her heart that it couldn't be true. How could Raymond's mystery woman be a criminal?

Sarah leaned forward and stared into Raymond's eyes. She could see his pupils moving back and forth horizontally. Then she suddenly realized what he was doing, and her spirits soared.

Raymond was reading.

He was actually reading the newspaper article. Sarah stood perfectly still, fearful she would distract him. After five or ten minutes, he looked up.

"It's her, isn't it?" she said softly.

Raymond's lips formed into a circle, and for a second, Sarah was uncertain if he was going to speak or just blow childishly at her. But he didn't avert his eyes and continued staring deep into her own, his lips slightly trembling. Finally he pushed the words out. "Yes," he said, a broad smile lighting up his dark face. "You . . . you found her."

Just then Sarah heard the phone ringing. She tried to ignore it, but she could tell it was annoying Raymond. Grabbing the receiver, she barked in the phone, "What do you want?" She was greeted with the silky smooth voice of Francis Hillburn.

"Oh," he said, "you must be the lovely creature who's been taking care of our Raymond. I'm sorry, darling, but I've forgotten your name."

"Our Raymond?" Sarah said facetiously, stretching the phone cord into the kitchen so Raymond couldn't hear. "What does that mean? You're turning him out on the street, remember? Isn't that what you told me the other day?"

"No," Hillburn said, "you must be mistaken. Why would I evict one of my most gifted clients? Raymond Gonzales is a genius." He paused and then continued, his speech lilting and rapid in enormous excitement. "We don't want to call him Raymond, though. No, no, my dear. We must always refer to him as Stone Black. That's the name we're using in our promotions."

Sarah was perplexed. Then she peeked around the corner to check on Raymond, and her eyes found the life-size portrait of Toy, the one with the outstretched wings. Of course, she told herself. Now that Raymond's subject was famous and the media was swarming all around her, there was no doubt that Hillburn would find a way to exploit the situation to his advantage. "I see," Sarah said slowly. "I gather you saw the article in the *Times?*"

"I don't know what you're talking about," Hillburn said defensively. "But look, while I have you on the phone, I'm sending a driver over to pick up Raymond's paintings for a show we're having this week. Please make sure he gets all of them and packs them properly."

"Raymond's paintings are not for sale," Sarah said.

"What are you saying?" Hillburn said angrily. "Who do you think you are, anyway? Certainly they're for sale. He's an artist. He has to sell them to eat, you foolish woman, and I'm his official representative. Who are you? Some little tramp he picked up on the street."

"Maybe," Sarah said, willing to accept insults as long as she had one of her own that was better. "But I'm the one in the loft right now, Hillburn, and possession is nine-tenths of the law. So if I were you, I wouldn't waste my time sending someone over here, because I won't let them in."

"I'll . . . I'll get you evicted," Hillburn snarled. "I'll take you to court. I own that loft and everything in it. You hear me? What kind of trick are you trying to pull?"

"You don't own Raymond, though," she said, "and you don't own his paintings." Then she promptly slammed down the receiver and smiled with satisfaction.

When she stepped out of the kitchen, Raymond was no longer sitting silently at the table. He had placed a blank canvas on his easel and was painting like a man possessed, stooping, standing, reaching. Sarah moved closer and gawked at what she saw. The faint outline of the angel with the flaming red hair was already coming to life in his rapidly moving hands, leaping from his brush straight onto the canvas.

THIRTEEN

When Toy opened her eyes again, morning light was streaming in through the window and a nurse was checking her vital signs. "Doing just fine," she said. "Ready for breakfast?"

"No," Toy said, "leave me alone. I just want to sleep."

Ethel Myers suddenly appeared by her bed, and the nurse vanished. "Good morning, sweetheart. Did you have a nice rest?"

"Who else is in here?" Toy said, not seeing anyone but wanting to make certain. She didn't want to see Stephen. Not now, not ever.

"Well, no one, honey. But look," her mother said, holding up a plastic bag, "all of these are letters. Letters for you."

"What do you mean?"

"They're fan letters. And Toy, they're from all over the world. Little children, older people, all of them saying the same thing."

"What? That I'm a baby snatcher and should get the death penalty?"

"No," her mother said, shaking her head and setting the sack on the floor. "I haven't read every last one of them, of course. I haven't had the time, but Toy, in all the ones I've read, the people think they've seen you, think you've helped them in some way."

Toy was astonished. This had to be another one of her crazy delusions. The only difference in this one was her mother was here to keep her company while she tripped through the Twilight Zone.

"Here," her mother said, holding a letter in front of her face, "I'll read you one. This little girl lives in Japan. She sent this letter by Western Union. She must be very smart, for she writes perfect English. 'Dear Angel' "—Toy's mother stopped and looked at Toy over her glasses—"Isn't that sweet? She called you angel. Okay, here we go. 'I was playing in the stream by our house when I fell in and couldn't get out. You came and pulled me out. You were so pretty. You had on a shirt with a big *A* and a halo. My mother said I be drowned if you had not come for me. I love you, Miss Angel. Signed Mitso.' What do you think, Toy? Isn't that darling?"

Toy didn't answer. She was lost in thought. She remembered something, a dark-haired child with the smallest and most perfect hands and feet she had ever seen, the stream, the strange houses, all of them so near the ground. When had she had that dream? she asked herself. She couldn't recall. There were just too many of them —the dreams, the children.

"Do you want me to read you another letter?" her mother said.

Toy felt warm and rested, at peace and restless at the same time. She propped herself up on the pillow and looked over at her mother. "I love you, Mom," she said. "No matter what happens, I love you and I always will. You're the best mother in the world."

"I love you, too, honey," she said. "But you didn't answer me. Would you like me to read you another letter? They're so cute and sweet. It'll make you feel better."

Toy studied her mother's gentle face. Didn't she wonder why these people were writing to her daughter? Didn't she wonder why her daughter was on trial for murder? Wasn't she the least bit concerned that her daughter could go to prison for the rest of her life? The answer to all those questions was no. Her mother was stooped over now, picking through the letters.

"Read them all," Toy said.

"What? Did you say read them all? All these letters? Well, goodness, there are so many. So-o-o very many. All of them from lovely little children, too."

"Read them all, Mom. We're not going anywhere."

Her mother smiled, bringing a whole handful of letters up from the sack. "That's just what I thought, darling."

By the time Miles Spencer's driver pulled up in front of Roosevelt Hospital Tuesday afternoon, there were at least fifty people lined up on the curb, many with large signs in their hands. Free the Angel, they read. A few people had signs that were more specific and referred to his client as not just any angel but the California Angel. As Miles squinted out the tinted window of his limousine, he realized that they had been drawn by only one television show, a few newsreels, a few articles in the papers. The whole thing was quite incredible. But, of course, he told himself smugly, this was Manhattan. There were lunatics on every corner.

As he stepped out of the car, a man with a long, flowing beard assaulted him, almost knocking him to the ground. "They crucified Christ. Now they're trying to lock up His angel."

Miles knocked him away, wiped his hand on his coat, and made his way into the hospital. At the reception desk, he had to fight through a long line to get to the front. "I'm here to see Toy Johnson."

"You and the rest of the world," the woman said. She had snow white hair that looked like a Brillo pad, and was dressed in a pink and white volunteer's uniform.

He turned around and looked at the people in line. "All these people are waiting to see Toy Johnson?"

"That's what they say. But you can't see her. No one can see her. She's under guard. She's a prisoner, you know?"

"Yes, I know," Miles said. "I'm her attorney. I have to see her. It's urgent."

She eyed him closely. "Don't lie to me," she sighed. "I've had a very stressful day."

Miles chuckled. She reminded him of his mother. "Here," he said, slapping his card on the counter.

Just then a heavy-set woman with dark bushy hair walked up to him carrying a suitcase, a frantic look on her face. "I heard you say you're Toy Johnson's attorney," she said breathlessly. "You've got to get me in to see her. I'm her best friend, and I've been waiting out here for hours. I have to catch a plane any minute."

"Excuse me," he said, giving Sylvia a look of distaste and turning to walk away.

"No," she called out, "I have to see her. Tell her I'm waiting. See if she can get them to let me come up."

Miles glanced back over his shoulder, but he didn't stop walking. Sylvia yelled out again, but he couldn't make out what she said. "What?" he said, annoyed that this strange woman was accosting him.

"Tell her I love her," Sylvia said. "Please, tell her I'm praying for her and that everything will be okay."

Miles kept walking and a short time later he was standing outside Toy's room, talking to the officer stationed there. Then he opened the door and walked inside, as nervous as the day he had taken the bar exam.

"Mrs. Johnson," he said, smiling briefly, "I'm your attorney, Miles Spencer." Then his mouth fell open and he gawked. The woman in the bed was so small, so childlike. Her red hair was fanned out on the pillow, her face void of makeup, and her eyes looked right through him. Suddenly he felt a chill and stepped back several feet from the bed.

"This is my mother, Ethel Myers."

"Pleased to meet you," he said, pumping her thin hand and then turning back to Toy. "Now, I have some good news. I bet it's the first good news of the day, huh?"

Toy and her mother both stared at him without speaking. On both their lips was a hint of a smile.

"We managed to track down Officer Kramer with the Transit Authority, and he verified your statement about seeing you the day of the fire."

"Isn't that nice, Toy?" her mother said, stroking her arm.

"Does that mean they're going to let me go?"

"Ah, not exactly. I mean, they'll release you eventually, I'm fairly certain, but it may take a few more days. We did manage to get the extradition hearing continued until Thursday due to your illness. The hospital assured me that you will be fine by then. We're in contact with the Kansas authorities, and they're sending their own man out to take Officer Kramer's statement, and statements from the hospital personnel. They also want to wait until their forensic people give them a report on the film clip."

"What kind of report?" Toy asked, holding her mother's hand now.

"They're having experts compare the image of the woman on the film to the footage they shot of you the day you were arrested. If the images don't match, then it will all be over."

"What about the case here in New York?"

"Yes," he said slowly. "I'm more than aware those charges are pending. I feel confident, however, that we can divert formal charges on that matter due to the child's statement. I plan to use her as a character witness next week. She's quite convincing."

"Lucy?" Toy said, her green eyes blazing. "Is she all right? I've been so worried about her."

"She's fine," Miles said tentatively, unable to take his eyes off Toy's face. There was something peculiar about her, he decided. "Mrs. Johnson," he said intently, "would you mind asking your mother to leave the room a few minutes so we can discuss your case?"

"Why?" Toy said. "You can talk freely. I don't have anything to hide."

"I—I, well, to be perfectly honest, I'd like to ask you a few personal questions."

"Oh, really?" Toy said, eyeing him suspiciously. "What kind of questions?"

"This is all so intriguing," he said, stepping to the window and looking down at the people assembled on the sidewalk. Either he was losing his mind, he told himself, or the number had doubled just since he had arrived. Even now new people were arriving in taxis or stepping out of cars and joining the group. "Why are they all standing there like that?" he said, talking without thinking. "Surely they don't believe in angels? That's asinine."

Toy exchanged knowing glances with her mother and then said, "Why is it asinine?"

"Well, you know," Miles said with his back turned, still peering out at the people, "angels are only fantasy, folklore. Anyone in their right mind would know they don't actually exist."

"Have you ever read the Bible?" Toy asked him.

Miles Spencer spun around and faced her. "Of course I've read the Bible."

"But you don't believe, right?"

The attorney's face drained of all color and for a moment he looked as if he were ill. "I don't choose to answer that question," he said huffily.

Toy was acting on instinct, but her instincts told her she didn't like this man. There was something about him that repulsed her, even though she couldn't put her finger on it. Then she suddenly saw it. Emanating from his body was a strange reddish glow, almost as if he were standing in a blazing inferno. Toy knew what it was instantly. It was aggression and cynicism, greed and malice. This man didn't care about her fate, any more than he cared about anyone's fate.

All he cared about was himself.

Stepping closer to the bed, Miles Spencer opened his mouth to speak and then closed it. A few moments later he tried again. "If you . . . know something . . . I, well, I want to . . ." He stopped stammering and stood there silently, as if he couldn't figure out what it was he had wanted to say.

Toy sat upright in the bed. "I can only give you a suggestion," she said. "You said you'd read the Bible, right? Isn't that what you just said?"

"Well, yes, I did, but—"

"How long ago was that?"

"Oh," he said, relaxing somewhat but smiling nervously, "when I was a child."

"Maybe you should try reading it again."

She didn't touch him, but Miles Spencer brought his hand to his face, almost certain he'd been slapped. She knew, he told himself. As of that second he was totally convinced that the woman he was representing was a mythical, magical creature. He was so convinced that he was ready to hold up a sign and join the growing crowd on the street.

She had seen inside him to a place no one had ever seen before—to the small, painfully shy boy whose father was a Methodist minister in a rural town in Pennsylvania. Visions of his father in the pulpit appeared in his mind, and he could feel the soft leather of the Bible he had always carried in his hands. Every Sunday when he had listened to his father preach his sermon, he had dreamed of the day he would become a minister like his father and have his own congregation. "Have you read your Bible?" his father would always say before he went to bed. Sometimes Miles would read the chapters his father selected, but then forget the message contained in them. "Then you better read it again," his father would say.

He had been so devout then, so caring and concerned about others. Where had it gone? How had he lost it?

Yes, he said to himself, Toy Johnson knew what he wanted to know, what he needed to know to save himself from eternal damnation. And she knew he wanted to know more than he had ever wanted anything in his life. Who exactly was this strange ethereal being who could appear in two places simultaneously? A creature who could inspire all these people? Where had she come from, and where would she go when she left?

She knew, but she simply wasn't going to tell him. She had somehow looked inside his heart and discovered he wasn't worthy.

When the attorney shuffled out the door a few minutes later, the guard looked up and did a double take, almost thinking one man had come in and another one exited. The man who had entered had a regal carriage: his head high, his shoulders thrust back, a look of authority and superiority on his face. But the man making his way down the hall was stooped, his face ashen, his feet barely moving as he crossed the floor. The officer opened the door, checking to see if anyone was still in the room. "Everything okay in here?"

"Yes," Toy's mother said politely. "You're doing a good job, Officer." The man's head pulled back and Toy's mother held a letter in the air. "Ready for another one, baby? My, my, this one comes all the way from Arizona."

Toy's mother left for the evening and Toy was about to fall asleep when the door suddenly sprang open and Sylvia rushed in. "Ssssh," she whispered, glancing back at the door, "I'm a nurse, see. It was the only way I could get in."

Toy looked at her friend and broke out laughing. Perched on the top of her head was a miniature nurse's cap with a big red cross on the front, and a small stethoscope was draped around her neck. She was wearing a white blouse and white stretch pants that were about two sizes too small. "Is that plastic?" Toy said, giggling and pointing at the stethoscope.

"Yeah," Sylvia said, picking it up and placing it on Toy's forehead. "Nope, nothing in there," she said a few seconds later, causing Toy to giggle again.

"Where did you get that hat?" Toy asked when she finally stopped laughing. "Did you steal it from a midget nurse or something?"

"Oh, this?" Sylvia said, grinning back at Toy. "They wouldn't let me in here, so I bought a kid's Halloween costume. When I couldn't fit into the dress, I used my own blouse and then found the pants at Woolworth's." She stopped and wiggled her hips. "Little snug, huh?"

"Just a little," Toy said, turning away and giggling again.

"Heck," Sylvia said, tugging at her crotch, "and they were on the bargain table, too. Thought they were a pretty good buy." When she finished speaking, Sylvia fell serious and dropped onto the edge of Toy's bed. "Missed my plane."

"Why?" Toy asked, concerned. "You have to go back to school tomorrow. Because of what's going on with me, someone has to—"

"Why?" Sylvia yelled, shaking her head. "My best friend is in a hospital, and the cops are charging her with murder. Why would I worry about that, huh? What do you think? I'm just going to go home and forget about you?"

"I'm fine," Toy insisted. "Really, Sylvia, I'm okay. They put in the pacemaker, so that should be the end of that problem. I want you to go back. I want you to check on Margie for me. I had a dream about her the other night, and I'm worried."

"Oh, yeah?" Sylvia said, narrowing her eyes at Toy. "What about the police and all? I went down there and gave them a statement, but they're pretty tough, Toy. They really believe you did these terrible things."

"They can't prove it," Toy said quickly. "I was in cardiac arrest at the time of the fire in Kansas. You were with me, remember? You told them, didn't you?"

"Of course I told them," Sylvia said, "but they don't believe me. They just think I'm lying, trying to cover for you."

Sylvia was silent for a long time. She finally said, "I've been thinking and thinking, and I just can't figure this out. The newspaper said there was a film of you saving that little boy. And the whole thing was just like you said: the fire, the school, even the field. How could that be?"

Toy just shrugged her shoulders, an impish look on her face.

Sylvia took a sharp intake of breath. "Oh, my God," she said loudly, "I'm sitting here talking to you like you're a normal person, but you're not. You were really there, weren't you?"

Toy nodded.

Sylvia immediately sprang to her feet and crushed Toy's head to her body, her eyes wide with astonishment. "I knew it," she said. "I knew it was some kind of miracle. I just can't believe you're my friend, that someone so special would want to be with me."

"I love you, Sylvia," Toy mumbled against her chest. The woman had her arms around her neck now and was practically strangling her. When she finally released her, Toy looked up. "We won't be together if you transfer to another school."

Sylvia instantly released her, slapping her hands against her thighs. "What are you talking about? Transfer? Did someone say transfer? I'd never want to leave Jefferson." She shook her head. "I was just kidding when I said that."

"No, you weren't," Toy said firmly.

"Yes, I was," Sylvia argued. "I love Jefferson. I love working with those kids. They need me. How could I ask for a transfer?"

"They do need you," Toy said. "They need someone who has a positive outlook and a good sense of humor." Then she smiled and added, "There's a lot of accidents at Jefferson, and you're pretty good at CPR."

Sylvia's chest swelled with pride. "I did okay, didn't I? I was certain I was going to clutch up."

"You did great," Toy said enthusiastically. "I owe you my life, Sylvia. I mean it."

Toy saw that her friend was crying and felt tears gathering in her own eyes. "Go on," she urged her. "If you leave now, you can still catch a plane back tonight."

"But I can't leave you," Sylvia sniffed.

"Go," Toy said again even more forcefully. "Please, Sylvia, they're going to need you at the school. We both can't be out. You have to go back."

"I want you to know I believe you," she whispered, clasping Toy's hand. "I've always thought you were an angel. I mean, not a *real* angel, but you've always been good enough inside to be one. Now all these people know, too, you know, and that's good. It's good that they know what a special person you are."

Toy leaned forward and kissed her on the forehead. Sylvia stood to leave but was hesitant. She made it to the door before she stopped and gazed back at Toy with a bewildered expression on her face. "Does this mean I'm not Jewish anymore?"

"I don't think so, Sylvia." Toy smirked. "Why would you say something so silly?"

"Well, if you're an angel and I believe you're an angel, I just don't know," she said thoughtfully. "The whole thing doesn't sound very Jewish to me."

"Look," Toy said earnestly, "I can't explain what's been happening to me. But I can tell you one thing. I believe there's someone at the wheel of this ship, Sylvia, and I believe that someone has a specific plan for all of us. I don't think it really matters if we're Jewish or Mormon or some other religion. Do you know what I mean?"

"Exactly," Sylvia said, a steely determination leaping into her eyes. "I know I've got to go back to that school and be the best darn teacher those kids have ever seen."

Before Toy could say anything else, Sylvia had spun around and disappeared through the doorway.

The next morning, Toy told her mother she wanted to see Stephen. While her mother went down the hall to call him, Dr. Esteban stopped by and told Toy that he would have to clear her by tomorrow to return to the detention center.

"I'm sorry," he said, "but I've stretched it as far as I can. They'll keep you in their medical wing, but . . ."

"I know," Toy said. "I want to thank you for all you've done."

Once he left, Toy pushed her tray over the bed and tried to comb her hair, put on some lipstick. She wanted to be strong when she saw Stephen. She wanted to look good.

* * *

Stephen was standing next to his wife's bedside by one o'clock that afternoon. Toy had been allowed to get up and walk into the hall before he had arrived, with a uniformed guard at her side. Now she was dressed in a bathrobe and sitting up in bed, pillows propped behind her back.

His voice was frosty, his face set. "You asked me to come. I'm here. Now what?"

"I left some things in the safety-deposit box at the hotel. When you check out to go home, please get them for me. There's a video-tape and I don't know what else, but please promise me you'll take care of this for me. It could be important." She stopped and handed him something. "Here's the key."

"Is that why you asked me to come?" he said angrily. "What? Do you think you're a celebrity now and I'm nothing but your errand boy?"

"I've decided I want to go through with the divorce, Stephen." Toy felt a jolt. She had finally said it. She tried to remain calm and spoke in a low voice. "I know you haven't been happy for years. I don't know why. I mean, I tried to do everything you asked of me. I guess it just wasn't meant to be."

He was silent, staring, his eyes opaque and distant.

"I won't destroy you or anything," Toy continued. "You can keep the house, the cars, everything. I just need enough money for my attorney and to get a new start."

"Doing what?" he said with contempt.

Toy didn't react. There was no use. The days for reacting were over. "I want you to know that I truly loved you," she said softly. "When I married you, it was the happiest day of my life."

His face softened and he shuffled his feet on the linoleum. "I still love you, Toy, but I guess you don't love me anymore. It seems like everything I do or say lately is wrong."

"I never said that," Toy answered, finding his eyes.

"Well, that's the way you act. I mean, I've only been concerned about your health. I knew something terrible like this would happen. Of course, I never thought you would be arrested for murder. If you hadn't run off like a nut, none of this would have happened. You should have stayed home where you belonged."

"See?" Toy said quickly. "That statement right there. Think about it, Stephen. You treat me like I'm an imbecile."

He slowly shook his head. "No, Toy, you're wrong," he said. "I think you're fragile, almost too good for the world we live in. I just get scared, you know. Scared that someone is going to hurt you." He choked up and had to stop, tears gathering in his eyes. "You give so much of yourself away that there's just nothing left. Must you hate me for wanting to protect you?"

"No," Toy said, sighing deeply. "I don't blame you. I understand, Stephen. Really, I do."

"Then why do you want a divorce?"

Tears were streaming down Toy's face now. "I just know it's time," she said, reaching for a tissue.

"Time for what?" he said.

She whispered, "Time for us to be apart."

"I see," he said stiffly. "Then I guess we'll be apart."

"I guess we will," Toy said sadly. "Can you hold me, though. Only for a few minutes. I just want to be held."

Stephen walked to the edge of the bed and took up a position next to his wife. Then he pulled her slender body into his arms. "Was it really that bad?" he whispered. "I tried to give you everything. We have a beautiful house, nice clothes, a new car."

"Yes, it was, Stephen," Toy said meekly. "What you didn't give me was the one thing I needed."

His face was twisted in anguish. "Tell me one thing you needed I failed to give you? Tell me?"

"You didn't believe in me."

Toy turned her head away while her husband pushed himself off the bed. When she looked back, the door was swinging closed and Stephen was gone.

The following day they transferred Toy to the medical wing of the detention facility. That afternoon she was allowed to have a visitor. Sitting in a small interview room, still dressed in her robe and slippers, Toy looked over at Jeff McDonald. "You want me to do what?"

"I want you to go on television," he said. "Tell the world everything you just told me, how you went into cardiac arrest and had these dreams. How these dreams turned out to be real-life events. We've rounded up people from all over the world. We're going to do a ninety-minute special on prime time."

The reporter leaned back in the chair and sighed. For all he knew, this woman was a dangerous criminal, or at the very least, a raving lunatic. The public didn't want to hear it. Like ET, or some other stupid fantasy movie, they wanted to believe she was an angel, so Fielder and the rest of the brass at CNN had decided to give them what they wanted. They wanted to see serial killers, they showed them serial killers. They wanted angels, they got angels. It chapped his ass. He'd done a dynamite job of investigative reporting and they'd turned it into tabloid journalism.

"No," Toy said. "I can't. For one thing, I'm in jail."

"That's not a problem," he said wearily. "I've already spoken to the warden. We're going to tape your portion of the program right here."

"I don't know," Toy said. She remembered this man the day she was arrested, remembered him with the cameraman. He'd been the man asking her to turn around so they could catch her face. Now he was sitting here asking her to go on national television.

"Look," McDonald said, leaning over the table, "this is your one chance to show the world who you are, to tell your side of the story." Then he paused. "This is your chance to prove your innocence. If these cases don't go to trial, no one will ever know if you were guilty or not."

Toy knew what he was saying. He was saying that she would always be the baby snatcher, the woman who had set fire to a schoolhouse full of children. No matter what she did or accomplished, this would always be hanging over her head. Toy wondered if she would lose her job, and if she did, if another school board would ever hire her.

"Okay," she said finally, "I'll do it."

"Great," McDonald said, standing and shaking her hand. "We'll get it set up. We'll probably shoot tomorrow. Are you up to it?"

"I guess," Toy said. "What do I have to do?"

"Just answer the questions and tell the truth."

"All right," Toy said, nodding her head, thinking. "But I want my mother there."

McDonald grimaced. Everyone wanted something. At least she had not asked to be paid like all the others. He knew if they didn't get her story aired fast, every studio in town would be trying to buy the rights for a movie of the week or a feature film. Right now she was the biggest story in the country. Whatever the woman wanted, she would get. "We'll see if we can arrange it."

When Sandy Hawkings came to work the next morning, more than two hundred people were lined up in front of the jail, all carrying signs that read Free the Angel. The NYPD had dispatched officers for crowd control.

"How long have they been out there?" Sandy asked the officer in the control booth.

"All night. They stood out there with candles."

"God," she said, "they must have heard they were filming here today. You know, everyone wants to get on television."

"Have you looked at these people?" the male officer said, staring out across the street from his booth. Not waiting for Sandy to respond, he continued, "There's little kids, old men and women, every walk of life out there. You know who that man is in the black trenchcoat? That's Senator Weisbarth. He's the latest to jump on the bandwagon."

"No," Sandy said, peering out through the glass, a cup of coffee in her hands. "What's he doing standing out there?"

"Swears the second he saw her, he lost all taste for alcohol. Seems he'd been battling the booze for years, and has a bad liver. Didn't you see the story on him? It was in all the papers. Thinks she saved his life or something. Don't that beat all?"

"Yeah," Sandy said, her voice peppered with cynicism, "mass hysteria. That's what's going on."

The guard spun his chair around and looked up at the tall correctional officer. "Can you get me in to see her?"

"Who?" Sandy said, her mind a million miles away, unable to pull her eyes away from the crowd of people across the street.

"You know," he said coyly.

She shook her head. "You, Zeb? Now you believe in this woman?"

"I didn't say I believed in her. I just said I wanted to see her. Who knows, maybe she is some kind of angel. If she is, I want to be sure and get my three wishes." The man laughed, but it was forced. He was serious.

"I think you're a little mixed up, Zeb. Angels don't grant you three wishes," Sandy said, thinking she'd heard enough. She headed out of the control booth to start her shift. "That's a genie, idiot."

Sarah read every story written on Toy Johnson in each and every newspaper and magazine, and then passed them on for Raymond to read. With every hour he was becoming more alert and lucid. He had spoken to her on several occasions, and he had returned to painting. In addition, the look in his eyes was far more alert and focused. Sitting on the floor in the loft with him and two glasses of wine and a half-eaten pizza, Sarah said, "We have to do something, Raymond. She's going to be shipped to Kansas and tried for murder. The hearing is tomorrow." She paused and looked over at him. "I don't know what to do, though. I've called the hospital and the jail, and they won't let me talk to her."

The newspapers were spread out on the floor and Raymond picked one up. "Look," he said, pointing at a picture in one of the articles.

"Yes, I know," Sarah said, leaning over his shoulder to see what he was referring to, "that's the boy she saved in Kansas."

"We have to call him," Raymond said, his eyes darting around the room frantically.

"Call the boy? He was injured, Raymond. What could he do?"

"He can tell the court what really happened."

Sarah ran her hands through her hair as she was thinking. What he had suggested really wasn't that far-fetched. If they could convince Jason Cummings to fly to New York for Toy's hearing the next day, they might not extradite her to Kansas. Surely, she thought, if any-one could convince the authorities that Toy hadn't meant to harm or kidnap a child, it should be the child whose life she had saved. "You might be onto something," Sarah told Raymond. "Here, give me the paper and I'll see if I can get in touch with the boy's parents in Topeka."

"No," Raymond said forcefully, standing and looking down at Sarah, "this is something I have to do on my own."

FOURTEEN

Thursday morning Toy was handed her lime green pantsuit so she could dress to appear in court. She was tense and frightened. She knew this wasn't a trial per se, but it was the first step leading up to one, and that alone was terrifying.

After riding over on a bus with several other female inmates, Toy was led through a maze of halls and corridors to a waiting courtroom. When she stepped into the room, there was an immediate commotion, many people springing to their feet and applauding as though she had just stepped out onto a stage. She spotted Miles Spencer standing stiffly at the counsel table, and then saw her father and mother in the sea of faces, Stephen seated right beside them on the aisle. She searched the crowd, thinking she would see Joey Kramer, but he was evidently not present. Her mother smiled at her and waved. Stephen looked embarrassed and uncomfortable.

"Order," Judge Antonio Valerio said, pounding his gavel and glaring out over the courtroom. "I said, order in the courtroom, people. If there's one more outbreak, the courtroom will be cleared."

Once they had moved through the formalities, Miles Spencer stood and addressed the bench. "We have several witnesses we'd like to call, Your Honor."

"Witnesses?" the older judge said. "What do you mean, Counselor? This is an extradition hearing. All we are going to decide today is if this woman should be released to the authorities in the state of Kansas."

"I realize that," Miles said crisply. "But my client has been charged with heinous crimes, three separate counts of homicide. I think I can prove to you that she didn't commit these crimes, that the state of Kansas doesn't have a case, and that my client has been falsely imprisoned. Mrs. Johnson has a heart condition, Your Honor, and just underwent surgery. To transfer her to a detention facility in another state would be a travesty of justice."

"I object, Your Honor," the district attorney said. "This is highly irregular."

Judge Valerio had his head propped up with one hand and started scribbling something on a piece of paper. Finally, he raised his head and rendered his ruling. "I think this case is unusual enough that we might move away from the norm here. Mr. Spencer, I'll allow you to call your witnesses. Just make it brief because we have another hearing scheduled after this one."

"The defense calls Raymond Gonzales," Spencer said.

The back of the room fell silent as a dark young man made his way down the aisle to the witness stand. Toy craned her neck around and then did a double take. He looked distinctly familiar, but she couldn't remember from where. She started to say something to Miles, but the attorney was fidgeting nervously and not paying attention. "This is going to be tough," he told Toy. "He's autistic and can barely communicate, but his girlfriend insisted he could testify."

Raymond was dressed neatly in a black blazer, a white cotton shirt, and a pair of brown wool pants. His long hair was swept back and secured in a tight ponytail at the base of his neck. Once he was seated in the witness box and looked out over the courtroom at all the people, he blanched and dropped his head in fear. But in his hands was the ruby-and-diamond ring that Toy had given him years before. He had been clutching it so tightly in his palm that the stone was cutting into his flesh.

Once he had been sworn in, they began.

"When did you first meet the defendant?" Spencer queried.

Raymond stared straight ahead of him and spoke without faltering. "When I was thirteen years old."

"And where was this?"

"In a Sunday school class in Dallas."

"I see," Spencer said, "and what happened that day?"

Slowly, painfully, Raymond told his story, forcing the words out. A pronounced hush fell over the courtroom. It was a momentous occasion for the artist. Sarah had hauled one of the life-size portraits of Toy depicted as an angel with outstretched wings into the courtroom, and it was propped up against the far wall for everyone to see. No one could fail to note that the woman in the painting was dressed in a California Angels T-shirt, the same shirt Toy had been wearing when she was arrested. And the likeness was remarkable. The painting was so lifelike and striking that most of the eyes in the courtroom remained focused on it while Raymond testified, allowing him to speak more freely.

Although the woman Raymond had searched for and painted obsessively all these years was right in front of him, where he could feast on her every feature, he was surrounded by a teeming mass of humanity. Voices, odors, and offensive colors swirled around his head. But he persevered. One glance at Toy and he felt strong and confident. She was real. She was here. Nothing could ever harm him.

He told how he had felt trapped inside a glass prison due to his autism, and how the woman seated at the counsel table had somehow freed him. With a voice laced with emotion and conviction, he stated that Toy was a mystical creature, an angel sent to him in his time of need. Knowing she was real, he insisted, had given him the strength to pick up the pieces of his life and go on, to continue painting, to speak to them as he was presently doing. Her existence on earth meant there was hope for the world, hope for the future.

"That will be all," Spencer said once Raymond had finished. It was a nice touch, he thought, and had brought some drama into the courtroom, but Raymond's tale could hardly clear Toy on the current charges.

As Raymond stepped down from the witness stand, however, the back doors to the courtroom opened and a noisy group of people appeared. Several of them were children, and one was being pushed in a wheelchair by a plain-looking woman in a purple sweater and black pants. Raymond rushed down the aisle to meet them, and then returned to speak to Miles Spencer. "He's here," he told him, his eyes drifting over to Toy and then back to the attorney.

Toy felt a vibrating sensation in her chest, as if merely being near the dark young artist was setting off some kind of alarm. But as she stared at his face, bits and pieces from that day in Dallas flashed in her mind. She remembered looking down at her body in the emergency room while the attendants worked over her, even though she was later told that she had been in cardiac arrest. It was as if she had been standing in a corner of the room watching it all. She recalled stumbling into the church, bewildered at why she was there. Then she saw his face, not as it was today, but as it was then. He'd been a child, the same as all the others, but here he was standing only a few feet away, a full-grown man.

"Fabulous," Spencer said. "I'll call him as my next witness. Is Lucy here?"

"Yes," Raymond said.

In the background, the judge was pounding his gavel, eager to continue the hearing. Raymond walked off, and Toy turned to Spencer. "I have to talk to him," she said excitedly. "After the hearing, you have to find a way to get him in to see me."

"I don't know if I can do that," Spencer whispered tensely, leaning over closer to Toy.

Toy gave him a stern look. "I'm sure if you set your mind to it, you can arrange it. You're an important man, aren't you? I'm asking you to do me a favor as a friend."

All the blood drained from the attorney's face and he began nodding. "Yes," he said, "of course, anything you want. I'll talk to the judge." He stopped and then seemed to be thinking out loud. "If I have to, I'll bribe the guard."

"Good," Toy said, patting him on the arm. "I'd really appreciate it."

Spencer looked down at his arm where Toy had touched him, as if her mere touch was electrifying. He seemed to forget all about the hearing and turned to speak to Toy, his voice laced with emotion. "I'm a good person," he said. "I mean, I used to be a good person. Surely I can make amends somehow. You know, before I die."

The judge started yelling now and Spencer finally snapped out of it. "We call Jason Cummings, Your Honor."

Jason Cummings was wheeled to the witness stand. His recovery was going well, but he was still too weak to walk independently and his left arm was swaddled in bandages. The flight to New York had been difficult for him, but he had pleaded with his parents to bring him. Once Raymond had called, the little boy was determined to come and no one could stop him. Exactly what Raymond had said to the child, no one would ever know.

"She wouldn't hurt me," Jason said once the first round of questions had been dispensed with. "I was on fire and she fell on top of me. That's what put the fire out, see, or I would have been all burned up. That's how I know she's an angel."

"Did she tell you who she was or why she was there?" Spencer asked formally.

"Mister," the little boy said, "I was on fire. It's hard to 'member things when you're burning."

"Well," Spencer said, "what do you recall about that day?"

"She told me a story," the child said eagerly. "It was a story 'bout a little blue engine trying to pull a bunch of toys over a mountain.

See, it goes like this," he said. "I think I can. I think I can. Then the little engine says, 'I know I can. I know I can.' " Jason paused and made a gesture with his hand, saying, "Choo, choo. This is the whistle," he said, making a high-pitched sound with his mouth. The audience broke out laughing. Then he started chugging like a train.

"You can step down now, Jason," Spencer said wearily. He could feel his reputation slipping through his fingers. He'd never presented testimony like this in a court of law. It was a farce, a circus.

The judge frowned at the attorney. "Mr. Spencer, this child is adorable, granted, but his statements didn't shed much light on this case. Perhaps we should move forward now and dispense with the extradition matter before we run out of time."

"There's one more witness," Spencer protested. The judge continued to glare at him, and he quickly added, "I assure you I'll be brief."

The judge sighed and finally nodded.

"We call Lucy Pendergrass, Your Honor."

When Toy heard Lucy's name, she jerked her head around, eager to see her. She didn't have to wait long. A beautiful little girl suddenly streaked down the aisle and leaped into Toy's arms. Her chair fell back against the bench behind her and the bailiff had to right it. Lucy was rubbing her hands all over Toy's face and hair. Then she started kissing her. She placed wet, sloppy kisses on Toy's nose, her forehead, the spot where she had a dimple in her chin. "My pretty angel," she said, patting Toy on the top of her head.

"I'm sorry, Your Honor," Spencer said apologetically. "As you can see, the witness is quite attached to my client."

"Can we proceed, Mr. Spencer?" the judge said sharply.

Lucy climbed off Toy and straightened her blue dress. In the back of her curly blond hair was a matching blue satin bow with streamers. Holding her back straight, she marched to the witness stand and promptly took her seat.

"How old are you?" Spencer asked.

"I'm nine," Lucy said crisply, "but I'm in the Gate Program. That means I know more than most kids my age."

"Can you tell us what the Gate Program is?"

"A program for gifted children."

"I see," Spencer said. "Can you tell the court how you came in contact with Mrs. Johnson?"

"Yes," she said, "but first I want to ask you a question." Lucy craned her head around to look at the judge and grinned. "Since he gets to ask all these questions," she said, "can't I ask one, too?"

The judge smiled down at her warmly. "I think you have a valid point, young lady," he said. "Ask your question."

"See, I don't understand what's going on," she said, deciding to level her question at the judge himself. "How come those bad men can come to my church and take me away? It was a church and it was Sunday. That isn't right, you know?"

"No, honey," the judge said softly, "that isn't right. Is that your question?"

"Almost," she said. "If the bad men aren't here for you to punish them, why is my angel here? Are you going to send my angel away and let the bad men keep hurting little kids like me? That isn't very smart. I thought judges were supposed to be smart."

The judge hemmed and hawed, trying to think of an answer. Then he simply smiled at her. "Mr. Spencer," he said, chuckling. "I'm going to let you take it from here. I think this one is too much for me to handle."

The courtroom exploded in laughter. This time the judge made no attempt to bring the room to order. He was enjoying himself.

Once the noise died down, Miles Spencer led his witness through the events of that Sunday, trying not to get mired in the details of the crime itself, but to center the bulk of his questions on the time Lucy Pendergrass had spent with Toy in Central Park. Then the district attorney stood and asked the judge if he could cross-examine her.

"Now, after Mrs. Johnson placed you in the back of the state senator's limousine, where did she go?" the prosecutor asked.

"She went away," Lucy said, jutting her chin out. "She had other things to do. When you're a guardian angel, see, you don't just have one kid to watch over, you've got a whole bunch of them."

"Let me ask you something, Lucy," he continued. "You're an exceptionally bright little girl. Why would a person who was trying to help you simply disappear? How did she know you would be okay, that the men in the car would take you to a hospital? If Mrs. Johnson had really been concerned about you, why didn't she go to the hospital with you?"

"She didn't have to," Lucy said confidently. "She knew I would be okay. Didn't you hear me? She's an angel. Angels know everything."

"Let's concentrate a moment on how she left the car. She dropped down on the floorboard and crawled out the door, didn't she? Where no one could see her, right? Only a guilty person who feared arrest would make an exit like that." The attorney looked up at the judge. He wanted to make his point. That in fleeing Toy had displayed the behavior of a criminal and was far from a saint.

Lucy was looking down at her hands, staring at Toy's heart locket. She opened it as she had done many times and studied the miniature photos of Toy and Stephen in their wedding attire. Then she looked back out at the audience and found Stephen's face in the crowd.

"Lucy," the district attorney said, "did you hear the question?"

"Yeah," she said. "I was thinking. Look, she didn't do what you said. She just went away. I was holding onto her neck, and then her neck wasn't there anymore."

"How could that be?" the prosecutor said. "Is Mrs. Johnson the invisible woman or something?" He laughed, but no one in the audience seemed to find his statement funny.

Every eye was glued on Lucy Pendergrass. This was the real story, the one they had come to hear. How could a woman be in two places at the same time? How could a person be anywhere, for that matter, when they were in cardiac arrest and technically dead? Thus far the issue had been carefully skirted in the courtroom.

"No, silly," Lucy said, scowling at the district attorney. "She's not invisible. She's an angel."

"Didn't you try to hold on to her?"

"You don't understand about angels," Lucy said firmly, wrinkling her small nose into a button. "Angels help you, but they don't do everything for you. Once they do what they have to do to make sure you're safe, they just fly away."

"With their wings, right?" the prosecutor said sarcastically. "Like a butterfly, perhaps? Lucy, do you think Mrs. Johnson is a butterfly? She's right here. Does she have wings?"

The little girl kicked out at the podium with her feet and her face turned bright red. "You're trying to make me look stupid," she said angrily. "I'm not stupid. I'm smart. You're the stupid person. I bet you kept butterflies in a jar when you were a kid. Ugh. That's disgusting and mean." Then the anger disappeared and she smiled brightly. "I'm not worried, though," she said, shoving a golden curl off her face, "because you can never, never catch an angel. No," she said, shaking her head, "no matter how big you are or how hard you try, you just can't do it. So don't even try."

"That will be all," the prosecutor said, taking his seat, wishing he had never decided to question her.

Lucy stepped down from the witness stand, smiled up at the judge, and then headed down the aisle. When she passed the row where Stephen was sitting, she stopped. "Here," she said, handing him the gold locket. "You lost your heart and I found it."

Stephen looked at the object she had handed him and instantly recognized it as Toy's. Their wedding date was even engraved on the back. "Where did you get this?" he snapped. "This belongs to my wife."

"Your picture's inside it," she said, giving him a peculiar look as if she were listening to someone on the other side of the room. Then she glanced over her shoulder at Toy. "She wants you to have it."

"Did she tell you that?" he asked, curious.

"Not really," she said, turning back to look at Toy again. "See, she doesn't need a heart anymore, but you sure do."

While Stephen sat there with an astonished look on his face, fully aware he had been chastised by a mere child, Lucy tossed her blond curls and walked straight out of the courtroom.

The judge asked Miles Spencer to approach the bench. "I heard there was a tape of this woman at the scene of the fire in Kansas? Is that correct? Do you have a copy of that tape?"

"No, Your Honor," Spencer said. "I mean, I'm sure we can get a duplicate from the television stations, but the original was accidentally destroyed at the crime lab. They informed me just this morning."

"So," the judge said slowly, "as of this date, there's no proof your client was ever in Kansas, and all the proof points to her being in a hospital here in the city."

"That's correct," Miles said.

"Fine," he said. "You're excused."

As soon as Miles was seated again at the table, the judge began speaking. "This is not a trial," he said, repeating his earlier statement. "What we are deciding today is whether or not the defendant should be released to the authorities in Kansas. Mr. Spencer, I'd say your witnesses were fairly credible, even if they are children." He paused and adjusted his glasses, glancing over at the image of Toy that Raymond had painted. "I don't know about this angel business, or how a person could be in two places at the same time. Perhaps there's a rational explanation that we have yet to uncover. All I know is these children are convinced that Mrs. Johnson's intentions were decent and in no way criminal in nature." He glanced over at the district attorney who was squirming in his seat. "Sometimes things happen that we simply cannot understand, Counselor, and as a judge, I must occasionally make rulings based on instinct in the absence of solid evidence. State Senator Weisbarth is a distinguished and well-respected man. He called me this morning and offered to testify in behalf of this woman. It's not a common occurrence that a man of his stature is willing to risk his reputation to benefit a stranger accused of a serious crime. In addition, I don't feel the Kansas authorities have a provable case. Their strongest witness, Jason Cummings, just testified in Mrs. Johnson's favor." He paused and took a deep breath, then rendered his ruling. "The request to extradite Toy Johnson to Kansas is hereby denied." He pounded his gavel, smiled briefly at Toy, and quickly exited the bench.

When Toy heard the judge's ruling, she was beside herself with relief. The audience went wild, clapping and applauding as reporters and photographers tried to push and shove their way to the counsel table to get pictures and statements from her.

Spencer tried to explain to Toy what the ruling meant, and other particulars about her case. The judge had basically squashed all criminal proceedings. He couldn't force the Kansas authorities to drop their charges, but he did have the authority to deny their right to extradite Toy to Kansas. They had the alternative of either taking the matter before a higher court or simply waiting until Toy was physically inside their jurisdiction.

The New York authorities were hot on the heels of two men who were possible suspects in the abduction of Lucy Pendergrass and had decided not to press charges against Toy.

"I'm free," Toy said. "I'm really going to be released?"

He nodded and smiled, pleased with what he had accomplished.

"Thank you," Toy exclaimed. "This is the happiest day of my life." The bailiff then told her it would be several hours before the paperwork could be officially processed, and in the interim she would have to be returned to the jail.

"Wait, don't take her yet," Spencer pleaded as the bailiff started to lead Toy out of the courtroom.

The bailiff shrugged his shoulders and waited patiently, holding the crowd of reporters and well-wishers at bay.

"I've decided to return my fee," Spencer told Toy. "I don't want to take your money."

"That's nice," Toy said, smiling at him. "But it was my husband who paid you, not me. Give the money back to him."

Spencer looked over at Stephen and then turned back to Toy.

"Maybe I'll just donate it to charity, then," he said softly. "That is, unless you have a better suggestion."

Toy patted his arm and whispered back, "You're learning." Then another thought crossed her mind, and she opened her purse and removed a white piece of paper. "These are the names and addresses of some needy families I've been trying to help. Why don't you send the money to them? Since I'm about to go through a divorce, I probably won't have the money to help them anymore."

"Of course," Spencer said immediately. "Anything you say."

"Anything? Did you say anything?" Toy said, giggling and clapping her hands together softly as though they were playing a game. "Why don't you add some money of your own?"

"Sure, yes, certainly," he gushed. "I shouldn't have a problem getting Raymond Gonzales in to see you now. I'll arrange it immediately. Will you remember me? Will you put in a good word for me?"

"That depends," Toy answered, not certain who he wanted her to put in a good word with, but deciding it didn't matter.

"What do you mean?" Spencer said excitedly, seeing the bailiff step toward Toy again. "Quick, tell me what you mean."

"It depends on how much money you're willing to part with."

With that, Toy turned around and faced the spectators, smiling and waving at them. Then the bailiff escorted her out of the courtroom and the hearing was officially over.

Toy was held in a small room at the back of the courtroom while she was waiting to be transferred back to the jail. She heard the key turn in the lock, and then saw the dark artist standing there. Quickly, she stood and straightened her clothing. There were so many questions she wanted to ask him, but for some reason, they had all disappeared from her mind. "Have a seat," she said softly.

Raymond stood perfectly still, gazing lovingly at her face. "You're exactly the same. You haven't changed at all."

Toy laughed. "Well, you're certainly not the same. You're about a foot taller and a lot more handsome."

"That's because I'm mortal."

"Believe me," Toy said, arching an eyebrow, "I'm mortal, too. So mortal, in fact, that I almost went to jail for the rest of my life. Pretty scary, huh?"

Raymond shook his head. "Don't you know that you saved my life? You were my savior. I didn't know the outside world existed before you appeared to me that day."

Toy was embarrassed. She reached over and took his hand, gently caressing it in her own. "I don't know what happened, Raymond, any more than I know what happened in Kansas. I guess as long as there were positive results, we shouldn't worry about the details."

She led him over to a chair at the small table, and then took a seat herself. Raymond extended his hand and opened it. "Do you remember this ring?"

"My ring," Toy exclaimed. "I can't believe you have it. I have yours, too, you know, but it's at my house in California."

"Take it," he said, "it's yours."

"No," Toy said, closing his fist around the ring, "I don't want it. I gave it to you. I don't give things to people and then take them back. Besides, you gave me something even more precious. You gave me your pumpkin ring. Do you remember?"

"Yes," Raymond said, dropping his eyes, "but it was nothing more than a worthless trinket."

Toy reached over the table and lifted his chin, looking him squarely in the eye. "It wasn't worthless to you, was it? You treasured that ring, didn't you?"

Raymond chuckled, recalling how the plastic ring had been his most prized possession. His parents had never bought him toys, certain he would only break them. He'd found the ring in the bottom of a cereal box when he was eight years old, and had carried it with him everywhere he went. Five years he had clung to a piece of plastic. "It was orange," he said. "I've always liked orange."

"Well," Toy said, "you were my savior in many ways. There was magic in that orange ring, Raymond. Every time I became depressed or troubled, I would put it on. Almost instantly, I felt better." Toy sighed deeply. "You have no idea how many times I put it on." Then another idea surfaced. "You know, you might run into someone one day who's having problems or confused about their life. If you do, give them the ring and tell them our story. Then what we experienced will pass on to the next person."

"I have someone now," he said after a moment of silence had passed. "A woman. She's beautiful and good inside like you. She's not like the others."

"Sarah?" Toy asked. "I met her at the hospital. That's wonderful, Raymond."

"Yes," Raymond said. "I had to paint, you know."

"What do you mean?"

"Because the old paintings are fading away," he said, his voice so low it was almost inaudible, "and there are no new ones to take their place."

Toy was lost, but she didn't question him. All she knew was there was something timeless about this man. He understood about questions with no answers. He might not know it, but Toy was certain he understood everything, probably far more than she did.

Just then the jailer came and told them that the bus had arrived to take Toy back to the jail. Raymond darted to his feet, closed the distance between them, and crushed Toy in his arms. He inhaled the fresh scent of her hair, brought his hand up and softly outlined her face with his fingers. "Don't leave me," he said, his voice cracking with emotion. "How do I know I'll ever see you again?"

Toy pulled away and kissed him on the cheek. "You don't need me anymore, Raymond. You have your work and you have Sarah. What more could you ever want?"

"We have to go now," the guard said impatiently.

"Besides," Toy added quickly, "you have all those paintings of me. I saw the one in the courtroom. It was marvelous."

"I won't have them for long," Raymond shrugged. "Everyone wants to buy them."

"Hey," Toy said cheerfully, "just paint another one. Or, maybe it's time to paint someone else." Then she smiled at him and stepped through the door.

Sandy Hawkings stuck her head in the door of the infirmary where Toy was being held while they processed her release. "Congratulations," she said, handing Toy a sack with her belongings in it.

"Thanks," Toy said. "Isn't it great? I'm going to be free."

"A newsman by the name of Jeff McDonald called," Hawkings told her. "He says they're sending a limo to pick you up once the papers are processed. Since you're getting out, they want to film the television show live from their station."

"Okay," Toy said, wishing she had never agreed to go on television. "If that car isn't out there, though, I'm not waiting."

The woman thought of the restless throngs of people lined up out front. They'd have to take her out the back or she'd be ripped to pieces. "They're sending the car right now. Oh, your father is here as well. He wants to tell you good-bye. I guess he's on his way back to Los Angeles. Should I send him in?"

"Of course," Toy said. She looked around the room. Even though there were several beds, none of them were occupied. They could talk privately.

When her father stepped into the room, Toy just stood there watching him. She was surprised when he walked straight up to her and collected her in his arms, for he had never been very affectionate. "I love you, Daddy," she mumbled into his chest.

He pulled back and appeared self-conscious. "Toy . . . I . . . I've been thinking a lot since you got sick. I'm afraid I wasn't a very good father to you."

"That's silly, Dad," Toy said sincerely. "You were a great father."

"I could never give you that much. I never made enough money."

Now Toy felt self-conscious. She had never seen her father this way, so sentimental. "You gave me everything I needed, Dad. Here," she said, "let's sit down."

They sat face to face in two metal chairs, her father leaning down over his knees, patting his shirt pocket, wanting to take out a cigarette. Then his hands fell to his lap. He knew he couldn't smoke in a medical facility. "I remember when you were a little girl and you used to dress up in those costumes. You were some dancer. Prettiest little thing I ever saw."

"Yeah," Toy said, fond memories swirling around in her mind. "Do you remember the time I fell off my makeshift trapeze and broke my arm? You know, right after you and Mom took me to the circus?"

"How could I forget," he said. "I drove you to the hospital, remember? Your arm was bent over backward. I didn't think you'd ever be the same."

"You were always driving me to the hospital, Dad. I was always breaking one bone or the other."

He chuckled. Then he became serious again. "I know you and Stephen are breaking up," he said. "I just wanted you to know that I never cared for him. He always looked down on your mother and I. Treated us like we were white trash or something. Just because his father was a doctor don't mean he did a better job of bringing up his kid than I did."

"You're absolutely right, Dad. Don't worry about Stephen, he looks down on everyone. You never told me you didn't like him, though. I thought you and Mother adored him."

"You never asked."

They both laughed.

"Well," he said, pushing himself to a standing position, "guess I got to get or I'll miss my plane. Your mother is all excited about this television thing. Don't think I've ever seen the woman so worked up."

Toy walked with him to the door, rang the buzzer, and then waited with him for the guard. "I might stay here in New York," she blurted out. "I might not go back to L.A."

"Oh," Tom Myers said, "that's fine, honey. Mom and I never saw you that much anyway. Tell you what. We'll just pretend you still live there, and we don't see you so often like before. As long as you think a person is close by and safe, you don't have to see them in the flesh."

Toy smiled at her father's practical approach to life. Then she touched his hand. "I'll always be close, Dad, no matter where I am."

"Oh," he said, "I thought I'd tell you. You know that artist that's been painting those pictures of you?"

"You mean Raymond Gonzales?"

"Yeah, I think that's his name. Said on the radio just now that he's having a big auction of those paintings next week. A famous art dealer signed him right in the courtroom, and people are coming in from all over the world." Her father paused and rubbed his hand over his chin. "I wouldn't mind having one of those pictures myself, you know," he said with a sly smile. "Think he'd paint me one? Not sure I can afford to buy one. Radio seems to think they're going to go for a lot of money."

"I'm sure he would, Dad," Toy said softly. "All you have to do is ask him. He's a really nice man."

The guard knocked on the door. Her father started to turn the knob, but he stopped and stood there, moving his feet around on the floor. "I . . ."

"What is it, Dad?" Toy said, seeing him struggling for words, an expression on his face she had never seen.

"I love you, Toy. I might not have told you over the years, but it wasn't because I didn't want to. I just thought you knew."

"Of course I knew," Toy said, fearful she was going to break down and cry.

He bent over and kissed her on the cheek. Then he stepped through the door, and the guard locked it behind him. Toy just stood there, awash in pleasure. It was the first time in her life that her father had ever told her he loved her.

* * *

Toy showered, washed her hair, and shaved her legs with the disposable razor they had issued her. She would have liked to put on some makeup, but she didn't have any in her property bag. The television station had requested that she come dressed in her navy blue Angels T-shirt. Finding it in the bottom of the sack, Toy pulled it on over her blouse. One of these days, she thought, she was going to have to wash it.

Now that she was dressed, she sat on the edge of the bed and waited. Suddenly she felt a wave of dizziness and nausea. Black spots flashed in front of her eyes, and she was certain she was going to pass out. She started to call the nurse and then thought of the ramifications. Another trip to the hospital. No way. Toy put her hand over her heart, the place where the little machine kept it ticking and ticking. Just calm down, she told herself. It had to be stage fright. A few minutes later, the sensation passed and Toy was relieved.

"Your car's here and the paperwork is ready," Sandy Hawkings said when she came in the door. "Hey, lady, bet you're ready to get out of this joint."

"Amen to that one," Toy said. Then she stopped. "They told me you were the one who gave me CPR that day. I never even thanked you."

"Say no more," Sandy said, looking away in embarrassment. "That's my job."

"You're good at your job, Sandy."

"Well, you're not so bad yourself." Sandy put her hand behind Toy's back and they headed out the door.

They walked down a long corridor, heading to the back of the facility. On one side of the building was a row of windows. Sandy walked over and Toy followed. "See all those people out there?" she told Toy. "They're all waiting for you. That's your job, I guess. Making all these people feel better, making them all dream the dream, so to speak."

Toy just shook her head in amazement. Then she followed Sandy to the back door, waiting to be buzzed through. The next thing she knew she was climbing into the backseat of the limousine. A lot of the prisoners had pressed their faces against the windows and were waving at her. Toy rolled down the car window, stuck her head out, and waved back.

The limo didn't pull up in front of the television station. There was another mob scene, people several rows deep, pressing against the police barricades. Toy watched the people through the tinted windows as the driver pulled in an enclosed parking lot in the back of the station. He got out to open the car door and Toy stepped out. Her heart was racing now and her hands were perspiring. Could she really do this? Really go on national television?

A pert brunette in a short black dress met her at the back door and escorted her down a corridor. "You'll have to go in for makeup in a few minutes." She glanced down at what Toy was wearing and then looked away, pleased that she was wearing the T-shirt as they had requested. "I'm going to put you in the green room right now. There's a television monitor in there, some coffee, juice. Help yourself."

"My mother?" Toy said. "I told them I had to have my mother on the show. She isn't here."

"I think she's in makeup," the girl said. "I'll go check on her for you."

Toy took a seat on a red vinyl sofa and reached for a magazine. She had no idea why they called the room the green room. There wasn't one thing in it that was green. Just as she flipped open the pages of the magazine, Joey Kramer appeared in the doorway. "Joey?" Toy yelled, thrilled to see him. "How did you get in here?"

"Oh," he said, "Joey can get in any place he wants. How you doing, kiddo?"

"Great," Toy said, but she didn't feel great. When she tried to focus on Joey's face, she saw black spots again. "I think I'm having a bad case of stage fright. Boy, I thought this would be easy. It's not."

"Nothing's easy," Joey tossed out. Then he changed his mind. "Well, there's some things that are pretty easy. You don't gotta do this, you know."

"I know," Toy said, "but I told them I would. I never like to go back on my word."

"Things are different now," Joey said, taking a seat on the sofa next to her. "You don't need to prove anything. The people that believe in you will believe in you. The people that don't won't. Why don't you just let Joey here take you for a nice cup of coffee?" He flicked his wrist. "Hey, what you need this TV stuff for?"

"But I can't simply walk out," Toy said. "Even my mother is here."

"Yeah, so what? She's your mother, she'll understand. Let her go on the show and tell them all about you. You know, a big star like you needs an advance person. Then if you decide to do it later, after you're rested and everything dies down, you can come back."

Toy was leaning close to Joey now, and she whispered, "You mean, I could just walk out the door and that's it?"

Joey laughed. "Yeah, you want to?"

"Really?" Toy whispered. She was feeling sicker by the minute. She didn't want to do this, go on television, make a spectacle of herself.

"Hey, we going or what?" Joey said, standing and smiling down at her. Then he took a pen out of his pocket and handed it to her, along with one of the magazines. "Tear off a page and write a note to your mom. Then we'll split."

All Toy wrote was, "Mom, sorry, but you've got to carry the ball for me. Enjoy. Left with Joey. I love you. See you later." She started to sign it and then added something else before scrawling her name at the bottom.

"Whadya add?" Joey asked. He'd been looking over her shoulder.

"Break a leg," Toy said. "Mom always wanted to be an actress. No one knew but me. Not even my dad."

"Oh, yeah? Well, dreams come true."

Toy leaned into Joey's body as they headed down the hall. "What if someone sees us?"

"No one's gonna see us. You worry too much. Just let Joey handle it, okay? I got the plan, see. Joey's always got the plan."

He yanked on the heavy steel door at the back of the station and they crept out like two thieves, giggling and making silly faces at each other. Joey didn't want to go anywhere near the crowds so they headed up a back street. "My car's up here," he told Toy. "Sorry. There was nowhere to park. Too many people around."

Toy looked ahead and suddenly saw he was pointing at a steep hill, like the kind of hills they have in San Francisco. "We have to walk up *there?*"

"Afraid so," Joey said, shrugging. "I don't got a limousine, Toy. It's just an ordinary car and I have to park in an ordinary parking lot. I'm not really even on duty today. I just wore my uniform so I could sneak in to see you."

"I'm sorry," she answered, catching up to him, huffing and puffing as they climbed the steep hill, perspiration streaming down her face, her neck, between her breasts. "I was acting spoiled. I just don't feel very good."

"It's not that far now," Joey said. "Can you make it just a little farther?"

Toy stopped, leaning over at the waist. She was so short of breath. Then she felt the pain and grimaced. "I can't, Joey."

"Hey, want me to carry you?"

Toy looked at him. "No," she said finally, "but if I didn't have that pacemaker, I would swear I'm having a heart attack."

He laughed. "You ain't having no heart attack. You're just out of shape. You've been sitting around too much. You need to get back to work."

Now Toy could see the crest of the hill. "Is your car right at the top of the hill?"

"Yeah," Joey said. "I told you it was."

"If you are lying to me, Joey Kramer," Toy said firmly, "I'm going to kick you right in the pants."

"What? Me lie?" he said, really laughing now. "Just a few more steps. Come on. You can do it. Don't wimp out on me now."

A few more steps, Toy told herself, panting and holding her chest. Just a few more steps and she could sit down and relax, catch her breath. She paused and looked back down the hill. No wonder she was out of breath. It looked like she was standing on top of Mt. Everest. Far down below, she saw throngs of people, still standing there waiting. Was it really right for her to be up here and for them to be down there? They had supported her and believed in her, and she had simply walked away. Oh, well, Toy said, turning back to Joey.

One last step would put her over the crest. Joey was already there, beckoning to her, a big silly grin on his face. "There," she said, standing right beside him, turning her head to look into his face. She felt like a marathon runner who had just passed the wall. The pain was gone and she felt weightless and free.

"Look," Joey exclaimed.

Toy turned her face slowly into a fragrant, gentle breeze. She felt the sun on her face, warming it, as the wind picked her hair up off the nape of her neck. Then the sun passed right over her head, and Toy was filled with awe. Beneath her was an incredible landscape. It was like she was in an airplane. The houses and buildings looked so small. Then she saw what looked like backyard swimming pools and suddenly came to the realization that she was looking at lakes, streams, oceans.

The entire world stretched at her feet in breathtaking splendor.

Joey was excited and pointing. "That's Big Ben over there. And see, there's the Eiffel Tower. Right there is the pyramids."

Toy smiled, a smile that entered her body and remained there. "It was you all along," she said.

"Well, yeah," Joey said, giving Toy a big wink. "Just a regular guy from Brooklyn. I did trick you a little on the car, though, I have to admit. But I'm not the *big boss*. I'm just a soldier."

As Toy looked at him, seeing him for first time, she saw that his police uniform was really a uniform like they paint on toy soldiers. The pale blue had turned to red and the coat was fastened with brass buttons. He made her think of the wooden soldier her father had been carving the day she had visited him in his workshop.

For a moment she was certain she was having another one of her dreams, her visions. "Joey, unless I'm hallucinating again, that's the whole world down there, not just Manhattan. That means you're an angel, not a soldier."

"Oh," Joey said, "we don't do wings anymore. People didn't take us seriously. See, it used to be kind of a battle. These days it's more of a war. The Boss runs a tight ship. He calls it His army."

Joey stopped and removed what looked like a portable radio, holding it up to his mouth. "Yeah, I see it. L.A., right? Yeah, I'll get someone right on it. I know. I know. I've been a little tied up." Joey turned to Toy. "This will be your territory soon. We've been a little shorthanded in California lately. Just not enough good prospects applying for the job."

Toy followed his gaze to a small corner of the landscape below them.

"You got a little advance training, Toy, because you'll be covering California for us and the Boss is extremely annoyed. This was prime real estate, some of His best work."

Joey looked and Toy could see long stretches of sandy beaches, shimmering blue water, palm trees swaying in the breeze. Then the scene shifted slightly and Toy could see a long, jagged crack which she realized was the San Andreas Fault. "If things don't get better soon," Joey said sadly, "the Boss might really get angry. But that's okay," he added quickly. "You're going to do real good, Toy. You're going to straighten these people out before it's too late."

They were back on the crest, walking down a narrow cobblestone path that Toy seemed to recall seeing before. On both sides of her were fields of blooming flowers, their fragrance so sweet and their blooms so perfectly formed that Toy was enraptured by their beauty. "Where are we going?"

"We're going to the mess hall. We don't work nonstop, you know. Tonight, after supper, we're having a dance."

Toy gulped. "Will the Boss be there?"

"No," Joey said, raising only one eyebrow, "*He* works full-time. That's what happens when you're the Boss."

In the distance was a large white tent, the canvas billowing out in the breeze. Beyond it the sky was awash with brilliant, dazzling colors. Toy could see people milling around and heard the soft chords of what she thought was music.

Joey's eyes were the bluest of blue. Toy's were the greenest of green. They looked at each other, met each other, this time for the very first time. Then he laced his arm in Toy's and they continued walking toward the tent.

"What about all those people down there," Toy said, "the ones who believed in me?"

"The Boss has a policy about things like that."

Toy was curious. "What kind of policy?"

Joey smiled before answering, his shoulder twitching with nervous energy, "Well, you know, the Boss has His own way of doing things."

Now Toy was really curious. "Come on, Joey, tell me the policy."

"It's pretty simple," Joey said. "The Boss likes to keep them guessing."

"Guessing?" Toy said, thinking it sounded so flippant, so callous.

"Well," Joey answered, "He calls it something else really. That's just my own interpretation."

"What does He call it?"

"Faith," Joey said, an enormous smile appearing on his face. Then he turned and looked off in the distance as a person walked toward them down the cobblestone path. "Well, whadya know, look who's here?"

Toy stood perfectly still, her eyes wide with growing wonder. Margie Roberts was walking toward her in the peach dress. When she saw Toy, she rushed into her arms. Toy crushed the child to her chest. "Oh, Margie," she said, tears of joy streaming down her face, "you look so beautiful, so strong, so happy."

"You're here," Margie exclaimed. "You're finally here. I was so tired of waiting."

"Yep, this one's a case," Joey said, laughing at the sight of Margie and Toy together, locked in a loving embrace. "Wouldn't leave me alone until I came down to get you, and I was plenty busy, let me tell you. You know," he said to Margie, shaking his finger at her, "New

York is a hard state to cover. Just wait until you get a territory, young lady, and then you'll see."

The moment he stopped speaking, Toy heard the sound of trumpets and suddenly saw legions of angels assembling beneath the big tent, chattering and giggling among themselves. They were dark ones, light ones, small ones, tall ones. Some were children, some were adults. There were no wings or halos, but Toy saw exquisite colors swirling around each being and could feel their overwhelming love.

Joey stood ramrod straight in front of the assembly of angels, every bit the soldier now. On the opposite side of him, Margie Roberts took up a similar stance, giggled, and then pushed Toy forward into a circle of brilliant light. Another trumpet sounded and the legions of angels saluted the new California Angel, formally welcoming her into the fold.